Shudders! Spasms!

And Shock Waves!

The Strokeless Orgasm

A Fun Tale By:

GABRYEL KEVYN

Copyright © 2023

The Cassie Publishing House

ISBN: 978-0-9801432-4-9
First Edition

Gabryel is an accomplished novelist, songwriter, poet, lyricist, videographer, and music producer. He lives in Pennsylvania.

Cover Design and Photo: Gabryel Kevyn
Editing: Gabryel Kevyn and Little Wosie

For more about Gabryel, including his music, please kindly visit him at GabryelKevyn.com

More Works by Gabryel now and upcoming!
Enjoy!

<u>Writings</u>:

'*Innocence Murdered*'

'*Absurdities*'

'*My Sensations*'

<u>Music</u>:

'*City Boy, Country Soul*'

<u>YouTube Videos</u>:

'*Everything Gabryel*'

Shudders! Spasms! and Shock Waves! The Strokeless Orgasm

Foreword - Author's note:

You are about to meet Darian, a middle-aged, average guy with a penchant for adventure. He works in corporate America and is a successful IT professional, yet he is very down-to-earth, maybe even a bit obsessive. We'll get to that.

As with some of us, and maybe most of us, his days are consistent with work, daily schedules, home stuff, and fun times with friends. He sees himself as a normal everyday guy, happily in a relationship with his girl, both who value their freedom and togetherness.

He loves sports, loves his home teams, and also is fond of history (mostly military), and psychology, a blend that suits his carefree and sometimes wondering attitude. He does occasionally entertain fantasies of what it would be like say to be a pirate, or a Roman warrior, or a discoverer, a pioneer, but these are just fantasies satisfied with the experience of movies, TV, and reading.

Darian, as again with many of us, though, never questioned his normality, his beliefs, his acceptance of what and how a guy (like him) should be, should act, should love, should play, and should see himself, to himself and to others. There was no reason to see anything differently, no reason to expect anything more than what was, nor did it ever cross his mind in such matters. Just simply no reason, since all was pretty acceptable, and as usual, normal.

Well, Darian, our hero in this tale about to unfold, suddenly finds himself inadvertently flung into a surreal, and a real set of unforeseen crossroads, questioning all he thought and felt about himself, and is deeply thrust, partly by his own will and partly not, into an imaginative, and some may say

Gabryel Kevyn

eccentric, personal and sexual adventure, a journey of self-identity, of what it really means to be a guy, a male, that completely tests all his preconceived notions of who he is socially, sexually, intimately, and personally, now and in a potential new and scary but seemingly advantageous future that entices him beyond his senses and drives deep into his desires and fantasies, finding more than he ever expected of himself, learning the difference between the individual and the group, and seeing and experiencing a new vision of masculinity, transforming him forward, more fully and deeper than the world he started at. All he has to do is conquer his fear.

We wish him well!

Tale Introduction ~

I couldn't believe it myself. I used to debate telling anyone. Kind of well, because, it used to be a bit embarrassing …well maybe not …well maybe …well maybe not *now*. But that was before my incredible journey. And any day prior to that journey would be a difficult day in my life expressing myself, like now to you.

And as you may well know too, how cautious (and possibly daring) the experience can actually be in expressing *your* true self to others, or maybe your inner *secret* self. Depends on the day, right? And how we choose to see ourselves, right? But as you will see, in the end it comes down to courage. And to my own surprise, I had made the decision that changed my life, as a person and as a male.

So, I'd like to share with you an adventure that fell upon me unexpectedly. But honestly, I somehow feel I drew it towards me. While at the same time, it seemed to come on its own (no pun intended, well maybe).

My name is Darian Dracco. I am full-blooded (some say hot-blooded) Italian-American regular downhome guy. I was born a male, with all the equipment. Still am a male I think, as there can be different interpretations and manifestations, but we can sift through that fun stuff later. Here's the part I used to struggle with… how to explain my unbelievable experience, and more fascinating, my learning. Yes, my learning. The real struggle always was opening myself up to how I treat myself, how I see myself, and in the end, with others, like here, with you. And none of this I would have *ever* considered before – *ever*. And especially as a guy. That must be made utterly clear. So, read on if you dare. I warned you.

What I do, what you do, what we all do, I learned is *not* fixed. There are

1

fantastic horizons to be discovered out there, as I have and others have, too. The battle used to be talking about it, as generally most of us do not – embarrassed, socially unacceptable, awkward – this, that, and the other. But it's too amazing not to. So, my decision is *onward*. So, please, have a chair.

In the beginning, God made man (that's the guy). Then, the female (um, the girl). Really fascinating stuff (lol). And then the female did a very bad thing and seduced (so we're told) the male to also do the very bad thing. Oops, now we have *knowledge of good and evil*, can't have that, so everybody, outa the pool! So, what really was that tree? That fruit? (If you want to bail, now is the time.)

It had to be *really good* to get kicked out for wanting it, and then actually doing it, knowing the dire consequences. Sounds like something you can get drawn into and once started, can't stop – *regardless* of the consequences. Since, no one really knows for sure, I'll choose…masturbation. Yep. Masturbation. She found it, did it, and loved it. It was so much better than the simple primordial wham bam from behind which she really didn't have much care for, so she brought her guy in and showed him, 'Hey honey, check this out! Look what we can do!' And he was, like maybe slow to catch on, okay, well this is good, ummm…really good…I can do this and that, and they were having a grand ole' time discovering the real power of their genitalia. Now both, after insanely cumming for the first time, felt that guilt we've been programmed and taught to feel, so they hid and grabbed those fig leaves and the rest is history, at least one history. Pretty sure it wasn't a granny apple.

Well, that's my take and hope we don't get bombarded by religious groups for *an opinion*. So, what's the point? The point is we are taught from the very 'beginning' that pleasing ourselves (whether together or alone) is wrong, guilt-ridden, stop doing that, or else! OK, so we're out of the *Garden* now and let's get to the real story. With all enormous credit to females, they beautifully forced a sexual revolution back in the 60's and 70's for respect, equality, individuality, and understanding, and it was great and needed! But there always seemed another part that never really caught up with that – not anyone's fault either (to be absolutely clear). The guy side – exactly!

Shudders! Spasms! and Shock Waves! The Strokeless Orgasm

So, here we are to explore what I learned and would say is.... insane, crazed *male* pleasure and the ultimate bloke's orgasm... *'Shock Waves!'* And of course, *The Strokeless Orgasm*. Can't forget that.

Once upon a time...

Episode 1 ~

"OH… MY… GODDDD!!"

I heard myself uncontrollably start to mutter between deep gasps. And the vocal repetition, as I tend to always do, continued to grow longer and louder (for short: OMG!!… OMG!!…) Never realizing how predictable I was.

And (as usual) my excitement grew more as I kept watching her writhe (always loved that word) below me, clawing me, clawing anything, face in ecstasy, voice approaching that screaming moment. I then proceeded from my slow deliberate gliding to deeper and more profound (profound?) thrusting. I was between soon-to-be explosion and analyzing her widening climatic insanity when she grabbed my ass by both hands and took control. And I let her because I was clipped by that sudden DEEP feeling in my cock (and balls – they tend to get forgotten) capturing my attention between my building insanity and her delirious craziness below me. I was watching both of us approach that feverish point of no return, of complete control loss! Looking at her beyond-ecstatic face, a blinding instant thought flashed by me and instantly disappeared… 'was she having more fun than me?' My thoughts flew back to my impending detonation…

My continuous calling of the Supreme Being coupled with the overwhelming, now uncontrollable, crazy climax overtaking me, made me retake control and pound at 96 miles per hour until I heard that unmistakable cry of release "I… I… OH NO!! YES!! I'M GOING TO CUM!! OH MY GOD!!" from my throat, and body, and with other things expelled, crashed down on top of her. And because my arms were really hurting.

After giving one final credit to the Supreme Being, I knew she had cum violently too (she was an expert at violent vaginal orgasms) and was huffing deeply as I lay slumped on her. As I propped myself up on my elbows to not crush her, I couldn't help thinking why I (do all men?) need to proclaim the obvious: "Yo! I'm a'cummin'! How 'U doin'!" And in that moment of final ecstatic male release, I came (not pardoning the pun) to realize that my own self-explosion had not blocked out her insane screaming of her own self-explosions! Yes, plural! So, I got one. She got, what, five? Ten?

It prompted me to proclaim, "my cum was fucking amazing!"

And I *emphatically* proclaimed it to the world, and the four walls, with pure self-confidence. I was feeling high in my own afterglow. (...afterglow? ...did I just say that?) Regardless. Period. I was good! No, I was *great* at this! Always overwhelmed me! And I knew *she* knew it, too. I waited for her confirmation of my proclamation! Which surely came.

"Hadn't noticed."

I heard words that didn't register in my 'afterglow' brain. Slowly, I said, "I'm sorry?" as I was desperately trying not to ask for ANY clarity because I did hear what she said. I did. All the while keeping my brain (and heart) (and ego) at bay with all the male armaments I could muster. But I did ask for clarity because it was too much to comprehend and of course, I know, I had simply, maybe, misread her. Hopefully.

She opened her eyes, looked honestly at me with sincere blue eyes, and with I think a small grin noting she had been busy, she lightly clarified: "I said, hadn't noticed."

Done. Shit. What? No way! Me? Not noticed? I noticed me *and* her. What the fuck! I blinked (not sure how many times) in disbelief. And then all my male armaments (which are supposed to keep us guys safe) failed and the hordes of reality's realities came crashing in.

Without caring about the sensitivity of the head of my dick, I promptly slipped out of her, looked back down one last time at her satisfied face (hoping it was from her 'better' orgasm and not cockiness of *believing* she was way better), and fell to the side wishing I had not slipped out so fast (the head of the penis thing). And the worst part was knowing full well, she might be right.

5

Could I ever experience what she (and women) experience? Was it true there are a billion more nerve endings in the clitoris than in the whole cock? Were our dicks just poor renditions of the clitoris? Were we poor men, who had to be pathetically taught how to masturbate in the *Garden*, doomed to average ecstatic-ness in comparison to the one who got us all kicked out in the first place? That was when I decided. I needed to know once and for all. Was I doomed? And then to be told "Hadn't noticed." That was the fucking kicker and you know where! I was dumbfounded. I didn't know which way to go or who to see or what to do, but I made a decision to find out or just simply get castrated to end it all.

Hence, the start of my obsession. Welcome aboard and warp ten speed ahead!

Episode 2 ~

So, I did what we all do when humiliated. Research! I started researching the difference between climaxes, the physical, the mental, the whatever *whatever*. All the while, wondering what the fuck was my infatuation with this whole thing. Was it the infamous fragile male-ego? Was it sheer fucking competition, gotta win, be better (or at least equal)? Somehow, that wasn't it – at least not for me (anyone looking to buy the Brooklyn Bridge?)

But honestly, it was more than that. I needed to KNOW, know for sure. Aren't you curious? Was I, were us guys, doomed to the forever lesser of the species' rapturous fun? Could we have violent, earth-shaking, blinding, infinitely prolonged ummm... 'experiences?' Who am I kidding. We wham it. We bam it. We (us guys again) probably would never have found that damn granny apple in the first place. Almost like an instinctiveness for girls. We just bumble and fumble along, hum de dum de dum, hunt, gather, roll the stone over the cave for the night. No! I couldn't accept that, but had absolutely no idea where to turn (or run). Sex therapy? No. Mental therapy? Maybe. Penis therapy? Definitely.

So, I did what I felt best, and safest, to do. Drink.

"Do you ever wonder if there is more to sex?"

"Oh no, what's going on?" Fred knew me well enough to know this was probably another one of my off-the-wall mental paths of trying to get the answers I wanted by cornering him. Of course, he was right.

"I mean it."

"More to sex? Sex is sex..."

"Exactly my point."

"What point?"

"I mean for a guy."

"You're seriously getting weird. Guys have sex. Girls have sex. We all cum – usually. Done. Next."

"You're making my point. Look, do you think girls, women, have better orgasms?"

"Than us? Of course. They're women, girls as you put it."

"Don't you think that's wrong?"

"What the fuck are you talking about," as he turned fully towards me taking a large gulp, downing his shot, and playfully banging the glass onto the bar

"You, I, all men, are at a loss when it comes to cumming. We just do it. 'Done,' as you so poetically noted. Didn't you ever think there may be more than just a shot?"

"Darian, my man, I think there's a lot more to a shot!" He smiled and pushed the empty shot glass to the bartender for another and turned back to the bar.

"Don't be a dick." I grinned at his pun.

"OK, OK, where is all this coming from?" He sounded genuine in his increasing drunkenness.

I told him what happened, in detail. I would never tell any other of my guy friends or girl friends for that matter. But Fred was different – which I was going to find out later – later part of the story I mean. (Still have your chair?)

"Well, that sucks," was all he said as he turned back to the bar. I wasn't sure if he was disinterested or embarrassed. Another point. Why can't men talk openly about their sexual details vs wham bam. Women do (I think). Maybe it's evolutionary. The more over centuries a certain sex talks amongst themselves about intimate sex, the greater the explosions become century over century. Some weird Natural Selection. Better yet, Natural 'Orgasmic Selection.' Thanks Darwin! You could have let your fellow chaps know!

I didn't care at that point how Fred felt. I wanted answers. I wanted some magical moment of all-knowing (yeah, like *knowledge of good and evil*).

Something like that.

Fred was still facing forward with his head slightly down like suddenly he was processing everything I was posing and maybe, it *seemed* he was more interested than he showed or wanted to show. Again, why do we, us men, (I know I'm obsessed) have such a hard time talking about our sex? Do we think somehow it makes us feminine – God forbid that!

"He says he has 'shock waves.'"

Out of my multi-tasking, self-debasing haze, I slightly looked over at him with a 'what the fuck did you just say' look – though my interest had peaked. 'Shock waves.' Is that what he just said? Who has 'shock waves?' What *is* a 'shock wave?'

"'Shock waves?' Who are you talking about?" I turned fully towards him, wanting him to face me.

"Zach. You know Zach."

"Zach? …Zach? …oh, Zach!" All I could picture was how many girls this guy has, gets, is with all the time, who all practically hang on him…well, they do hang on him. And his always cocky smile. Which I guess is warranted. Reminded me of Salty Deke, a sly ladies-man *and* mastermind yet good-natured seducer friend I used to know. My nickname for him was 'Salty Deke *The Sex-Demon.*' He could seduce anyone any time, even men if it served his purpose and poly desires. I never liked him. I mean Zach.

I always admired *The Sex-Demon* for being something I never saw in myself, especially his *mischievous curiosity* of his soon-to-be lovers, the demon part driving his good-natured seductions which all his 'victims' loved in the end, even the guys. Everyone loves the taste of salt! (lol was my little saying!) But was Zach the same in a different way?

"Yeah. My golf buddy. Adamant, too," he muttered not looking at me. I couldn't tell if he was bullshitting me.

"OK then, what the fuck is a 'shock wave?'" I figured I'd play along. But something in Fred's demeanor made me think he was actually for once being serious. Probably the alcohol. But what has he opened up? Pandora's Box?

Didn't that release all the evil in the world? Wait, wasn't that the granny apple? I'm confused. So, I waited.

"Hell if I know." He cocked his head towards me all the while playing with his glass. I knew my friend well enough when he starts doing that. Like when he was *almost* getting divorced years ago. "He claims it's the ultimate in cumming, in a guy cumming, and he can do it. Ya know, I think he's just fucking cocky and makes shit up."

I couldn't read his damn poker-face. He was good.

Making up or not, I was thinking, could there really, maybe, be more out there, somewhere in the vast universe I was missing? Who would make that up? Well, Zach would. I wondered if I needed to upgrade my equipment somehow. Did Zach sell upgrades? Surgery? OK, stop...

"Dude, he's adamant. Get him drunk and he'll spill it, I'm sure. Probably don't even need to get him drunk. He'll love to talk about it either way."

Still couldn't read his poker-face. But wait. A guy *wanting* to talk about it?

"Have you?"

"Me what?"

"Had 'shock waves?'" He's playing with me now, I thought, and the whole thing suddenly seemed bullshit. Then I got a feeling he was hiding something. I was all over the place.

"I don't think so," he replied with a look like not having made the team, while at the same time had swallowed the canary. "Probably not, because I don't know what it is, and *I don't care.*"

Well, I knew one thing. I surely *did* care if there was such a thing. In fact, anything more would do just fine. Maybe position myself differently? Stick something up my ass (just kidding!) Anyway fellow inquisitors, my hopes were rising that there may be hope for us beleaguered descendants of Adam other than "Oh, oh! Boom! Done!" Back to our show...

"Maybe it's the girls he gets. Maybe they have some technique or magical superpower. To their *superpower!*" Fred toasted his next shot and downed it.

Shit, hope that's not true! I didn't want that everything came from our opposite sex. Then they hold the keys to it all. And I mean no disrespect. There must be something we have special to us, something we can do. I was beginning to think I was going a little mad and overboard on this whole thing but Melissa's matter-of-fact "hadn't noticed" brought me back. I was going to find out one way or another. And of course, whether he knew it or not, Fred got me going even more.

I ordered two more shots. And then our typical Uber.

For days after, all I could think about was what I (and all us guys) were missing. I really enjoyed a good slow intimate fuck, I'm good at it, using my hips to get that co-rhythm to it all, to then take control (now starting to doubt that) of the whole act (act? Did I just say *act*?).

Maybe that was it. I was just *acting* the same role over and over again. Nothing unique. Always the same. Nothing sending my cock and balls through the cosmos and back. Nothing more than "hadn't noticed." I knew I was getting *perversely obsessed* but fucking didn't care. Hang in there. There's shit more to cum (I mean come). Can't let every cat out! Come on, ya know, a little suspense here...

So, is that what she possibly thought? What all women thought? Men = Utilitarian. Period. Just get her started and she'll do the rest. I knew I wasn't being fair but it kept crossing my mind — *because* she HADN'T NOTICED! Fuck. Fuck. Fuck, again.

And the worst part is we think we're awesome. We have fun don't we? But it may all just be 'putting up with us' because we have certain equipment, and muscles to use said equipment (versus a dildo which takes up extra female effort). Was that the difference between a dick and a dildo? And batteries?

I was in a swirl of indecisiveness and lost in a whirlpool of wondering. I had to know what kind of total consuming ecstasy blinded *a woman*, to the faux greatness a guy felt and especially, obviously, his complete inferior abilities to gain anywhere *near* her 'normal' clitoral explosions. Ever? Was I the *only one* who cared? Did anyone even *think about it*? Any psychoanalysts out there?! Help!

Shit, no help. Thanks a lot everyone (lol). Meanwhile, back at my delirium...

But my culminations (*culminations?*) felt awesome. BUT *hers* were infinitely more! At least that's what it appeared. Was it programmed and literally unachievable? Was there any truth to male 'shock waves' (whatever that was but sure sounding good) or just another perceived, pathetic, ego-driven wish and fantasy.

Keep the men-folk believing they have 'it' and they will fall in line and follow in step. Girls: "You were great honey!" Guys: "Thanks babe, hope it felt good to you, too." Of course it did! We were being duped, I was seriously beginning to believe. Not viciously at all. Meaning no offense. Simply, matter-of-factly. You made the team! Of course, just second string. Forever.

On the flip side, I enjoyed playing with myself (doesn't everyone? Come'on, admit it!) – and sometimes better than the good slow intimate fuck. Maybe there's something there I'm also missing. *When* does Zach have these 'shock waves?' I had to know. I concluded: this ain't fragile male ego (of which we will discuss later). This is male *hunting and gathering*. Better yet, pirating! To the ships men!

Episode 3 ~

So, as you will see, I set out on my iniquitous journey to prove to myself, and to her, that we had 'it' too. Not *believing* we had 'it' but really *having* 'it.' Far beyond anything we could have dreamed of or been taught through the years of no one really caring. Our first touch of a soft breast, the slipping of the hand down her jeans, the surprise wetness and warmth. Her light moaning. Finally, full board sex and years of congratulating each other that we men had 'it' never really knowing what 'it' was. How can that be claimed 'fragile male ego' when we don't *even know* anything more? In my current state, I was fully convinced it was all a setup to keep us men in our place. And then just tag it as 'fragile male ego' and close the book. Thanks guys for having the dick! And here's how you play with yourself. Oh, sorry babe, we also lost paradise. Oh, well…

Now, my searching, calculating, evil mind was planning, scheming. On to our mission! Get together with Zach somehow without looking weird or stupid. "Hey, Zach! How's your 'shock waves' these days?!" Yeah, that'll work. Well, Fred said get him drunk. OK, that's the simple plan. Back to the bars! Alcohol is going to save our souls! I'll bring the rum maties!

Took some time to get Fred on board as I knew he felt somehow it would come out to Zach that he let me in on it all and would appear a setup. Of course, it *was a setup*. Just set it up! Fred finally agreed because he knew very well I was never letting it go. He offered me Zach's number and do it myself but I tossed that out as I didn't know him that well, really didn't want to know him that well (part jealousy, part disgust), and needed a buffer zone. A la Fred.

So, it was set. This Sunday. After their round of golf, Fred was having friends back to his place. I and Melissa were invited as usual though at first I thought just me, Fred, and Zach at a bar but that finally seemed too weird being it would have been the first time we ever did that together, just us three. Fred saved the day with his invite. Plus it kept him safe. Now, how do I get Zach alone and drill the shit out of him without appearing the Spanish Inquisition or *worse*, appearing to come on to him sexually.

I told myself to stop over-thinking and get on with it. I thought a game of Truth or Dare but then all would know my intent. And it would be really fucked up if it was all a joke Fred was playing on me — which sadly, he has done before and really well. Just somehow, I didn't think this time. I was really getting to myself. Shit. It was really only sex. Is it that important?

"Yes! It's that important!" I howled at myself in my bathroom mirror. That's the WHOLE POINT! We DON'T make it important!

Captain! I believe a storm is fast approaching! We're heading right for it!

Episode 4 ~

Sunday finally arrived. I was still majorly overthinking everything and couldn't stop. I sincerely apologize to you all for being completely possessed by my insane obsession, but Melissa's comment really struck home to me. Fred's note about Zach having all the male-climatic answers we ever wanting struck home with me. Feeling inadequate up against a woman's struck home with me. And why didn't us men seem to *even care* struck home with me. Is sports' excitement all we get? That's great but is there more?

In the end, are we being drugged by our very accepted and craved activities that we have become completely utilitarian, disinterested in other facets of life. No! I cannot accept that. We at least need *some* answers and if in the end, we *are* just utilitarian, then back to sports, cars, tools, guns, and whatever else any one of us uses to keep our male-ness happy. Yeah, I apologize to you guys out there. Just getting antsy. I blame Melissa (lol).

"I was meaning to ask you," started Melissa with a tone I knew so very well when she feels something is not right and is looking to prepare herself for whatever it may or may not be.

"Yeah," I replied in my best calm, nonchalant voice. Could she also read my mind?

"Are you still upset about my comment?" She glanced up quickly from the bed and then back down again while she was slipping on her thong undies.

'Whew!' I thought. I was sure it was going to be about Fred's unexpected, short-noticed gathering.

"Naw! It was nothing."

My mind said: "YEAH! You bashed me in the balls with it!"

"Oh, okay, just checking because you've been really weird since then."

Again, the glance up and down.

"Men and women are obviously different," I shot out a little too quickly.

"Of course, we are!" she exclaimed as she stood up just in her red thong which I saw first before hearing her comment. "We're better at sex!" she stated matter-of-factly but with conviction, and a big smile, as she patronizingly patted me on my shoulder twice, walking past me into the bathroom. Don't you find that shit annoying? Anyway, I couldn't tell if she was just playing. And I'm actually really good at poker. Poke-her? OK, forget that.

I stood there motionless feeling the fool I was feeling, and speechless, until I blurted out, "well, maybe not!"

"What did you say?" she asked with brush in her hair as she peeked out the bathroom.

"Nothing," I almost whimpered, still feeling the fool. I backpedaled fast because I knew I didn't have enough or the right ammunition to support my claim. Corporate management taught me that at least.

She shrugged and disappeared back into the bathroom. I decided to hold my tongue until after I had my pow-wow with Sir Zach, the apparent 'knight in shining armor of the legendary 'shock wave' kingdom.' I continued getting dressed in silence.

She popped out of the bathroom, hair flowing and gleaming, tight breasts pouting, toned thighs strutting, passing by me as the red thong disappeared between her strong, shifting cheeks.

As she disappeared into her walk-in closet all I heard was, "guess you'll have to prove it!"

Cocky bitch! She had heard me! Game on!

Episode 5 ~

It was a brilliant sunny afternoon. Melissa's golden long hair swayed and glimmered from her highlights as she started walking from the car to Fred's, what I would call, really big house. This was *her* style and *her* world. Being in fashion and designing her own line went perfectly well with her air of sophistication without any snobby-ness. It's what I loved about her, and she loved my acceptance of her unconditionally (except possibly recently) and gave me more attention than I actually needed (albeit her comment). Everybody we knew and even folks we just met always complimented our relationship as carefree yet committed.

We could joke about anything without ever hurting feelings – though the recent conversation had unlikely, unforeseen tension in it. In the completely uncharacteristic quiet ride over, I sense I may have crossed some boundaries not ventured before in her feelings and thoughts. Almost as if I was challenging her to defend herself about something she never thought before to defend. Uncharted territory for sure, I mused. And maybe also her newfound hidden struggling with trying to understand where I was coming from and possibly more importantly, where I was going. To be honest, I didn't even know.

But I did know that when I was pissed or upset with her, I turned cold and my iciness she knew too well and reacted in the same way – cold but with growing anger until something broke the ice and it all melted away. For now, icicles had definitely formed.

We followed the noise of talking and laughing around the side of their stately home, following the carefully gardened stone pathway, and entered the spacious grounds which amazingly had tents, bars, bartenders, food stations, and music all set up for a quick get together. Fred could just snap his fingers and ta da! Instant elegant outdoor party!

I noticed Zach immediately with his always two female companions. Somehow, he seemed more dressed for a party than for playing golf where they had come from. I wondered if the girls were part of the golf outing, or were here on their own, or had waited in his car, or had descended from heaven upon his arrival.

Fred slapped me on the back out of nowhere.

"Yo buddy! You made it!" he exclaimed as he hugged me from the side with one arm. I knew he fully knew I was going to make it since the majority of this gathering was him helping me out. At the same time, I knew Fred never needed a reason to throw a quick yet awesome event. And I also think he has had eyes for Melissa for a long time even being married for 10 years. I didn't mind the eyes as long as they remained eyes. Jealous male fragile ego? Or Arthur defending Guinevere?

"Yes, I did!" I intentionally over did it.

He whispered in my ear, "he's over there" as if some kind of clandestine sting we were about to commit.

I whispered back, "I know" in my best secret-agent-voice.

There always was an underlying fun between us since we met and became great friends, joining the same company at the same time. He advanced faster in his product department than I in my IT department but both were still pretty much equals. Our respect for each other both professionally and socially kept us closeknit. And honestly, I always liked his eyes for Melissa knowing she was mine (as far as I could tell, I joked to myself). I pushed out the sudden thought of spouse-swapping.

"Darian! Mel!" I knew the voice of Katie, Fred's beautiful wife. If anyone was the life of any party, it was Katie. Some thought she was overbearing. I thought she was passionate. The thought of swapping or as some say 'sharing' came back in my mind, which I had previously toyed with, and which sometimes seemed like the natural course to take being such great couple-friends. Yet, it never materialized. The thought of a foursome rose and I quickly shut that one out, not wanting to think of the same-sex part, and not sure why. I surely wasn't homophobic. Maybe just not ready. OK stop.

"Katie!" Melissa belted out.

"Hey, Katie," I replied with just enough enthusiasm.

"Glad you could come in such short notice! You know Frederick. Any reason to throw a party…"

As she continued, I stopped listening as I eyed her short sundress and her firm, feline legs. I glanced at Melissa's sundress and the same admiration. The sharing thought came back pretty quickly. I held off on the foursome. In the meantime, back at the…

"You're looking awesome today," I sincerely complimented her. "You and Melissa could be sisters!" I was being honest at the same time feeling Melissa's gaze burning holes through my skull. She was definitely the jealous type even with the sophistication. I hugged Melissa from my side hoping to cancel the laser beams.

"Well, mingle! Get a drink! Let's catch up in a bit!"

"Thanks Katie," Melissa replied in a sweet tone. She always was even-keel even when maybe not.

Katie bounced away with Fred. I motioned to the bar and we proceeded.

"You know I love you," I whispered in her ear and kissed her cheek.

"I know you do and I love me, too," she whispered back with a sweet touch of venom.

Could a simple discussion of who had better ones cause such a passive-aggressive attitude?

"Then we're in agreement!" I said a little too enthusiastic I thought. She hugged me closer as we walked and I know it was her way of letting things go…for now.

I saw Fred now with Zach and knew he was prepping a way for us to meet. I suddenly wished Melissa wasn't there. At least for the next hour maybe.

Episode 6 ~

As we strolled, I noticed there were about twenty or so people there, all dressed very summer-y. Khaki shorts, sundresses, miniskirts, blazers, and all as one might think of on a warm summer sunny day at an outside party at Fred and Katie's home. Idyllic to say the least.

The corner of my eye kept watch on Fred as Melissa and I ordered our drinks. After tipping, I looked up and they were coming over, with the girls.

'OK, this is it,' I thought. How was this going to happen? I suddenly felt like a panicking George Costanza! I just wanted information from a male about his orgasms. I almost choked holding back my laughter while taking a sip. Melissa glanced at me hearing my choke and I could tell she was making some connection about them coming over to us. Nice job Darian!

"Boy, Zach really does it up, don't you think?" I asked, looking to cool down what I wasn't sure needed cooling down. Just was hoping it did.

"Yeah, he does," Melissa added coolly. I decided to ignore that and focus on the matter coming straight at me, like a freight train.

"Hey guys!" Fred announced boisterously as usual.

"Hey."

"Hey."

"Wanted to introduce some folks you haven't met formally before. This here is Zach my old-time golf buddy. He's a very successful retired Realtor if you never need one. And these two gorgeous ladies are Sam and Maxie!" Fred sounded like a game show host. "And these are my longtime friends Darian and Melissa."

"Hey guys!" Zach exclaimed hold out his hand to me first. Then, holding Melissa's hand, he gently brought it to his lips and added a very soft kiss before gently returning it. I knew that would endear her and saw the same as she lightly curtsied never taking her eyes off his. It struck me that this was somehow revenge or real or both. The image of 'Salty Deke *The Sex-Demon'* returned.

Zach lightly hugged his sexy girls on both sides of him and they demurely glanced at him, and then effortlessly turned their heads back to us, in all I can say was a bit witchy and amazingly sexy at the same time. Sam was a light complexion angel and Maxie was a dark complexion angel both complementing each other's astounding beauty. I had to admit, they just may be the reasons for 'shock waves!' How was I to find two like them? Was that the plan or even maybe them? Mmmmm crossed my mind forgetting Melissa until Fred broke my dreamy fantasy.

"So! Who wants to talk about orgasms!"

What!? Whoa!! My head went reeling as I knew my mouth dropped wide open as was Melissa's. She recovered faster than I did, probably thinking it was a Fred-joke as usual to break the ice. As for me?! My ice was broken, shattered, melted, dissolved, as was my brain. How could he blow my cover in front of everyone!

Melissa shot me a double laser death-glance that simply said: "this is your doing!" Then suddenly, Melissa broke out hysterically and convincingly laughing and exploded with: "I'm IN!"

I turned and looked at her, knowing the look was somewhere between incredulous and shocked. Was she in on this somehow?

She continued after completely composing herself, and looking at all the smiling faces (except mine), she spouted, "Sure! Let's! Who's going to start?!" Right at that moment Katie appeared. I didn't even see her approach, knowing even more so the potential nightmare that was now about to unfold. And all with Fred stating that out loud, all for my sake mind you, which I sorely didn't want out! I only had wanted a fucking side conversation with Zach and now...

I took a deep breath and smiled, knowing no one knew it was my topic. Yet. I hoped.

"What's going on?" Katie asked honestly not knowing — or was also playing the game.

Silence. We all looked at each other and after a forever moment, Fred, obviously a bit drunk, pointed to the Gazebo and started walking over to it. We all looking like disciples followed. I heard Sam and Maxie whisper something to Zach but couldn't make it out.

We sat in the circle of the Gazebo, drinks in hand, and waited. Zach looked so completely at ease that the image of our mischievously confident *Sex-Demon* once again appeared in my mind's eye. It was consuming. His look. The look of complete satisfaction that everything was going according to his cunning, 'evil' plan.

Fred, as usual, broke the low-level tension.

"So! Let's begin folks! Who has better orgasms!"

My mind screamed 'What THE fuck, Fred! Can you friggin' tone it down!' I felt everyone could see through me.

But there was only silence.

I shifted in my seat trying to not be noticed.

"I think we do!" declared Katie.

"*We* do?" asked Fred. "You mean me and you or ladies?"

"Us girls, of course!" she clarified. I still wasn't sure she was being serious.

But I did notice the slow grin creeping on Zach's serene face and he somehow suddenly appeared contentedly excited to let this fray unfold without a word.

"Well, how do you know?" came out of my mouth before I could stop it.

"Silly question!" Katie replied. "We are girls! The clitoris says it all!"

I knew Katie wasn't the brightest star in the sky and her reply made me chuckle, which I knew Melissa heard by another quick laser beam glance, which was beginning to get annoying to me.

"I agree with Katie," Melissa said matter-of-factly. No glance this time.

"OK, OK, my turn," Fred chimed in. "I think it's different."

"Of course, it's different," Katie responded immediately. "Ours are so much better!"

"How do you know?" I finally asked firmly, now being fully in the game, and still well aware Zach and his girls were just silently smiling.

"Because! We're girls!" Katie reiterated.

Again! Hey, why is the sky blue? Because, it's blue. But *why* is the sky blue. Because, *it's blue*!

"Let me explain," Melissa began with a partial grin of self-assurance. I couldn't wait, but I actually could have waited…forever. "It's a scientific fact that there are more nerve endings in the clitoris than in the whole of the penis. And forget the balls."

"Depends on the size of the penis!" Fred interrupted laughing.

"Right," she replied with a 'just shut up for just one moment Fred' tone. He completely missed it looking at Zach's calm face, still chuckling at himself, looking like a little boy. "It's a fact, and therefore it's impossible for a guy to have more pleasure, aka orgasm, than a girl." She sat smugly. "Not our fault," she finally added with a tone of exoneration yet subtly saying "too fucking bad!"

"What about women who are ice cold, frozen, what's the term?" I added and the fucking death-glance again.

"You mean 'frigid'" Melissa chimed back, with a tone of 'you idiot.'

"Yeah, yeah that," I said glad for a small win. Or at least I thought I won.

"They're not part of this discussion," Katie replied, playing the judge somehow.

"Why not?" Fred asked with more serious tone.

"Because they sway the balance," Katie declared again with her 'I'm the judge and that's it!'

"OK, take them out of the equation, how can you all be so sure women have more fun?" I challenged once again leaning forward, feeling exasperated on a topic I didn't want to discuss in a group. I just wanted to beat the shit out of Fred. And I was so going to pay for this later. Waiting for their next answer, I was looking back and forth from Katie to Melissa.

"Because they're right," said Zach.

Episode 7 ~

Silence, and then...

"SEE! Even a man can see the truth!" exclaimed Katie victoriously, though I still felt I heard playfulness in her tone. Was she being serious or just having fun?

Melissa folded her arms smugly and apparently refused to look at me, not even with the laser-death-glance. And I knew she did it on purpose - not looking. I knew her too well that it was also her victory pose.

Fred, also seemingly playful too, stared at Zach incredulously (which I couldn't tell was real) and with what I saw as 'how can you betray us in the middle of battle!' I had the same feeling.

"Why would you say that?" I asked trying to avoid defeat in my voice.

And are we seriously talking out loud about people *cumming*? I didn't want to be in this conversation and at the same time losing poorly! And topped off with Zach's betrayal?

"Yeah, why!" came from Fred right after, which again seemed overly played.

"Because he's a smart man and knows his place," Katie said as if a teacher actually putting someone in their place. I caught her wink at him.

What the frig was going on?! Why all the feelings of something behind the scenes was going on. Was it my paranoia, my insecurity, my whatever?! And why was I questioning the validity of this whole insane conversation. Because maybe... it was friggin' insanity to talk about? OK, back at the ranch...

Both Fred and I glared at her and I knew this conversation was beginning to definitely go awry — at least for me. I turned back to Zach and for just a brief but decipherable moment, saw a knowing stare at Katie then it was gone.

Serene face again.

"Well, if we are speaking of the vast majority of the male population here on this Earth, the ladies are absolutely correct." Zach's response was so matter-of-factly given, I couldn't find a rebuttal...yet.

"See!" from Katie.

"See!" from Melissa, who from the side I could see her face change with the realization and understanding of the words 'vast majority.' "Wait, what do you mean by 'vast majority?'" She folded her arms, waiting.

Zach smiled knowing it hit home, at least to Melissa.

"Vast majority," he reiterated. I looked at Sam and Maxie. Both were ever so lightly nodding their heads with small smiles. It dawned on me that they were in agreement with Zach.

"So, wait, let me get this right, you believe there are some men out there, some males on this here Earth, who actually have greater orgasms than women?" Melissa's tone was both slightly shocked, challenging, cocky, and aggressive. That's my girl! Go get 'em!

"Yep, absolutely."

"And where are these men?" Katie added folding her arms.

"Right here."

"Where?" Katie added again, playfully looking around. But I knew where.

Zach crossed his arms like them and replied with a very confident smile.

"Me."

Episode 8 ~

"Him." Sam and Maxie both said nonchalantly in unison, each with one palm up pointing at Zach.

An uncomfortable pause led to a snicker from Katie and then a short burst of laughter slipped out. Zach sat stoic with a calm glare at her, then at Melissa.

"Fred, he's joking right?" Again, something bothered me about Katie's tone.

Fred looked at her with the look of 'why are you asking *me?*'

"He's not joking at all. It's amazing!" Maxie said. Sam nodded in agreement.

"What, do you have some superpower?" Katie pressed obviously not accepting this at all. But again, I felt she was playing a role in it all. I couldn't shake it.

"Nope. Just technique and learning how it all works."

"I'd like to see that!" Melissa uncharacteristically retorted and we all could see she immediately regretted it.

"Actually, we both agree. It's equal to if not better than ours." Sam chimed in with Maxie nodding.

I looked steadily at Fred waiting for that 'Fred-moment' when he cracks up laughing and enjoys getting over on us all with his huge fabricated lie and the fun of bringing in special characters, especially with such a topic. It would be so Fred-elaborate.

And I also wondered how they were able, the three of them, to compare and gauge the *level* of pleasure, and maybe even duration of pleasure. My mind, outside of the 'getting a hold of what was going on,' and with their unwavering almost annoying confidence, started an immediate wondering of 'could this all be true' and was this the 'shock wave' thing Fred had related?

Guys! This could be the answer to the universe! Well, maybe…(lol) Anyway, I was definitely intrigued at this point since it was now all on the table about us guys and absolutely wanted it to go further. I noticed Melissa's sudden silence until…

"OK, OK, let's say for sake of argument," she began in an analytical tone with a tinge of 'you're full of shit' added in, "that you have some guy superpower and these ladies are right, too. Can you, say, show little Darian here how to achieve such *things* you confidently claim?" She sounded like a lawyer in a trial. My trial!

And… little?! What the fuck! She did the same palm up gesture towards me as they had towards Zach, obviously mocking it all. I was beyond surprised and getting a bit (a lot) angry with her for first: pointing me out in the midst of all this, and second: for insinuating that I was inadequate somehow…or that's how I took it in that moment, and third: professing that I was 'little' – which my dear friends, I am not! (Just so you know for future reference.) If she then mentions she 'hadn't noticed,' I was walking out and cutting my own throat with the nearest dull butter knife. I wanted it messy.

"Sure can, if Darian wishes."

"Huh!" was all that came out of Melissa's huffing mouth. It was pure sincere disbelief, not a question. Her fangs and claws were out.

"No one said I needed anything," I heard myself say and then regretted it. On the damn defensive and Melissa knew it, planned it. Again, *my* girl, though I was seriously contemplating… Then my thought was cut off.

"Actually, less is more when it comes to this, pardon the pun," Maxie grinned. Her beautiful dark face beamed.

"What does that even mean??" Melissa asked a bit riled, but then pretty much recovering back to her poise. Amazing skill, I thought.

Maxie glanced at Zach for what appeared to be a 'go ahead' permission. He grinned and slightly nodded.

"What I mean is 'The Strokeless Orgasm,'" she noted with a confident tone.

"Um, the what?" Melissa muttered, starting to lose her poise again. I think I made my best Robert Dinero smug face at that (wishing I had a mirror). I liked it. A lot. It was getting to be fun. Sorry, Melissa.

"And the 'Cumless Cum,'" Sam added in.

"See, less is more!" Maxie reiterated with a big smile.

Silence until...

Episode 9 ~

"OK, this is getting deep," Fred finally blurted, appearing to see Melissa's distress and knew it was time to diffuse and save her. I could finally tell, this was not a Fred-joke. They were serious. And all because I asked Fred to have a *private conversation*, mind everyone again, with Zach about damned 'shock waves!'

Fred had obviously lost some control at the moment and I think (still wasn't sure) this was all new to him, too, outside of *hearing* about 'shock waves' before, which I don't think now he knows what they are either. Or he was an excellent actor – which constantly kept crossing my mind. Now we're at 'The Strokeless Orgasm' and the 'Cumless Cum' *on top* of 'shock waves'... seriously? I acted like 'what the fuck is going on!' though I felt like 'this is so cool!'

After the short jolt of hearing this, I went into further intrigue-mode. Inspector *Darian* at your service! The comedy of it all was really becoming enjoyable but, if this stuff was all true, and this guy actually has found some 'fountain of male pleasure' unknown since before the *Garden*, this could be the new sexual revolution. Yeah Guys! Our revolution! Mount your tanks! I was seeing book titles, book signings, a movie...even though I wasn't a writer. May have to take writing up I joked inside – or at least be one of the actors. OK, back to reality...

"Are you a sex therapist?" Melissa asked, this time in a more serious tone. I knew her well enough that inside she was struggling to comprehend without asking too many questions for fear of the answers.

"Uh, no. I am not. I am retired."

"From what?" I asked, also seriously. "Is this part of Real Estate?" I sarcastically followed up with, not meaning to sound that way. The conversation seemed to be turning towards general sex therapy talk, I hoped, and also hoped not.

"Pornography, of course."

"Seriously?" I asked, somehow hoping it was true.

"He's fucking with you!" Fred exclaimed.

"Yeah, I am fucking with you, but only on my past career," Zach said with a little boyish chuckle. "Sorry, it was too easy with the current looks on all your faces."

"So?" Melissa asked with an annoyance tone obviously not happy with Zach's last humorous remark.

"Stockbroker. Then Realtor."

I saw Fred nodding and figure it was true.

"Trainer now."

"Trainer?" Melissa asked, looking bewildered.

"Yes, trainer. I think I'm going to get a new drink. Be right back."

With that, he left us. Fred said he needed to look in on the catering and pulled me with him.

"What the fuck is going on Fred?" I whispered firmly. "All I wanted was to have a brief conversation with him and *solely* to see if there was more I may be interested in about this 'shock wave' thing. That was all! Now Melissa's obviously pissed at me probably thinking I or should I say we set this whole thing up because of her and my private discussion which I'm sure now she thinks we discussed." I heard my distinctive uncontrolled rambling.

"We did my friend."

"Yeah, but she doesn't know that. And it's all your fault. You are the one who had brought up the whole 'shock wave' thing at the bar and got me wondering. But not this fiasco! She's going to crucify me for days."

"It's not that bad. It yeah, got out of control I'll admit —"

"Out of control?! Seriously?" I heard and felt the exasperation in my voice.

31

"A bit," he smiled calmly at me, "but you have to admit, you are intrigued. I saw it in your face with your always poor poker-face." He knew me too well. "Look, I honestly asked Zach to come so you two could have a chat like we planned. But when we all grouped together, I couldn't help myself! It just seemed less obvious to open it up jokingly to everyone rather than you huddling in a corner with him. I'm sure Mel would have questioned that. Now you are just another victim of my insanity."

Somehow his explaining was making sense to me. He had protected me from deeper questions from Melissa, albeit I would have probably taken a slightly different route than his. All for better equipment functioning. Well, I wanted to know more. Fuck it.

If there's more out there for us guys, or even just for me, we have a right to know! And defend our manhood! All for one! And one for... oh, forget it (lol).

I just wanted to know. And this guy, with all his debonair and sleekness, was sure-as-shit confident about it. And were there really that many more nerve endings in a clit? If so, we definitely needed something to level the playing field. Can we *add* more nerve endings?

And I just don't know if most guys gave a shit at all anyway (please put your comments below). Wham, bam, and all that shit. But guys, what if, just if, we *could* really peak so high that it *would* blow our minds and hook us in. Or maybe, again, we've been so desensitized from birth and peers and parents and ads and media, over so many years that we lost touch with our own real masculinity and what we can actually *do* and *feel*.

I told myself I was talking like a pseudo-psychoanalyst, but I didn't care. At least I was hooked now and somehow I knew I was pushing forward no matter what. My curiosity was peaked. I had to find a way. You're welcome to come along. And come with me on the ride home because I fucking *dreaded the ride home*.

"OK Fred, I'll buy your reasoning though pretty fucking poor." We reached the house and he led me to his huge oaken study. I looked him straight in the eyes and asked, "let me ask you, after all you just heard, do you believe him?"

Awkward pause.

A look of confidence grew on his face. "Yeah, I do believe him."

"And you knew nothing about this whole strokeless thing ahead of time or even before?" I felt I should put a blaring light right up to his face with my interrogation.

"Dude, no, I wouldn't do that. Maybe," he added with a grin, knowing he was leaving me hanging. "Plus, you know me, I would have told you that shit. And I'm gonna get a load of shit from Katie you know. So, why would I not have told you before?"

I couldn't tell if he was being brutally honest or conning me. He was that good.

"OK, then. Do we further the conversation or look to bag it and change it."

I heard the floor creak.

"Hey, guys. Can I join you?"

It was Zach.

Episode 10 ~

He had a look of 'hoping I'm not interrupting but I'm coming in anyway,' but not in a bad way.

"Hey Zach, come on in," Fred offered but I could tell he wasn't finished with me and didn't want an interruption. "Helluva back and forth out there, don't you say?"

I was watching Zach as he approached and what his response was going to be. No matter what, he always appeared very poised, confident, and at ease.

"I think it's going well. We should never be inhibited in discussing anything. Open dialogue and comparing ideas and thoughts is very healthy, even if at times it may be embarrassing for some or even intrusive." He sounded more like a psychoanalyst now but I happened to agree.

"We were just discussing to, kind of, shut it down, I mean the whole conversation as I, we, think it's getting under the girls' skins…I, I mean we, mean our girls." I tried to sound even keeled but felt it sounded like it was getting under *my* skin.

"No problem. We can easily change the subject. I just thought Fred here wanted me to discuss these things, especially for your sake because you were interested. That's what Fred had told me. I just didn't think it was going to be a group session." Zach appeared to be very honest and even concerned. He continued. "It's just if the conversation opens up, I'm not going to back down unless told to. I guess this is the telling me to back down part. And I had thought that you wanted to discuss this, and my impression was, more like one-on-one." Zach pointed to me.

"It's all my fault," chimed in Fred. "I got carried away and rather than try to find alone time for you two among everyone, even though that was my initial goal, I figured just throw it out there for all and see where it went."

"It's all fine," I added. "It was kind of fun." I smiled knowing it was fun for me but not so sure about Melissa and Katie, who I think felt they had to go on the defensive. Why is sex-talk always so emotional, especially between males and females, I wondered.

"Look guys, I meant *everything* I said and it's all true — at least for me. I think for now I agree to shut it down and change topics. But Darian, honestly, this is what I do now. I train guys to find the highest excitement they *never knew* they can get. And even more things than that."

I tried not to stare at Zach as I realized now his comment before on being a trainer meant this! I thought it was something like in a gym or golf or whatever — but not …a what would you call it… a "male-increase-your-orgasmic-pleasure" seminar? Seriously?

"And us," he was pointing at me again, "right now, doing a private pow-wow would not be beneficial." I nodded. "So, here, here's my card and my business. Think it over and give me a call if wish to discuss further. I will just say that it's an innovative and over-the-top type of training that not many guys will go through due to how we still view ourselves. And it's affordable and by invitation only and by *referral only*. Since Fred referred you, I'm inviting you…if you are openminded enough and willing to have a discussion first and then the evaluation seminar. Nothing to lose except once involved, you promise to give it your all."

I was agreeing inside and was also wondering what was 'my all.'

And I was watching him closely, waiting for the laughter of the joke being played but he was serious. I glanced at Fred who was just looking at me, waiting for my answer. Is this fucking for real? And what the hell happens that most guys wouldn't go through it? And how do I know it's really worth it? What's going to happen? How much does it cost? What's an 'evaluation seminar?' Do I get naked? Is there a money-back guarantee if I can't *explode* wildly more than ever before? Does it involve another guy? Or those two girls? Is it legal? Where's the proof? The questions flooded my brain.

Zach chuckled. "I know all your questions you're having right now. It's normal for a newcomer, pardon the pun. Take my card. Call me if you wish. Keep it confidential. I'm going back to my ladies and this beautiful day. Thanks so much again Fred for inviting us. Golf was fun, too." He was obviously being funny about the golf. I took the card without even looking at it, shoved it in my pocket. He calmly walked out.

"We need to talk buddy," I pressed to Fred, "but not now. We gotta get back. I need a drink."

"So do I!"

Episode 11 ~

We both did a bourbon shot and got our drinks. As we walked back, I looked at the card and stopped in my steps. Fred walked right past me until he noticed I wasn't next to him. His gaze was forward, then back to me. I showed him the card.

"What the fuck?!" was all he could say. There was a lot of 'what the fucks' going on today I thought. He was now looking forward again.

"Yeah, this is surreal."

"Weird I'd say. Put that away. Let's go."

We finally got to the gazebo and now I saw what Fred was gazing at. Zach, Sam, and Maxie had stood up and appeared to be taking their leave. And they were.

"Ladies," Zach said in a very James Bond gentlemanly voice, "wonderful to have met you and hope our conversation wasn't a bit too risqué. Sorry, have to leave but got a call inside about something I need to address right away. Thanks again for all your hospitality Katie …and Fred," he said as he noticed us now back.

"It was our pleasure. Sorry to see you leave. Let me get you all some food to go," Katie offered. It may have been their leaving that caused her to regain all her original poise. "Yes, sorry you gotta leave buddy," Fred added. Wasn't sure he was happy or sad but I knew it would definitely end the conversation – at least with them not here. I hoped.

"Thanks so much!" Sam and Maxie said almost in unison. It was getting a little creepy I thought but if they are part of some of this 'training' well…

"Take care and no thanks about the food. We'll catch something later. Bye, for now."

I noticed the ever so slight glance at me and then it was gone. And then they were gone.

I felt the card in my pocket and decided that's where it was going to stay, for now.

"Well, they are quite a trio don't you think!" Katie was obviously back to her bubbly self.

"Strange people. Like, too happy. And what is all this crap about *your* damn fucking orgasms? Who the fuck cares. Fred, you started it! Did you on purpose?" Melissa shot me a glance and back to Fred. "Did you know about 'them' and this stuff?"

"Me? No, I mean I knew Zach was retired and we met through golf buddies and been friendly, like having drinks with the golf guys and all."

He sounded stuttering, looking for the right words.

"Come on, Fred! You are a lousy liar!" Katie blurted, cocking her head. I for one knew he was an excellent liar. And actor, too. "Why then would you EVER say: 'who wants to talk about orgasms!'" she pressed. Again, her playful smile made me feel like a preordained act.

"OK, OK, I knew somewhat..." He paused. He was obviously gathering his words to get out of this interrogation by his wife, who was definitely enjoying it, "...that he was involved in I think experimental sex therapy ...that... was somewhat interesting and had come out a bit, back at our last post-golf bar hop with the guys." I saw clearly he was uncharacteristically stumbling but couldn't tell if it was on purpose.

"So, today, I had asked him how his 'business' was going – not really knowing much about it – and he mentioned nonchalantly that the *pleasure* business was doing very well. Well! That took me aback and thought he was kidding. So, sorry, I blurted it out to everyone thinking it would be a fun topic..." He trailed off.

"Fun. Right," Melissa said in an almost whisper. "They're insane and there's no way it can be better than ours. But whatever."

Again, we're back to who's better, I thought. Guess it wasn't going away.

"Well, I'm sorry for bringing it up and can we drop it. I'm hungry. Anybody else?" Fred motioned to the food stations.

"Fine! Let's eat. And no more sex talk." Katie rose stiffly, paused, and walked past him. Did I see a wink?

Fred gave us a look of 'whew, that's over' and quickly followed her.

"Hope you're happy now," Melissa looked at me with revived, reloaded dagger-eyes.

"Me? I didn't do anything."

"Oh yeah sure. You really, I mean *really* want me to believe you had *nothing* to do with this Zach being here and this whole conversation? You're the one with the dick issue. Always thinking with it. And you act just like a girl with all this sex talk." She also stood stiffly, didn't pause, and walked past me.

That simply pissed me off. I was obviously no way going to admit I had wanted to talk with Zach based on Fred's recommendation and helping hand, and I was also no way going to accept I have a problem. And I'm not acting like a girl! Why can't a guy simply want to know more? Why is that wrong? I just want to know more. What is this barrier I keep feeling and experiencing? I just want to know what more there may be (don't you?) and if that's thinking with our dicks, then so be it. The hunt is on. Me and my dick are going to find out, together. And of course, you, too. The curiosity now is too much.

I *have* to know! (…getting seriously obsessed …may even be *possessed* by my own personal, mischievously curious, rising *demon!*)

I felt the card in my pocket and walked slowly to the food.

Episode 12 ~

Cold wasn't the word. Frigid wasn't even close. Eternal ice age was getting there. The desolate emptiness and Absolute Zero coldness of the vast space between galaxies was pretty much the ride home. Nothing had worked out except a card in my pocket and a new Ice Age.

Melissa just stared out her side or down at her phone, never looking over at me. I, in turn, was furious of how everything turned out and now this. All I had wanted was to satisfy my curiosity and Fred had just been Fred – though I should have been more prepared to what and how he would proceed. I knew he was just thinking about me, and probably thinking I was insanely obsessed about something I should just let go. But I can't let it go, I am fucking obsessed, and guess what, we're all in this together!

Or maybe he was like all of us – not willing to explore, to see what's under the covers, try it differently (whatever that means), and stop being so led down the path of same o' same o' – and not just 'accept this was our fate.' Eve was the star of the *Garden of Eden* and we just friggin' fell in line and held out our hand for that damn apple, pear, peach, whatever… a banana (lol). I would have preferred an olive and a martini. 'Yup, honey, sure anything you say. I'll take a *sip* for you!' I had nothing against Eve. I had it against *myself* for being such an awkward weakling.

We arrived home, walked in in silence, and I went out back to have a cigar and a cordial. Wasn't tired. Needed quiet space. We both did. This wasn't unusual when we fought or one was pissed at the other. Just this time, Melissa seemed removed more than usual. And I wasn't in the mood to care enough to try to smooth things out. Not right now.

Part of me felt it was silly. Just forget it and let us travel through the vast unknowns of our pathetic crotches. Simple. Right? Not! Well, we're going to see this shit through to the finish…whatever that is!

'So, Battle speed, men!'

I had Zach's card in my hand, turning it over and over as if some magical piece of knowledge or a hot genie girl would appear. Should I rub it? Nothing happened except my final conviction that to end all of this wondering, I was going to contact him. Just to put it to bed (and absolutely no pun intended). I found some laughter inside. Part of me wanted to forget the whole thing, and the huge rest of me couldn't. I wasn't recognizing the person, the guy, I was starting to become. Or was it more the guy I may have been hiding from and who was always there. What the fuck.

And how the hell was he able to claim such incredible abilities – as a man, as a regular guy? Dudes, what are *we* missing? I couldn't stop thinking of it. What was it like? Do we pass out? Levitate? Wasn't it our right to know? What did *he* know that millions of guys didn't? But it was his calm demeanor, his absolute air of supreme confidence, and in no way unsettling his fellow female friends in any such way, as they held their own confidence. That gave me hope, hope that I too could be super-cock-man. OK, getting weird. Well, maybe not…

Wait! Did this require a super huge cock? Did they find a way for guys to actually increase their equipment if they wanted to? Like an abnormally super gigantic colossal 22 inch long 6 inch girth fat monstrosity? Come on down! Monster Cocks for all! Take this pill and watch it grow! I literally laughed at my growing insanity and imagination (and where did I get those measurements?). Sorry folks. Getting back from my wonderful fantasy imagery…

So, to top it all off, I had stumbled and stuttered idiotically the whole time. What an incompetent idiot. But was this a scam? Just a stupid scam to cash in on? Couldn't be, I thought. Fred was Fred but he was acutely aware of everything and extremely savvy with people and seemingly knew Zach well. I forced the thought of a scam out.

Maybe it wasn't a pill. Maybe it was all drug-induced. LSD, heroin, cocaine, meth…all the typical ones crossed my mind. Or maybe it was some unknown hallucinogen drug Zach was using which simulated amazing, until now unknown orgasms that were merely the effect on the brain and not of the cock (and balls, sorry keep forgetting those). And then we get hooked on the drug and he ended up just being a dealer. A scam after all.

I vowed if I did this that to make sure I didn't drink or eat anything and would be constantly watchful. The fear of drugs still didn't push me away. I was beyond just curiosity now. I was on an adventure. A cryptic secret journey into the unknown depths of depraved pleasure that I *had* to experience or face that I may never enjoy sex again. Zach was now my *White Whale!*

I finally took a good look at the card for the first time. I realized it was actually a folded card with the flap somehow attached by some adhesive making it feel like a single card. Mmmmm…suspenseful. I liked it. The outside read only…

(By Invitation Only)

I had held off looking at it, afraid of what it may say or state. But this wasn't so bad. I slipped my nail between the flap and it easily separated. I looked inside to see if my suspicions of something insane would appear. I wasn't far off. In fact, I was right on the money. In raised bold lettering, it read…

"SHOCK CUM!"
School of Sinfully, Sensual, Scintillating Delight and Satisfaction for All!
(Guy Version)

OK, was this for girls, too? The intrigue was amazing. Why invitation only? If so great, why not publicize it, put it on TV commercials. 'Learn to shoot like a Superhero in no time at all! No obligation! Just call the number below on your screen!'

All seemed a bit obtrusive and over the top but what the hell. Getting to know Zach a bit better with each step I take. But a school? A physical school? Something to teach? Zach had alluded to that – but a formal, real school, with formal real teachers? Were they men teachers? Female? Both? Robotic? My mind was reeling with images. Was this in a group session? Individual? The weird ideas started to appear. And I let them... the bit of voyeur in me. Don't tell anyone.

But the main message I received from the card, outside of the title's sounding like Shot Gun! (no, not a sexual inuendo at all), was the ending *'Guy Version'* There was a weird sort of satisfaction in that ending. We were being sought after and someone really cared. Awwww... Sure, for good cash probably, but still.

There was also a taste of macho I felt in reading it. A proudness. We had taken control of our sex lives fearlessly, men! On to our soon to be glorious orgasmic moments (what?), without reproach, without peer, and finally, finally have achieved total and complete victory over our mundane petty wham bam status! I'd like to thank the Academy...

'Onward!' I proclaimed inside. This better be fucking good! And I secretly liked to see the 'Girl Version,' too. But for now, guys first. Sounded weird but I let it go.

At the bottom of the card simply was the word Zach and a phone number. That was it. That was enough. At least for me. Was enough to take the next step. Fuck the cost. Fuck the method. Fuck what anyone thought. This was mine.

I planned to call Zach the next day.

We'll see now.

Episode 13 ~

Melissa had already left for work. The morning had brought calmness. We were back to our normal, almost normal selves. Had a nice breakfast conversation, told her I was working remote today, and we planned to meet later for a nice dinner together.

All good, I thought. I didn't mention the day before, nor did she. It was the past. And knowing her so well, it was definitely the past for her. Well, I hoped and played along if it wasn't.

By mid-afternoon I had some free time and decided to make the call.

I felt like a horny boy stealing his dad's *Penthouse*. Excitement slowly rose with the impending feeling of doing something bad, something prohibited. Thoughts of Catholic school passed my mind. But this was obviously no Catholic school...at least with no pedophiles and predators. I can never fathom such horrible acts. I digress.

The apprehension was like right before an important job interview where suddenly your mind goes completely blank. Or deciding to slip unnoticed into a strip joint. It all was irresistibly wrapped around scintillating nervousness. Would I dial and then hang up. My number would show. Would he call back? Then I'd look foolish or afraid. But I was afraid. I consider myself a strong personality, a strong male personality, no false ego, just me, a guy, and confident. Yet, this was blowing that all away.

The conflict of macho vs being called a girl rose suddenly into the spotlight of my fighting brain. Was this just the realm of girls? Am I stepping over a forbidden boundary reserved only for the female part of our race? What would the guys say at the bar if they knew? What would the girls say? I pictured laughter. I felt laughter. Laughter at being called out as a girl and caring about sex more than I should, more than society norms allowed, more than I'd be able to take if widely known.

"You fucking coward!" I said out loud to myself.

I never backed down from anything I wanted. Never. I found a way always. May not have always been the best approach at times, but I always found a way to get what I wanted, what I desired, and took any heat with the satisfaction of winning my goal.

"Time to pay the piper!" I reproached myself with a crooked smile. Fuck the laughter! If I get this, this possibly astounding ability to rock my rocks more than seemingly ever possible, and every other guy remains in the mundane of not caring, well then bring on the laughter. I look forward to becoming Zach! To becoming *The Sex-Demon*, or at least one of his sex-crazed junior demons. Seeking ultimate pleasure. And possibly with such ladies as Sam and Maxie partnering with me all the time. I pictured horns on them.

I loved my friend's *Sex-Demon's* imagery. Where he is absolutely fearless, flaunting himself to anyone, seducing, confidence beyond confidence! They would never realize the seduction until too late, yet they absolutely adored the seduction! I smiled thinking how much Zach actually came across as a disguised *Satanic being* ...and maybe in real life, too. Did *Lucifer* actually care about us humans? Was on our side to show all aspects of living? Challenging us to break away from conformity, to taste the forbidden? And in the end, recognizing that it was never really forbidden in the first place? Well, I decided I was going to bite into a different kind of forbidden fruit this serpent is offering.

Wasn't that the original premise in the *Garden*? Taste what is forbidden?

I called the number.

Episode 14 ~

I could feel my heart thumping as it rang. Then it picked up.

"Hello, how may I help you?" It was not Zach's voice.

I paused, not sure what to say or do.

"Hello?" the voice repeated.

"Uh, yeah, I'm calling for Zach, he gave me his…"

"Oh, hi Darian! I'm Brad. Nice to meet you! Zach said you'd be calling!"

The enthusiasm caught me off guard, as well as knowing it was me. Didn't anyone else call this number for this ummmm …service?

"Uh yes, how did you know the call was me?"

A chuckle. "Because this is Zach's private line and he only gave it to you recently. He said you were a special customer." Enthusiasm continued unabated. I thought this could be a 'cult,' some weird coitus demonic cult. Led by who else but… Zach, my *New Sex-Demon*.

"Oh, OK, good," was all that came out of my uncertain mouth. "Well, I was hoping to talk with Zach. Is he there?"

Why was I a special customer?

"Yes, he is but he is in training. Can he reach you at this number?"

The word 'training' stuck with me. Images flooded my head. What was going on? What the fuck was he doing? What am I getting into? "Yes, he can reach me at this number."

"Great! I'll let him know when he is free! Take care!"

The bouncy-ness was unnerving. Started to think this actually may be a cult or something where everyone is a happy idiot brainwashed into submission, all having crazy orgies all the time which makes them constantly upbeat. And probably really exhausted! I smiled at my new evaluation of the situation – of which I still had no idea. OK, I promised myself to zero in on Zach when he called and to get the complete story, end-to-end, without exception. Or I am bailing. Period. Maybe.

Almost an hour later, my phone buzzed. Same number I called.

"Hello? Zach?"

"Hey guy! What's up! Glad you called! Ready to discuss?" The enthusiasm was annoying and contagious at the same time. Somehow his voice, his tone put me at ease like I've known him forever. He had a trusting voice. Little flags went up in my brain and I let them stay up. Needed focus, as I knew we were going to talk man-to-man about men's cumming in detail and it was just not a 'normal' guy thing to do. Really strange but here we go...

"Yeah, I think so...well, at least can we talk about how this all works and all?"

"Absolutely! That's the plan! Are you sitting down?"

"No, should I be?" Now getting a bit tense.

Laughter. "I was just kidding to lighten the mood! I can tell, as normal, that you are very apprehensive about all this and dude, that's totally normal. We are not conditioned, programmed for such discussions between us guys. So, honestly relax and let me begin – OK?"

Again, his tone and even his joke, put me at ease. He was good.

"Yes, I agree with you totally," I replied, "it's a bit unnerving to discuss this."

"OK, good. It would be. So, let's start. I run a private, very private you may say school for guys like us and really only guys that can take it or at least willing to try. There is a counterpart school for girls but let's stay on track. The hardest part, pardon the pun, is what I'll call 'the wall.' You know it when it's brought out, but on a day-to-day, us guys ignore it. It's 'the wall' our upbringing, our societal rules and conditioning, our western culture, our media, our own friends, family, and peers keep up. We each have it. Things we *never* speak about. Things that sorry to say would make someone think we're acting like girls. Some would actually horribly misuse the term 'gay' to ridicule. It's just terrible how some people categorize and stereotype so horribly. In fact, it's our gay friends who actually tend to be so much more open about themselves and their sexuality and their feelings and therefore we erroneously stereotype them which helps immensely to keep our 'wall' up amongst ourselves — and against ourselves, sadly."

"OK, I get it so far," I interposed. "So, really, what is this 'wall' thing?"

"Fear."

"Fear?"

"Yep, fear."

Silent pause I think he intended.

"Fear of what?" I finally asked.

"Fear of ourselves." Said very matter-of-factly.

"What do I fear then?" I was trying to really understand.

"We fear our deep feelings about ourselves. We put up images to hide and protect these feelings. We are programmed to do so as males. Push them down, keep them quiet, maybe only think about them in the middle of the night. Put up a strong front and when we all put up a strong front together, it keeps all those deep feelings down. Togetherness makes it easy. Togetherness keeps us safe. And then when maybe, just maybe, a deep emotion comes out or even a curiosity or a hidden desire, we are labeled. May actually even be called a girl or acting like a girl."

I'm glad he couldn't see my face. I had firsthand knowledge. He continued.

"We not only can't express our deepest feelings to others — guys to guys *and* guys to girls — but we can't even to ourselves. We fear our own *self judgment* — because we have been conditioned to do exactly that."

He paused. I waited, thinking what has this to do with my crotch.

"I'll tell you something," he continued. I felt like the student already. "It's exactly how you're feeling right now and I'm sure have been feeling when something triggered your emotions, your curiosities. Something triggered your false ego of yourself to peak. And that causes an immediate want to hide, forget, not me, I'm a guy."

False ego? Is that what I had?

"False ego?" I asked not wanting the answer. "You mean the infamous 'fragile male ego?'"

"Absolutely not! I mean your *false ego*," he emphasized. "The false belief of how you see yourself – both as a person and as a guy. The real Darian ego, or better yet, the real Darian self, is deep inside behind the false ego we've created to sustain the 'wall.' A topic discussed well from many writers. Does this make sense?"

It did and at the same time I was wondering again what the hell this had to do with orgasms and 'shock waves.' I went for the jugular.

"OK, OK, I get it and see your point. I think I need to digest all of this."

"Oh, yeah, you do. We're just getting started – if you wish to continue. You see, this is both information for you and a screening for me."

Screening? He's screening me?

"So, you screen guys to see…if…they what? Qualify for the program?"

"Exactly."

Episode 15 ~

He continued. "Darian, this 'wall' we have up from our false ego is extremely strong. Picture it deep set with concrete. Not every guy can see it, even when shown and explained. We are unbelievably conditioned. Remember the 'wall' is *fear*. How many guys do you know will admit fear, real fear? It's not in our creed. Especially, fear of ourselves and what's beneath. I need to be absolutely sure you or anybody who has been initially invited is openminded enough, at least somewhat at first, and curious enough, at least at first, to let down their guard, to be vulnerable – just a little. Believe me, after doing this a long time, I can tell."

"You can tell? About me?"

"Absolutely. From the moment Fred told me and especially and secondly, the moment I saw you, and thirdly, the moment we all spoke together. And what's in your face, too."

He's been screening me step-by-step from the start!

"That's why *this* 'training' is by invitation only and this one is for guys. Just again to be completely open, there is a training for girls. They are separate. And it's real training – to learn how to really know yourself, trust yourself, believe in yourself, the real you hidden inside. Only then can you then learn to trust your feelings and allow – big word here – *allow* yourself the pleasure you already have but don't know nor willing to see. This is both sexually *and* emotionally – which by the way, they go together. A wham bam doesn't have emotion. A 'shock wave' and more, does. But that's for later." He chuckled a soft almost endearing chuckle.

"Have I passed?" I was definitely intrigued now, and still somewhat apprehensive. Or was it fear? My head was spinning with all of this and I understood why I needed to take it away and let it digest and really look at myself, who and what I really am, and who and what I really want to be. Which at that moment, I had no fucking idea. I just wanted to hear more. And how does the sex fit in with the training – which I still wasn't sure I wanted to hear.

"I'm still talking with you," he laughed. I knew he wasn't mocking. "Honestly, I wished all of us guys would get together in a room and let it all out. Just ain't gonna happen. It's a one-by-one thing. Sad to say. But anyway! Question time!"

I knew I was on now.

"OK, first thanks for talking with me and *screening* me," I said a bit cockily but knew he took it right. "I am definitely curious and have been for a bit. Do I need to tell you what triggered…"

"Nope," he interrupted. "Only if you feel you wish to now or another time."

"OK, good. Another time. So, how does this 'training' work?"

He laughed.

"Well, it's a bit complicated and we assign trainers tailored to the person and their ability to trust himself or learn to trust himself. We will need to get into more detail on that in person – if you still wish to proceed after taking alone time to think through what we talked about today – and I mean next time in a *discussion*, not…" he trailed off laughing again. I could see his smile through the phone.

"OK, fair enough. So, there's a cost."

"Yes, and it's a bit hefty but I believe fair. I do have to make a living."

"OK, so, how much then?"

"Nothing. No money."

"Nothing? I thought you said at the party that there's a cost involved."

"I did," he answered and I could again see his smile through the phone.

"I don't get it." I actually didn't get it but was pleased to hear 'nothing' though my instincts said there's something of a cost.

"OK, honestly, I do not need any money. I am extremely well off. I cover everything and it's my pleasure to help us guys, and girls, become greater than we are, and in a way, I wish to start the second sexual and societal revolution. But there is something other than money."

I knew it! Always something! I waited. He paused knowing I was waiting and continued.

"Your cost, every person's cost who comes in, is completely letting your guard down. Dropping every veil that our upbringing, our peers, our parents, all of society has firmly held in place. Opening yourself up like you have never before. Becoming truly *vulnerable* like you never have before. It's the only way to then become so strong in your person that everything looks different all of a sudden."

"And that's where the door opens for not only astounding physical pleasure but everything about you. Think of the early seventies with the first sexual revolution. Women had to dig deep inside, to open themselves up from the chains that were holding them down. And take huge risks. And they DID! Same thing dude. It doesn't mean you lose any of our masculinity at all. We actually increase our masculinity a thousand-fold. We take ownership of our masculinity and each of us in our own way."

"Taking a step into the unknown and willing, willing to take the heat for it, as women did back then. And guess what? It then becomes the norm. But can you take the cost of such vulnerability? Can you take the crazy risk of things about ourselves we won't even look at? More scary, and maybe more costly, than losing money I would think."

I was silent, digesting all he was saying, all of this whole premise. I finally spoke. "So, you're saying that the only cost is my fear of breaking down my own 'wall' which is fear of looking at my real self inside that I hide or may hide? And once done, there's no going back to the former view of myself? Like an enlightenment. And as a huge benefit or prize, I get 'shock wave' craziness never known before? And trained also ...*sexually?*"

"You got it."

"Simple enough."

He laughs. "Don't think it's so easy. I have not found any guy who found it easy. And honestly, the physical part is absolutely *integral* – it's not a 'side prize' at all. Trust me."

"OK, so how many guys bail?"

"To date, once pass the starting gate? None."

Episode 16 ~

This all was more than I expected. Do I want to change myself? And in seemingly such a dramatic way? What will I become? The damned image of 'Salty Deke *The Sex-Demon*' kept friggin' coming back vividly into my mind's eye (…and did I just say 'damned' and *Demon* in the same sentence? Are we damned for wanting 'to be better than we are?')

And he has no fear at all. None. He did what he wanted, and got what he wanted. And in fact, he is probably more masculine than anyone else. Could this really be possible? To rise above the norm and become a new norm? For me? For us guys? The thought was digging deep into me and gaining fast traction. Just, was it real?

"You there?" he asked knowing I was and knowing somehow that my inner wheels were wildly churning.

"Well, I'll have to say Zach, you present a helluva case and prospect."

"Yes, we do."

The 'we' sank in.

"So, what is it? Classroom? Bedroom? Others involved?" After I asked, I realized that he knew I was going forward. And I still kept thinking, what else does he and they get out of all of this. A place in the history of pleasure? I need more than that. I logged that for the next time when I could see his face.

"We'll get into more detail soon. Let's take it step by step and all your questions will definitely be answered. Trust me."

Something about him just made me trust him. "OK, fair enough," was all I could say. He continued.

"I know there was a trigger in you that caused your wanting more or solving something intimate that is really bothering you. I don't need to know what. I'm telling you I know it was something strong. And I wish more guys would open up about things to each other like you did with Fred. Don't want this to sound condescending, but I'm proud of you and every guy like you. Takes courage to take a first step."

"Well, yeah there was something. And you're right about something else. It has more to do than sex. It's..." suddenly I really understood all that he had been saying "...about how I see myself." I stopped, not wanting to continue. At least not at that point.

"I'm glad," was all he said.

I immediately wondered about Fred and if he...

"May I ask about Fred?"

"I keep everything confidential. You wouldn't want me to discuss you, would you?"

"No, I wouldn't."

"All I'll say is that Fred as you may know, is a very unique individual. Everyone is different. There's no cookie-cutter."

"OK, fair enough. I'm still interested. What's the next step?" I could feel a subtle vulnerability after I spoke my words.

"We meet in person and if okay, with a couple of other guys who have completed the process. Helps you get the big picture and feel confident it's not just me."

I noticed he said 'process' not 'course.'

"Are there females involved?" I had to ask.

"Yes, at times, but that's all I'll say right now. You need to experience."

I felt better at his answer. And then I felt embarrassed that I even asked. I pushed the wavering confusion and fear aside.

"OK where? When?" The 'other guys' part had me a little worried but I let it go for now. I wondered how females were involved but something in me said the 'process' was more a coed thing – whatever the fuck that meant. Were guys going to touch me? I was a little scared and intrigued at the same time. My need to know outweighed my inner fears. Onward I professed inside! The adventure, Captain, *is* a go!

"Where, is at the school. It's very private and we will arrange how you get there. That's only for the first time. It keeps it secret until our first in person. When all of us as a group trust you are sincere, because it's not just me to decide, then you can come and go as you please. When, will be whenever you're ready and we can set up an appropriate mutual time for everyone. Again, this is just for the first gathering together. It's very informal. I will call you with more details. When's the best time to reach you?"

"Just text me times in advance and we can lock in."

"Perfect. Well, I hope this talk was good for you and hopefully if all works out, you'll be astoundingly happy!" I was drawn by the word 'astoundingly.'

"Yes, it was enlightening, though there's a lot more I wish to know and understand." I tried to keep any tone of apprehension way down. Or was it just fear. Then I thought of his description of the 'wall.'

"Absolutely. That's what the first gathering is for. Bring all your questions and concerns after you have taken the time to digest and deliberate. Let's look at next week some time. OK?"

"Yeah, that's fine." I was thinking rapidly and the one thing that kept popping up was 'what the hell do I have to lose!' I had already lost my virginity many eons ago. Seemed now another 'virginity' was about to be lost, probably more destroyed …hopefully nicely.

"Great! Remember, it's a matter of trust."

"One last thing, if I may. I'm not buying you do this totally for self-gratification of helping the human race, specifically us fellow blokes. Or get a kick out of it somehow. Be straight with me. What's your deal? What's your goal?"

Silence. I knew he was debating on letting me know something. He finally replied softly but firmly.

"Repayment for someone who had changed my life."

Episode 17 ~

I stared at my phone for a while after we hung up as thoughts crisscrossed my mind and I felt a little breathless. And I wasn't sure why.

I broke my stare and placed the phone down. What the fuck was I getting into? Was this for real? The conversation was actually surreal while at the same time *felt* real. Again, all the same questions, yet with each moment and discussion, I find myself drawn into it more and more. Maybe it was just curiosity, maybe a get-back at Melissa to show her, maybe wanting justification that I'm better than I knew, maybe, maybe, maybe.

One thing was for sure, Zach was serious. I couldn't image anyone taking such great lengths and being so avid and sure of himself, *and* asking for no money at all. Just some personal 'repayment.' What does that mean? But then again, that was his business and really didn't affect my taking on this whole venture.

The only other thing I could think of was him wanting to become the leader or the face of some new sexual revolution. The modern male sexual liberation advocate. He had said he was well-to-do and didn't need any money. What else was there in life when the need of money is completely gone? Fame. And power that goes with it. So, is it just an ego-trip after all?

No, I told myself. My gut says differently. Yes, he may want fame but somehow after that long conversation, my feelings were he really cared about us guys and gals. He has a vision that I kept reading into. Are there still magnanimous, well-meaning people in the world? Willing to share for the greater good? Was this the revival of hippiedom? Was this the revival of chivalry? *Sir Darian! The Italian-American Knight of the Courageous (and Obsessive) Order!* (hee hee! …okay, okay, trying to be serious…)

Well, at this point, I had nothing to lose, except maybe sheer embarrassment of myself and others seeing me in a different light forever. Lose my friends thinking I'm nuts and acting like a 'girl.' That one got me. How the fuck am I acting like a girl?! I don't even know what that means. And maybe, it's what's needed. To have some balls AND act like a girl! I laughed literally out loud. Just gotta *have balls* to *act like a girl*! Seriously.

I told myself to get some friggin' courage! I shook my head and smiled. Well, I knew I was at a crossroad. At least *that* I knew. And I have been at crossroads before in my life. Half the time taking the right road and the other half not taking the right road. Shit! I was only 50/50? Well, it is batting .500. Yeah, that's reassuring when my dick, balls, and manhood are on the line.

I thought to forget the whole thing. Chalk it up to a whimsical hurt feeling of not being noticed, that I was insignificant, not capable of anything more or greater, just fall back into the mundaneness of a wham bam, sorry, I 'hadn't noticed' for the rest of my miserable life. I smiled again at my drama. And stop fucking whining! Sorry guys, you know how I can get (and I'm *not* whining! ...maybe).

But what if Zach and Sam and Maxie and all the others are right? What if there is an enormously better way, higher self and self-image? I've read enough self-help books in my time. See life differently! Set your goals! But I never read... *Achieve 'Shock Waves!'* And try our new and improved *Strokeless Orgasm*! And as an added bonus, what do we have for our fine fellow guys, Johnny?! That's right! Your own personal *Cumless Cum!* Say goodbye to semen forever! Free for all who are nuts enough to do this! Stay tuned for a message from our sponsor, the honorable Zach himself!

OK, I'm better now.

But if true, what does all of that feel like? I know I have never come close to anything near what these things seem to mean. And don't pardon the pun. Well, maybe.

And the added benefit of higher self-esteem, confidence, strength of conviction to find my true self, *whatever* that was, was definitely drawing me in. And conquer my fear of being a person hidden inside, standing up to potential criticism from my girl, my friends, my colleagues, my whole world. But what would I then be? A real-life whimsical pansy or a real-life powerful *Guy-Sex-Demon*? Damn I loved that image — oh, to clarify, I meant the *Guy-Sex-Demon* image, not the pansy (lol). But you knew that, didn't you?

In the end though, I knew deep inside I wasn't really happy with myself. But I honestly didn't know why, nor would EVER admit it. I would never admit before that I wanted to learn more about my sexuality, about a guy's sexuality other than wham bam (and maybe a blow job). But I think most guy talk is wham bam bravado. Don't you think? It's fun and yet demeaning to girls. I knew that wasn't right.

When do we ever sit around and discuss our intimate desires, our fears, and our needs and wants, and even *techniques*. Discuss maybe better ways of doing it — with girls and even alone. 'Hey Johnny! Can we discuss the last time you played with yourself and what you exactly did? Oh and how did it feel?' Never! Ever! We never will let our guard down. We never will let...

I paused in my thought. I remembered what Zach said. We won't let our 'wall' down. Our 'wall' of fear to look inside, to really look inside and drag out our vulnerable self. To tear down our false ego. To go against *everything* we've been taught — at least for me and probably all who I hang around with. And be unafraid, even extremely willing, to talk about it among us guys. Not just sex, but vulnerable feelings. I see that perfectly now this 'wall' even though I still have no inkling of my true self... But I now see the 'wall.'

I paused again. Somehow all this discussion and after thoughts made me peek inside. Made me glance quickly, and then quickly away at my fantasies, at my need for something more, even something *different*. But what more? What different? What did I see? How can you feel a need and not know or understand the satisfaction of that need? Was I the only one? Anyone in the studio audience?

I knew now it wasn't all about physical stuff, though that new need (or old need?) of *exponential climatic moments* was definitive (...never thought to

59

use those three words together). But I wanted that and to experience the highest ecstasy possible. Com'on, aren't you curious, too? And maybe it even keeps getting better (hence exponenti…never mind).

But again, why not? Is it that I can't have that, and find out how, because I walk around with a dick and therefore I *shouldn't* think of it, or want it? It's not a guy-thing! No! I will not accept that anymore. We should be able to be open about our feelings to each other, our wants and desires, and stop thinking it's not a guy-thing!

Shit! I was sounding like Zach. Damned good brainwashing. Or maybe damned good enlightenment.

And I knew not all guys were this way. There were men who showed their vulnerable side out there — though I surely didn't know any. Not Fred. Well, as far as I knew. Mmmmm. What if…

The thought creeped in that absolutely ALL men are actually *vulnerable* (you and me) and in need of more than what we have, but deep, deep inside we cannot ever look at that. And if we can't look at that, then we can never fix it, we can never achieve more, out of pure fear, even pure embarrassment. Keep our macho up! The 'wall' will remain standing. Forever.

Now I started to really understand what Zach absolutely meant. And why Sam and Maxie really aren't concubines but actually equals in a new and different world of being. Sexual and *more*. Promoting a new society one person at a time. And maybe the plan or goal is some nuclear explosion of the accepted norms being blown away like dust, and openness and acceptance of our true selves becomes a reality and we all feel free to express ourselves in ANY WAY we choose. What we do, how we dress, what we say, how we fuck, all that good stuff. Guys and girls, together. Well, that would definitely be 'fame.'

I asked myself, 'are you fucking done analyzing the shit out of everything you fucking psycho?! Huh you fucking raving maniac?!'

'Yes sir, Mr. Dracco… I think so.'

'Fuck off!'

'Yes sir.'

So, after getting my much needed personal reprimand, I thanked myself and told myself to now shut the fuck up.

OK, OK, I know I rambled out of control and it's all a bit friggin' weird but bear with me. I'm just trying to keep my balance between all this shit, as all I can feel is that my safe world was now barreling straight for a mammoth upheaval of galactic proportions, with my mind swirling uncontrollably between what I knew and what is coming at me like a freight train, again. And folks, we're gonna find out together.

Either way, any way, every way, I made my decision.

Episode 18 ~

Melissa was looking as wonderful and sexy as always. I knew I loved her and she me, even with our little spats. We always get over them and resume our fun and pleasant times.

She smiled at me looking up from the table she had chosen. It was nice and private in one of our favorite local pubs. The large wood beams and pillars projected strength along with beauty. That went well with my girl and her ways.

"Hey!" I greeted, leaning down and placing a soft kiss on her glossy red lips.

"Hey, honey!" she replied with the same enthusiasm.

"Sorry, I'm late. But..."

"You're not late. I'm early. Left work a bit early to just unwind from a very busy, hectic day. But all good. Glad we can have some quiet private time away from everything." She took a sip of her ruby cabernet.

I didn't know if she just meant 'away from' work or the weekend. I brushed it aside, not willing to take that deep dive. "Well, my day was slow but fruitful." I wondered why I said 'fruitful.' Of course, she caught right in on it.

"Um, fruitful? When do you ever say 'fruitful?'" she asked but pleasantly with a beaming smile. I knew she was playing but still questioning what may have happened for such a description of a day. I thought maybe I'm just reading too much into everything anymore. Really? OK, be cool, I told myself. And stop saying 'fruitful!' Sorry guys.

With light, fake, laughing, I answered, "I have no idea why I said that. It just came out." Definitely hiding behind my façade, peeking through.

"OK, but never say that again," she kept smiling. "You sound like a girl."

Took all my strength to keep my pleasant smile as I sipped my water. I wanted to bite the glass and swallow the jagged pieces.

The server had arrived and I ordered a gin martini, dry, olives. He wrote it down and disappeared.

"Gin martini? Gin? You never order gin."

"You know I love gin. It just doesn't love me," I chuckled and this time meant it. "Felt something different and just one."

"Suit yourself. It'll be your hangover," she said matter-of-factly, knowing full well only two drinks give me a hangover: gin and red wine. One glass and boom, instant hangover. I could mix anything with anything and then with anything else in one night and have no hangover. Add a touch of gin or red wine? Done. But at this point I really wanted that taste of gin because regardless of hangover, I loved it. Definitely treating myself to my gin and hangover after 'you sound like a girl.'

The rest of the dinner went enjoyably after the initial fun little tiffs. Well, fun for her. But we always jab back and forth in entertaining ways, always playfully challenging each other without ever meaning any harm. And I knew her well enough that she meant no harm or derision at all with 'girl,' it's just she just didn't know the effect. I surely was letting it go…for now.

Who the fuck am I fooling. It was sticking deep in my side like a hot spear as yet another one of her innocent but brutal stabs, but who's counting. Don't answer that.

"Dessert?" the server asked.

"Um not for me." Looking at me, she continued, "want an after-dinner drink?"

"Yeah, sure. What's your pleasure m'lady?" Yep, I was definitely going for cute chivalry as the blood viciously poured out of my side.

"Amaretto, neat."

"Two. And a double espresso, please."

I glanced at Melissa with an asking look 'you, too?'

63

"Naw, I'll just have the Amaretto. Thanks," she replied, smiling up at our server.

After he left, we sat in silence, in our own thoughts. It was not unusual for us to sit quietly together, while a lot of times it is uncomfortable between other couples. I did feel we had a mature relationship in place after these two years. My worry right then and there was, can something like recent events and statements start to erode a relationship this young? Was there enough built-in strength to survive the starting of differences of opinions or viewpoints that had never come up before?

I looked at her as she watched people walking outside the window. Damn she was gorgeous, and pretty, and cute, all at the same time. The curve of her mouth and lips drove me crazy, among many other physical features. She was perfect for me. Small pouting breasts, slim waist, not too big ass but definitely tight, and thighs I kissed, licked, and caressed all night! I felt the pressure grow in my crotch and vowed to not say ANYTHING to hurt the ride home and the frolic soon to come...and sorry, not pardoning the pun. 'Come' is such an easy pun. I'll try to refrain.

I also prayed she wouldn't bring anything up, especially yesterday's party conversation. If she did, I wasn't sure if I could hold back after my long talk with Zach. My adamant feelings were solidifying and I was going to protect them. And I also wasn't going to lose her. The pendulum keeps swaying...

At the same time, I felt an ever so slowly growing conflict that I was holding something back from her with my decision to proceed with investigating my... manhood? (is that what I'm doing?) ...and the boundless possibilities Zach and two lovely goddesses promised. And there was always the fear of finding, with the possible guy interactions (whatever that means), that I may be a hidden bisexual from it all, though I never consciously ever thought or felt that. Does everybody have that concern, fear, thought?

And I am not homophobic at all. There was this feeling that somehow, some way, other men will be involved or another man, and maybe with a girl, or whatever. But the lingering thought was there if I follow through. Was this one of my actual 'walls?' And was it the *fear of*, or the *being of*? Do all straight men have this hidden fear they never look at? Straight girls, too? We'll take callers now (lol) the lines are open!

Can we just simply play with all combinations of sexes, and not only be excellent at it, but also love it and it be completely natural to us. Does every 'straight' guy and girl, barring any inner fear of bisexuality, also have, *maybe*, some curiosity about it but would never admit it? Since we guys can't suck our own dicks, and must believe every guy thought about it at least once in their lives while playing with themselves, just use another guy's as a surrogate dick? Or try it out? Maybe just once? I smiled inside, musing, 'what was the truth?' And I really never thought of another guy (or did I?) Maybe more just my *own stuff*. What if we were well-endowed enough (lengthwise) and could *do* ourselves? Any of us secretly try? It would be right there.... just to try once... twice...? What if girls could actually lick themselves, too? We'd all never leave the house! Crazy shit this Zach has me thinking. And you too, Salty Deke!

But therein lies that 'wall' again of fear. To me right now was the fear of the *unknown* and Zach had a way of keeping the curiosity up and running hot. We can call it: *Curiosity foreplay*. I lightly shook my head with another internal smile, trying not to show my thoughts. I was definitely curious though of what heights of extreme pleasure lurks unknown inside us and at the same time *feared* every bit of taking that journey of no return.

Did I ever tell you of my little sexy angel who lives near my ear? She talks to me...

Okay, I'll try to get help... anyways, back to...

My little sexy angel was whispering in my ear: 'Courage! Courage!' I heard it clearly in my mind and could only say to myself once again...onward, into the unknown...

Our drinks arrived, bringing us both back to reality.

I don't know for how long, but Melissa was staring at me. "What the hell are you thinking?"

"What?"

"Um like your face is somewhere else with that weird grin. Like you're laughing at something inside."

Damn she knew me too well! I suddenly felt like running away.

"Oh, it's nothing. Just thinking about some weird shit that happened today on a call. A work call," I clarified realizing that doing so made it sound like a lie, a coverup.

"Are you still thinking about yesterday?"

"What about yesterday?" Another flub. I felt her claws coming out.

She laughed a genuine laugh, with no malice (I think) but was disturbing. "You are!"

"No, I am not," I replied as calmly and steady as I could, hoping it would go away but I knew her better.

"You want to know more about this Zach guy and what he's talking about. I can see it in your eyes and your face. You want to actually do it? Get this 'training' if that's what he's offering? Seriously?!"

I broke down.

"I don't know. It's just weird. And that whole conversation. Was like a battle of the sexes." She was nodding in agreement though I didn't mean it. "But you have to admit, it's curious stuff. What if..."

She cut me off.

"No way. Honey, it's a fraud. Did you see those two 'ladies?' she said with sheer sarcasm. "Bimbos, dear. Hanging on his every word. Like they were drugged or something. You really can't be serious to even think of contacting him or even doing this weird thing. Men are men. It only goes so far..."

Hold the fucking horses! I cut her off.

"What do you mean 'men are men?' And 'only goes so far?'" I heard my voice rising and called out the Marines to controlled it.

"Honey, I've never in my life met a man, a guy, who had any better 'fun' than the rest and it's pretty much the same every time. Yeah, some get more excited, and others seem to just want it to be over with, and honestly, most cum and go. Flop over, done. Period. That's it. I'm sure it's fun and pleasurable, but from my point of view, and trust me from every girl I know or have known, we all see the same thing. Wham bam baby done! Give me a fucking beer!"

Seriously?! Is that what we really portray? Or are we just not trained enough to fucking know any better? My mind was reeling. Her whole dissertation, though I firmly believe she was being completely honest with again no malice (maybe), and actually trying to 'teach' me *reality*, was in total conflict with Zach's dissertation earlier in the day. How could two such points of view even exist? Were we actually physically *incapable* of greater gratification, incapable of longer amusement, incapable *scintillating* decadence as the card read? As she just *said*? I was beyond obsessed. I, we, us, need to know if we are only using 10% of what we got in our equipment. 90% is a big friggin' missing piece!

Or…were we actually inadvertently brainwashed into believing this, and then it manifests into reality as 'That's all folks!' You're done! That's all you get! Now stop bothering me with your broken, fragile ego! Us girls own the *ultimate orgasms* and they go on forever, multiple in one act, just keep it going long enough with your utilitarian rod and your tired tongue!' At this point, even blowjobs were suspect. The weird thought entered that maybe guys give the best blowjobs as they know… I called in the drone airstrike to squash that thought. And the fiery battle continued.

The funny thing was I sat there not blaming anybody. Not girls, not guys, not my little sexy angel, not even *The Sex-Demon* himself. Well, maybe him. But all I saw was perception vs reality. And the complete mundane world of current male *performance*.

Guys, we are duped! No wonder we play with ourselves so much. Was it just machinery or are we always searching for that ultimate long-lasting insanity for us conned guys? Keep working at it, you may get there someday! And if not, then maybe it 'Cums in a Bottle!' 'On sale now!' 'Get *yours* while they last!' I smiled, feeling my own internal sad, pathetic laughter.

"Well, maybe since you're so sure and maybe, you are completely right..."

Cuts me off.

"I am."

I continued with a smirk. "...and maybe, just maybe, he actually has something, knows something, and can teach something. And maybe..." I paused dramatically, tilting my head, "...just maybe you are completely wrong and don't want to face it. Can't that be possible?"

"You're actually going to do this, aren't you?"

There it was. It was out. What I feared and tried to stay away from the whole time. Amaretto glasses still full. Her face a bit contorted, waiting for a reply like waiting for the jury's final verdict. We find the defendant ...guilty! I couldn't speak. Nothing I could say would work. Except the truth. So, I lied.

"No, I am not. Too weird. Just he and they were so confident, and then you think, could they really have something there, being so confident." I heard my mumbling tone but my latent courage rose to the top. "I mean, come on, even you must think – *possibly* – is there really something there. Wouldn't that be worth the try?"

"No, I don't at all. We're talking *stupid* orgasms. Who fucking cares. You're done in ten minutes anyway. And I think he's a charlatan. An egotistical charlatan conning men into giving up tons of money for nothing. No results. Maybe just a better way to play with yourself." I bit my tongue knowing there was no money needed but saying so would reveal my contacting him and our discussion. And was she right? It was only *stupid*...?

...in ten minutes?! Guys, need help here! Call in the calvary! Call in the missile strike!

"OK, each their own opinion. I'm entitled to mine. I think there may be something there. That's all." I sat back and took hold of my glass and sipped it slowly, looking straight into her eyes. I saw her mouth force a smile and knew she knew not to press me any further. She knew when to stop battling with me and to push my limits. It could get nasty, as some times it has when she keeps it on. She sighed and took her glass and sipped, too. Then she smiled genuinely. I tried the same.

"Well, ok, each their own opinion. Would love to know Fred's." She was diverting the conversation on purpose to end it. I appreciated that from her. I did love her, pain in my ass!

"You know you're a pain in my ass," I claimed, truly smiling.

"Someone has to be," she smiled back and then winced an adorable snarl at me. A snarl just the same.

"Maybe you can teach me something?" came out of my mouth, seeing the words cross the table towards her, sending my soldiers in without air cover.

"Maybe. Let me know when you get a clit," she laughed again, genuinely. "Just kidding. Enough of this talk, let's go see what we can conjure up!"

Whew. Beat the hangman...for now.

But I loved the idea of getting home and making love. And I was going to time it! I'll let you know. And I was already trying to think of how to somehow teach myself the 'Zen Ways of Zach' on my own. At least was going to try...

We finished our drinks, chatting about other things and finally were very relaxed again. Paid the bill and we left arm in arm.

The ride home was quiet but not unnormal.

The sex was good as ever. Meaning the same as ever. At least for me. Oh, twelve minutes. She was wrong! Didn't make me feel any better. Damn. Fuck. Please add in your own 'expletive' in the space below.

When done, she got out of bed, heading for the bathroom. Before closing the door and not looking back, the fucking 'badda bing bombshell' came.

"You know, if you do ever try it, we're done. I'll leave."

Episode 19 ~

What the fuck. I wanted to say "thanks honey, and the sex was good, too, if you had noticed," but of course me the coward was silent. I lay there staring at the ceiling, trying to process those words and that ultimatum. I wasn't a person who accepted ultimatums. Are you? But her tone was as forceful as it was calm. No bullshit here. I believed she would. And I believed I was going to try. The trick was how to avoid the prior and achieve the latter. And somehow have a happy ending. And 'shock waves.' And hopefully no electrodes were involved.

"You wouldn't leave me," I finally stated as confidently as I could. I had to know for sure the risk I may be taking. Keep my love vs gain a whole new person of myself (maybe).

"Yep, I would," she came back, smiling down at me.

"Why?"

"Why? You need to ask why?"

Here we go, back into battle again...and being outflanked. Girls are good at that.

"Yeah, I do. You would literally leave me for something I may want to do? What happened to our agreement we would never interfere with the other's wishes?" I needed to invoke our code we agreed to upfront when we knew we would live together.

She paused, sitting on the bed, looking exhausted and not from the sex.

"Honey, you're absolutely right. I have no right to deny your wish. It's just weird, and I wouldn't stop you, but on the other side, I want no part in it. And who knows what goes on. What diseases. And thinking you are having sex with another, and probably a lot of others, in this delusional 'training,' would just tip me over. I'm sorry. You in turn need to respect that is my wish. Would you want me to do something like that and then still be with me?"

She had a point. Hadn't thought of it that way (aka being outflanked). But I knew my answer.

"Yes, absolutely. I would not stop you but I also wouldn't leave you for it. I'd work with you and see together what it's all about and see if it *is* delusional," I said though I firmly didn't think it was delusional. I also knew that she couldn't come with me. And therefore she would only know things filtered through me. Probably an issue, too.

"Tell you what," she started like the beginning of a speech, or the opening statement of a trial, my trial. She sat straight up turning her head, looking at me on the bed. "Compromise. Do what you want. Just don't tell me nor tell me anything about it. Let's see how that goes. And if it all makes you happier and freer and feeling more manly with greater whatevers, which I doubt, good for you and I'm ok with it. I'll just have to decide as we go. And use a condom."

Pause. She turned her head away and then back again, meaning here's the time to give my response to the jury. 'More manly?' That surely wasn't how I was seeing it. 'See how it goes?' That surely meant she hadn't and probably would never buy into any of this. 'I'll just have to decide as we go?' That surely meant the door was open for her to walk out any time.

Why the fuck was this so difficult for her or any woman (if you are so inclined) to understand that maybe, just maybe, a guy may want to see more into himself, and not always present a macho or stoic hard front and at the same time NOT be seen as girly!

And the worst part was it was being done unconsciously, innocently. Almost a robotic social response to conditioning over the millennium back to the *Garden* where the poor guy just 'accepted' the fruit without question from his hot naked girl. No blame here. Reminded me of strip joints where us guys (admit it!) try not to show our ogling of those naked seductive girls and we probably accept any 'fruit' visual or tactile we can get without question. Are we just friggin' programmed to be goo-goo eyed weak blobs of protoplasm when in the presence of our dream lovers?!

I tried not to let the laugh out, as that surely wouldn't help my case.

"OK, agreed," I lied. I didn't like the subtle toxicity that was happening but it was either toss the whole thing out the window, which I wasn't going to do, or lie that her conditions were acceptable – and *that* was not what I was looking for in any type of support. But I knew how things were in the world and it was the best that was going to happen – at least right now.

Maybe I'd be the one leaving. The risks were clearly out there. And I was clearly taking the step into the unknown of myself, trusting people I just met, and taking a big risk of looking completely foolish, idiotic, and worse, unmanly, girly, or whatever derisive term will and could be used against me in a court of law. And of course the eventual 'I told you so' would be devastating. I would have no choice but to lay down my sword (dick?) and flee for the hills. Leaving my supposedly fragile ego in complete ruins. I suddenly felt like a virgin. But a virgin of what?

"Good! Now let's forget all this and get some sleep," she closed the conversation, learned down, and kissed me on the mouth and slipped under the covers.

As the light went off, I stared into the confusing, quiet darkness.

I need reinforcements. Told you it was going to get hairy! Please stay tuned...

Episode 20 ~

I stared silently, unmoving in that darkness. Why couldn't I just let this go? Was it hurt feelings from 'hadn't noticed?' No. That was only a trigger.

Does any other guy out there feel the same way? That we are programmed to hide all this 'stuff' inside and project an air, a façade of some kind of show, in essence to, in the end to, hide all this 'stuff' inside. Going in fucking circles!

I'm a normal guy I told myself. Well, as normal as the next normal guy. I'm full-blooded Italian-American macho-man all in one, with an added touch of psychoanalysis crap (my apologies to the psychoanalysis community). But that was my credo. My mind paused. What the hell is 'normal?' All kinds of 'normal' out there. I thought of things I do, things I like. I like sports, going to bars and watching the game with my buddies, not a beer drinker but give me a rum and coke and all good. And a shot or five. Love a good mostly raw fat thick steak. Does liking bearnaise sauce tip the balance away to not being so masculine? Hell, nobody is *exactly* the same! I play a mean rock guitar solo and a lot of people can't even pick a string. I like history, especially studying wars (as you can tell). And I like poetry. So, what? We all have our added extras, and idiosyncrasies, and okay, differences we all accept of each other (do we really?) But the mainstream 'guy-ness' still remains. Or at least I think it does. Does it?

But the question lies, and this is where I'm at and my *fucking* crossroad, what is really underneath it all? Anything? Are we really hiding inner most secrets we would never tell another guy? Probably never tell a girl, either?

I was trying to think of a really taboo guy thing we would never talk about. It came back to me in the quiet darkness and I don't mean to belay the point but hear me out. I remember reading somewhere that most people are *actually* bisexual and don't know it or at least somewhat bi-curious. I firmly believe that *that* is a huge straight guy-taboo to even *think about*, less discuss openly. I can't remember EVER speaking or talking about the possibility of it at a bar with my friends. Hey Joe, you ever think about sucking Johnny's cock? Or even your own? I held back the chuckle of the probable response. And I thought, what are the other taboo guy things? Why do things have to even be taboo?

What about just really sensitive feelings? Vulnerability? A wanting of a sincere hug for no reason. To cry for no reason. Where the fuck was I going with this?! Damn Zach! And fuck Fred, too! And all the psychoanalysts, you're no help! I really had to hold back the smirking laugh by biting my tongue visualizing actually fucking Fred! OK, scratch that.

OK, OK, time to stop you silly girl! Also read or heard somewhere or maybe it was girls talking, that guys need to be more sensitive. Let their inner female out. Shit! Ain't no guy I know going to let some inner female out let alone admit there even was one. Switching from the devil to the my sexy little angel on my other ear, I heard: 'why not? Do you have an inner female? Come on! Admit it! She's in there! Look at her! Let her out!' The devil on the other ear quickly responds: 'if you do and I'll cut your balls off! You don't have any such thing inside and you know it! You're a guy damn it! Stop this silliness!' A stifled chuckle came out. Melissa didn't move. Good. This little devil-angel battle was actually fun.

But then again, why am I going through with this whole thing? For unbelievable heights we have never experienced before? Rock my fucking balls? That *is* why! Why can't I? Where is it written I can't? Surely, that falls in the guy-realm, doesn't it? We have dicks, don't we? They do pretty well for us so far. I heard my dick comment: 'yep we do! Don't mess with us!' Now it was three-way. Devil: 'got that right!' Sexy Little Angel: 'you know there's more!' Dick: 'prove it!' Devil: 'what?!' Sexy Little Angel: 'game on!' Devil: 'fine, outnumbered. But no touching by another guy!' Sexy Little Angel:

'game on!' Dick: 'I'll decide!'

They all paused.

I thought my dick won. Thoughts? Review the instant replay in the booth!

So, I asked the arguing trio, "can a macho-man be a sensitive guy? A vulnerable, delicate guy?" The thought scared me. Delicate?! What the fuck... What am I thinking?!

Silence. I had a strange sense their eyes were on me and how fucking weird this all was. Well, whether or not some inner female comes out or is even in there, whether or not I become a real sensitive guy, whether or not I find a whole new person inside, whether or not there's any truth to guy and girl bi-curiosity and whatever that brings, whether or not I lose some macho-ness for some more real me in return, I made the final decision. Final answer...

I'M GOING ON 4TH DOWN! FOR THE WIN!

Everyone was pleased.

Episode 21 ~

The next day the date and time were set. Didn't say a word to Melissa. Going to follow the rules we set.

Since I worked remotely at will, it was safe to set a weekday and keep it under wraps. When the day came, I didn't know what to wear. I was a bit shocked I even cared. Business casual? Casual with jeans and tanktop? All sweats for easy removal? I figured it didn't matter as the adventure was kind of fun and the unknowing was building excitement, and fear, at the same time.

Fear. The 'wall,' came back to me.

Again, it didn't matter to me at this point. It was a bright sunny summer day and I felt I was going on safari! Sounded threateningly dangerous enough for my adventurous, scared self. I decided on business casual to be safe while not really knowing why it was safe when I knew dick-shit about anything, except a guy named Zach who has two astoundingly sexy girls. It occurred to me that the girls were lures for unsuspecting guys like me. It was working.

I waited outside on my porch. It felt like waiting for an Uber with destination unknown. But right on time exactly, the fire-glow red Corvette pulled up the driveway. It was Maxie. Thank God I whispered that it wasn't someone I didn't know or guy. Damn, stop being so homophobic, even though I wasn't! I told myself it was a stupid macho-thing and tried to hush it away. Didn't want to have any predispositions on my journey even though a guy possibly touching me just kept lurking in my insanity. Nor any other conflicts, though they were surely there, as this journey was making me think in so many different ways and ways I hadn't foreseen.

Maxie's dark glistening long hair shined in the sunlight and she and the Vette appeared as one, each sensually complementing each other. I forced my stare away and walked to and opened the passenger door, saw there was no back seat, and almost fell into the extremely low Vette. I heard Maxie giggle. She beamed a smile.

"Nice low car," I smiled back. "And hot," I meant her, too.

"A bit," she replied, "and thanks!" I think she knew I meant her, too. Too fucking cute! Well, it was starting out pretty damn good. "OK, first welcome to a new beginning!" she said enthusiastically. "And please put this on." She handed me sunglasses. I was, OK, I can do this. The image of a blindfold in bed crept in.

When I put them on I realized I couldn't see through them. Well, I was warned about this for the first trip. And it beats a real blindfold in public, though having Maxie put a blindfold on me in a bed would be... (sorry, I get fixated...but you know that).

She interrupted my fantasy.

"No cheating, hear me?"

"Yes, ma'am!"

"Good, cause if I catch you, and I'll be looking, we turn around and you'll be home."

"I won't cheat." I said the truth. It was too cool this suspense. In my darkness I thought, could a lovely lady commit some horrible crime and bury me in some park, never to be found again? Wait! That's exactly something that could happen! I just met her and knew squat! I pictured the bed scene instead and pushed out the crime scene.

"OK, here we go!"

She backed out of the driveway with a jolt, screeched to a stop after spinning the wheel to be facing to our left down the street. The roar of the Vette was so deep and powerful to push me into the seat like the feeling of an airplane taking off.

It took about 45 minutes I assumed since I couldn't look at my watch. I could feel her eyes ever glancing at me and I refused to cheat and cause an end to all this before it even began. I was going full board and was in it now.

Somehow, being finally in it both relaxed me that I had actually followed through and made me even more excited. I just heard my little sexy angel say, 'I'm proud of you my little boy!' Yeah, she calls me her 'little boy.' I'm still seeking help… back to…

What the hell are they going to do to me, to my equipment?! Or maybe for the first time, they would just tell me and allow me to run out screaming.

Before I could think to laugh, I could feel Maxie spin the wheel and like on rails, the Vette perfectly turned right. I could then feel a gravel road the tires were now tearing through. After a couple of minutes, she veered right again and came to a sudden stop. I felt the Vette slide on the gravel with its power exhausted. I think it came – just kidding. Well, this story *is* about sex, so you have to bear with it. It's game time!

After the complete silence of the ride, she exclaimed: "We're here! You can give me those." I took off the glasses and handed them to her but was looking out the window. What the fuck?!

Episode 22 ~

I knew full well I was gaping. I slipped out of the car. Before me stood a huge mansion of what appeared to be from the Victorian Era with a medieval castle touch. It was literally massive. The only description I could think of was 'strength.' The gables were large and gracefully adorned the building. The front door was enormously stoic and apparently oaken with big black iron hinges and knockers. A long, flowered path led curving from the driveway, sided by black iron ornate railings. All the windows were expansive and tall and had long drapes blocking any view inside. There were flags hanging with various colorful royalty designs and crests. It was all a picture out of a history book but real.

My eyes shifted from left to right, from up to down, capturing all the splendor. And then I noticed the security cameras carefully hidden within the exquisite adornments but once noticed, I could feel the eyes...

There was a parking area ahead of us apparently for guests or more likely for 'students' enrolled in this endeavor. I could see partially behind the mansion. My eyes fixated on a tall white fence that seemed a bit out of place with the rest of the outside imagery. A simple arched sign was above the gate and I could only make out the word 'Your...' My ears then fixated on the sound of talking, laughing, and splashing. Splashing? Must be a pool area and from the length of the fence I could see, maybe multiple pools. The sounds were extremely festive and I wanted to check it out. But knew better.

The rest of the grounds expanded far until ended with a long forest tree line which seemed to encapsulate the entire premises past the fence. A mansion-castle hidden within a forest! I couldn't think of a more interesting and eerie place, and even more so how it may be at night. I promised myself if anyone looked like a crazed insane bloodthirsty torturous murderous diabolical fiend, with bulging bloodshot eyes, and blood oozing everywhere, I was running for my life. (trying not to be over-dramatic…well, maybe …who me?)

I finally noticed Maxie looking demurely at me with a look of 'take your time, I know it's captivating' without saying anything.

I took a deep breath and asked, though I knew the answer, "so, we are going in there." I pointed to the huge door but I wanted to point to the fence area.

"Well, honey, I don't see anywhere else to go. Are you ready?" Didn't she hear the party going on?

I paused only a moment, got my courage up, nodded my head, and lifted my palm for her to lead the way. She beamingly smiled and with a flamboyant twist, turned and slowly glided towards the imposing door. I followed somewhat close behind, ready to bolt at any moment. The only way to describe my feeling was scared and excited at the same time, with a sense of weakness. I felt as if being drawn in and wasn't sure if it was my own curiosity and commitment, or some evil power pulling me into the chasm of horrors unknown, or both.

"Interesting place for a training center," I muttered loud enough for Maxie to hear. Without turning around nor interrupting her stride, she replied casually.

"Sure is."

OK, she didn't take the bait. The door loomed high above us. What I couldn't see from the car, hidden by the ornate wooden overhang, was a crafted plaque right above the oaken door. The writing was in block lettering clearly stating its message boldly with flairs of some kind of medieval decorations. It commandingly read: 'NO FEAR, ONLY COURAGE' followed by underneath, the statement: 'to all who enter here'

I hadn't realized I had stopped to read the powerful plaque. Maxie, again, waited patiently and I knew she had expected me to stop. She smiled and opened the heavy door with complete ease.

"Shall we now?"

"Yeah, sure," answering and not being sure of anything anymore. The suspense was fucking spooky.

Right at the threshold, before finally entering the mansion, I took one last glance back outside expecting to see an audience and some narrator say: 'Darian is journeying into the unknown, the unknown of... *his insane mind!*' with some crazy creepy music. But no one appeared. There was no audience. Almost disappointed for then it would be just a fictional tale – and I'd be the star.

Somehow, I did feel like a star.

I turned forward and watchfully entered.

Episode 23 ~

Not stopping again but slowing down, I took in the panoramic visual around me. The mansion's inside hall rose high all around with ornate gold serpentines seemingly slithering up the huge marble pillars. Everything was adorned with gold and silver, thick wooden banisters and wall carvings in oak and teak, floors of marble surrounded by wooden inlays, long thick satin and velvet drapes appeared to caress the tall windows, large and small oil paintings of what looked to be real impressionists' works with highly crafted frames carefully positioned to be gazed at but unobtrusive to the whole vista of an opulence in disguise, as the feel of the place was comfortable with Roman styled lounges and appealing cushioned kingly thrones.

Not realizing until now, I had had the predisposed image of finding nude paintings and naked woman statues of a *Playboy Mansion*-style décor. But not to be – somewhat to my disappointment. There were statues on marble pedestals but were more Greek and Roman style, many of ancient warriors and others of medieval knights. Everything articulated 'strength' in an extreme commanding manner. I also had the distinct feeling of both masculine and feminine, though I couldn't pinpoint it. I couldn't help feeling both relaxed amongst it all along with a growing wonder and awe. And all in the middle of nowhere. At least this wasn't fake, I comforted myself.

I hadn't noticed that in the middle of my gazing, I had actually both stopped and turned around a couple times. As usual, Maxie was waiting.

"Shall we?"

"Yes, of course," I answered with true enthusiasm. Now, I was intrigued for what was next. All this drama for orgasmic exhilaration! *'Grab your balls and go!'* I screamed in my head. Well, I didn't really grab my balls...yet (...if I did, wouldn't tell anyway…maybe… lol) Back to the tale…

Had to be more than this show but I simply told my adventurous self, go with the flow. Onward men!

We passed a couple of very large rooms on both sides, each with a different feel, color, and expression. I wanted to stop and explore each one but Maxie kept her stride, as I had to also in order to keep up.

She made a right down a corridor, turning with such grace, I more watched her than where we were going. All I could think of now was the word 'classy' for her and for everything surrounding us. Suddenly I heard him.

"Hey! Darian! You made it! Welcome!"

Zach appeared out of nowhere and was suddenly in front of us, holding out his hand to me. I shook it and he pulled me in for a quick front hug that was not intrusive at all, almost like Roman soldiers would do greeting their fellow warriors. Strangely, I wanted to give a Roman straight arm salute for fun but didn't. I had to admit, he had this down so far. And, again, for some sex training? Seriously? Gotta be more.

"Yeah, I guess I did," came out of my mouth and knew it sounded a bit lame. "Maxie here has been the perfect hostess and really great, though a bit of a crazy driver," I smiled a smile at her saying was just messin' with her and she smiled back knowing. "Though I have no idea where I'm at." I tried the bait.

"Soon enough! Soon enough! First, coffee? Tea? Some snacks before we begin?"

Coffee sounded excellent and I agreed. Just didn't know what 'begin' was.

He turned and took a couple steps, stopped, turned back to us and with his long arm, motioned to enter the room to our right. We did just that and he followed behind.

The room was small compared to the rest of the mansion but spoke of comfort. There was a circle of seven chairs on a beautifully crafted, plush Persian-style rug, all facing inward as if a group session. But what was a group session needed for? My intrigue heightened and I knew inside that I was probably the subject of the session. 'Duh,' I said inwardly. Was this an interview? An intervention? A séance?

Zach motioned to a large table which had coffee, tea, water, donuts, pastries, and other sorts of small finger foods, multiple meat and cheese boards, as well as a large bowl of beyond-jumbo shrimp, another with cracked lobster tails and claws, crab claws, and raw oysters. It dawned on me that we may be here a while. I took some coffee…for now…as the rest really appealed to me but thought to lay low. And also, not to make a mess and fool of myself as I was apt to do…well, sometimes. I kept wondering who the chairs were for. He was a master of suspense.

"Seriously? You're not indulging in any of these delights?" Zach comically reprimanded me.

"Um, not just yet but definitely will, trust me. And thank you for this and your hospitality." He smiled accepting my thanks. His face and smile for an instance reminded me of a disguised *Satan* again, wanting my poor soul. I looked away.

"Good! So, let's have a seat and get started. Anywhere is fine."

He and Maxie waited until I chose a seat and I instinctively knew they waited so they could position themselves accordingly. And that was exactly what they did, but not as I expected. Zach sat to my left and Maxie to my right. For a moment, it was uncomfortable until the others walked in.

Episode 24 ~

I had wanted to talk about the mansion with Zach first but knew that would have to wait as I watched three guys and two girls casually stroll into the room. All were smiling and for an instant I felt it all a bit cultish. OK, I'll play along I told myself for the millionth time. I eyed the door for any escape attempt.

The guys looked like average everyday guys I knew and were friends with. All were casually dressed, even more casual than me. One was a handsome black guy with a dark beard on a crafted strong face, wearing a dark flannel shirt with the sleeves rolled up tight. He was slightly taller than the others and was obviously a bodybuilder. Another guy was slim and the medium height of them all. He had a pale complexion with light stubble on his boyish face that gave the appearance of a surfer boy, and a cropped head of medium length dirty blond hair with piercing blue eyes. And the third was Hispanic-looking and had a stocky toned physique. His hair was long and wavy like in an 80's hair-band with an amazing handlebar mustache that added a wild western-look with a movie star handsome smile. All were pleasant looking guys, very diverse, all with the same air as Zach – confident and casual at the same time.

Now the girls. I had to take a deep breath when looking at the first girl. Slim, small breasted, wearing a very short midriff blouse with obviously no bra, showing off her tight waist, with a miniskirt so short I only had to lean down a bit to see if there were panties. She appeared very fair complexioned of Irish or English background and her hair was blonde, cut in a short bob (a very 60's pretty hippie-look), picturing flowers in her hair. I kept my posture as my eyes finally watched her lithe but muscular legs stride themselves to the chair next to Zach.

The other girl was Asian and appeared slightly older than the rest though had an amazing youthful look. She was dressed more conservatively, almost in a business casual way. She wore tight fitted jeans with a light sports jacket and was definitely in great shape. Larger breasted with a slim waistline. She had an air of sophistication reminding me of Melissa. Her hair was dark and full, just touching her shoulders. She approached Zach and smiled. Zach stood and gave her his chair. I wondered if she was his partner. I had also expected Sam but she was not there.

The guys took the other chairs. I was nervous and calm at the same time if that was possible. I wondered if I got to choose which lady. But the sense of me being the target of all of this was a bit unnerving, like an unprepared job interview that you knew was going to go awry. Deep breath Darian, deep breath.

"Great! We're all here!" started Zach, standing behind the chairs, looking more comfortable standing. "Well, I guess introductions are in order." He spoke almost like a gameshow host but better. He motioned to the one next to me in Zach's seat.

"Darian, I am Denise, nice to meet you." Her tone was businesslike but sexy soft, was all I could think.

"Hi, Darian, I'm Teri!" with an unexpected husky voice. I had expected a British accent but none. She turned to the bodybuilder next to her. I tore my eyes from her legs. Calm down boy, I told myself. Focus.

"Hey, Darian, I'm Don," with a deep full-bodied tone. He turned to the next, smiling.

"Yo, Darian, Jason here," from the hair-band guy, his voice sounded like a tenor.

Finally, surfer boy. "Hi, Darian, very nice to meet you. My name is Josh." His voice was smooth and even, crisp and at the same time soft.

"Nice to meet everyone," was all I could think of, though a thousand questions wanted to spurt out.

"Great! And you know me and Maxie. So, let's start," Zach began. "We know you are probably a bit confused by all of this and this place and that's where we will start." He moved around the back of the chairs a bit, to more face me directly.

"Everyone here is both a trainer and a graduate from this school. Now, I say school because that's exactly what it is. It's a learning center, physically, mentally, and emotionally. When I say 'physically,' yes, I mean in a sexual manner with ways to highly increase the sensual, intimate experience. With 'mentally,' I mean that in order to achieve the physical, the mind must be conditioned and a lot of times, reconditioned. Have you ever heard that sex is mental?" His dark eyes were beaming into mine.

"Um, I think so," I answered, not being sure. I thought I had heard that before and also knew that if one wasn't in the right mindset, the sex did suffer.

"Good, because it totally is mental. Think of it biologically, sex is driven by nerve endings and nerve endings are driven by the brain. Therefore mental, being very simplistic of course." He paused with a smile.

"And, finally, emotional. The foundation of everything comes from our emotions and how we feel and experience them; and as you will see, how we hide them. More to come on that."

"So, obviously you chose to be here, at least for this initial session as I had mentioned. We have already met and discussed the possibilities that you want to investigate." He said 'investigate' slowly. "Are you still of that mindset and willingness to proceed?"

"Yes," came right out of my mouth, a bit too fast I thought. A sense of the Spanish Inquisition went through me.

"OK. So, this session is a double interview and assessment. Double meaning that we are interviewing you and more importantly, you are interviewing us. And then definitely time for any and all questions you have. But let me continue for a moment." He paused again, seemingly gathering his thoughts, but I felt also for the dramatic, too.

"I started this school seven years ago with the intention of helping guys *and* girls, of all adult ages and orientations, attain a higher existence of life and this includes obviously sex as well as higher self-esteem, greater insight into their hidden desires, and to genuinely provide ways to pull those out, *drag them out* if necessary, to really look at these desires and emotions and understand them and realize that this is more of *who* we are – and in the end, have the sheer confidence to be ourselves, our true selves, to all our friends, family, workmates, the whole world – without fear, without worry, without regret. For the greatest regret is never knowing your true self – whatever that may be – *and*, it is different for each of us. Hence the beauty of it."

He had slowly strolled back and forth, never taking his eyes off me. Then, long pause, eyes still on me, I suddenly pictured a Mafia movie when the unexpected 'hit' occurs. I quickly pushed it back.

I couldn't say anything because I was in awe of both his words, his aura, and his powerful passion. Surely, he must have been a motivational speaker, an *awesome* motivational speaker.

I looked around the circle and all eyes were on me instead of him. They were all sincere eyes and it didn't bother me. Zach continued.

"Almost all guys and girls who come here, and I say 'guys and girls' regardless of age for we are all young inside, come here by invitation only, and they all started with wanting greater sex and fantastic ecstasy they only read about. And trust me, they get it. And I can say also get an added bonus of finding themselves in ways they never thought of, or hid from, that can be so deep down, they don't even know it, or won't ever look at it. Think of the inner unknown *effort* to constantly and always keep things hidden – from not wanting to see, but mostly out of pure fear. We live in a society of normality, of stubborn conformity, subduing the *individual* – 'be like everyone else and then make fun of or curse those that are naturally different.' And surely, some actually do find their differences and embrace them – and show them. It will be the most difficult part of this journey – as well as opening up yourself to your true sexuality and physical abilities. It all goes hand-in-hand. It's simply more than sex."

Pause.

Wow, I thought, not exactly what I expected but again the intrigue of such a larger sphere of 'training' was very appealing. Many thoughts were running through my mind.

"OK," he continued, "definitely will have time for your questions but first let's play a little game and then let's let our friends here speak a little, if that's okay," he stopped and waited, but really not giving me any choice.

Not having anything else possible to say and definitely wanting to know more, I simply said, "OK."

"Good. Here's the game. Look at everyone here carefully. First the guys. One is straight, one is bi, and the other is gay. Who's who?"

I hadn't expected that! I knew I had the 'how the hell do I know' look on my face. He read it.

"It's OK. It's just a little experiment of how we prejudge people and in a way, how we prejudge ourselves. Please, go ahead. You won't hurt anyone's feelings. Believe me. Oh, and when done, same with Maxie, Denise, and Teri. One is gay, one is bi, one is straight. You're on!"

The gameshow host imagery burst in again. I took a deep breath and hoped for the best. Part of me already made those decisions as I felt I was pretty good at seeing through people.

"OK, here I go!" I exclaimed more enthusiastically than I wanted to but saw everyone sitting waiting with smiles. It was pleasantly disarming.

"Don, straight. Josh, gay. Jason, bi." I turned to Maxie and said, "bi." To Denise I said, "straight." I turned to Teri and not wishing it but it was my instinct, said, "gay."

They all started to applaud! I felt extremely satisfied and victorious!

All said at the same time, "wrong!"

Episode 25 ~

My eyebrows lifted. I felt my mouth slightly open and I promptly closed it. And I just looked around the circle and saw chuckling and some giggling. Somehow, it was endearing, if I could use that word (which I don't think I have ever used before, ever). Then they all regained their composure.

"Sorry!"

"Yeah, sorry."

"So, sorry, didn't mean to react like that," Teri apologized softly, head slightly down, eyes on me.

The others were nodding in agreement. Zach just stood there looking at me with arms casually crossed. He began.

"Yeah dude, sorry, too. We never had anyone guess completely wrong across the board. You took us by surprise. Really, apologies. You see, and will learn, we are extremely open here. No fear of each other."

Still stunned, I tried to speak. Finally, I laughed and with a smile blurted, "you dirrrrrty bastards!" All knew I was kidding and smiled back. "OK!" I started, a bit too boisterous but feeling good taking some control back. "Let's have it," I motioned to Denise and they went around the room.

"Gay," she said with a smile.

"Bi," Teri whispered, I believe intentionally.

"Gay," said Don with a broad smile.

"Straight," said Jason, flipping his long hair back.

"Bi," stated Josh with a cock of his head.

"Obviously now, I am straight," voiced Maxie matter-of-factly.

Again, my mouth was slightly open. I told myself to shut it and I obeyed. How could I have been so wrong! Everyone wrong! Point made.

"Point made," I finally said. "Way off."

"So, can we ask why you chose what you chose," asked Josh with his boyish smile.

"Um, OK, let me see," I started hesitantly. "Denise, the way you are dressed and hold yourself, I was sure you were straight. Teri, with the short bob hair, totally gay and butch-y. Maxie, you have the air of free spirit, so I figured go both ways."

The guys all waited.

"OK, I apologize, but Don you look so masculine that you had to be straight." I immediately wanted to take that back, knowing masculine didn't define orientation. "Josh, with the boyish look, definitely gay. And Jason, like Maxie, 'free spirit' look, and added rock 'n roll air, I went with bi."

Silence. I thought for a moment they may gang up on me. But all still had a pleasing understanding smile. I felt like suddenly they were brothers and sisters. Then I realized the whole time they were all communicating somehow with each other. Maybe it was their being together long enough and their crazy openness, though it was a bit unnerving. It was like a union of thought which led me to guess that maybe when all 'walls' are eliminated within a group, every part of them, even body expression, is honest and therefore easily read amongst the group. My thoughts mingled between Heaven or Hell, angels or devils, some superhuman, devious power flowing here. It was eerie and attractive at the same time. The intrigue pulled me in.

"Lesson One," Zach stated firmly, "never judge by looks or attitude or voice or anything. *Never.* Because when you are wrong, it inevitably isn't good. You'll learn this more and more. The straightest-looking guy you may know, and judged because of looks, can be completely gay and you don't know it. Why? Probably because he won't let you know for fear of the repercussions. So, we hide it. And that is just sexual orientation. So much more. And you were willing to put yourself on the line in front of complete strangers and was seriously curious at the same time without any malice. You have passed."

Passed? What? I did? Passed what?

"I'm sorry, passed?" I asked almost meekly and feeling weird about it.

"You may begin training anytime. We can get more into how that works but you are an open individual and honest and we all can see that. First prerequisite, my man. Congrats."

"Thanks, but wait. What would have constituted 'not passing,'" I posed truly wondering.

"Easy. For one, if you didn't want to play the game. If you put the game down. Said it was stupid. Ridiculed it. Things like that."

"I don't get it. Why?"

"Because you wouldn't be ready. That's all. Wouldn't mean not possible at a later time in your life though. But without honesty and the willingness to be honest in the face of six fellow humans, being vulnerable, and being fearless of the repercussions, how could you ever start being honest with yourself – and *those* repercussions. Which is the whole reason you are here – and of course, the sex." He smiled broadly when saying 'sex,' like it was a slice of apple pie. (Or maybe a granny apple?)

The smile was charming and inviting, yet mischievous. "Trust me, 'Shock Waves' will blow your mind as well as The Strokeless Orgasm," he spoke calmly, like saying the sky is blue. "As well as the Cumless Cum and much more. Lot's to take in. But that's later. Trust me. More than you had thought, I'm sure. Just need a bit of courage, that's all."

His last comment '...that's all' sounded ominous with a playful twist, like 'you're gonna need it!'

The guys were nodding their heads and the ladies were just smiling.

So, I was in! And being happy to be in ...in something I still had no idea what it was or how it all worked. Was this just a huge orgy? Who touches who? My mind was now reeling knowing if I continued, it probably was a journey of no return. These folks, being genuine, were also very serious about it all. Definitely more than your typical sex therapy.

And the guys here, seemingly like me though now I wondered my own judgments, appeared committed and so damned confident! Don gay? Never

92

would I have thought, nor had a problem with it. I was just so fucking off. I was really embarrassed, too. How could I judge so easily like that! What the fuck do we humans really think? It was all so new and at the same time I was beginning to question everything I thought I knew. And that was only orientation. What about everything else about each of us? Point so made. I wanted answers now. I could tell as usual, Zach read my face.

"Let's have everyone tell a bit about themselves and how and why they are here. Then, QA time and all yours!"

Episode 26 ~

Each gave a brief summary of the reasons they came here, who invited them (since it is by invitation only), what they gained by it and still do, and why they chose to be 'trainers.'

The common theme was feeling lost or incomplete. Feeling not being their whole selves, and more so, that something was missing in their lives, even though they all seemed to have full lives now. And of course, something missing in their sexuality too, their identity, their inability to express themselves, and finally, how it all had brought out their deepest, hidden fantasies, desires, and feelings – sexual and nonsexual. And now each had an aura of complete fulfillment, complete wellbeing. Without it being said, the confidence exuding from that room was contagious, almost intoxicating. Could such things actually be gained in life? And by anyone?

I thanked them all. I knew it was my QA time. But two interesting things kept bothering me. Why hadn't Zach spoke more about himself? And why wasn't Sam there? I knew I couldn't ask either question, so I tucked them away for later.

Before I began, Melissa came to mind, amid all the room's festive atmosphere to put it mildly. I couldn't think which way she would think if she was here. Probably that this was all crazy still and even if was true, would think it too weird to participate. And obviously, Zach had screened me at the party along with Sam and Maxie, and the final screening here. To have honesty. Have no fear. And along with it all, which he didn't mention but I knew – courage. My cowardly-self would be proud! At least at this point.

"This may take a while," I stated hoping for a positive response.

"Take your time." "We have time." "Reason we're here" and around the circle it went. OK, here I go.

"Right. I guess I'll just pose my questions to the group and anyone can answer?" I proposed.

"Perfect," Zach answered for everyone. I thought of Jonestown and made a note not to drink any cool aid on that table if there was any. I smile at myself and began.

"Honestly, I thank everyone for opening up as you did, but is this really worth it — whatever it is in the end? Are you so much different...I mean better, better than before?"

All emphatically said "yes!"

"OK, that was easy. And this costs no money? No anything? All paid for?"

Same answer.

"And I can stop at any time?"

Same answer.

"Um," I hesitated to get this one out but had to, "um, is there touching involved?"

Laughter. A big "yes!" and some "of course!"

I paused and looked around. Faces showed 'you silly boy!' I think they knew my next question.

"Touching by whom...I mean by a girl? ...a ...guy?" My last word dragged out without control and I hoped it wasn't a game-changer. And it may have been for me, but at the same time, my rambling mind didn't know either way. And what if it was somehow necessary. Then I can just bail for no good reason — or even *if* a good reason. I couldn't make any judgments as I didn't know *anything*. It was a question I wanted to ask. I needed to ask. So, I did. Moment of truth...

I saw them looking at each other with the look of who wants to answer it. After looking at Zach, Teri spoke up. She looked me directly in the eye with a very serious look, immediately replacing the girlish childlike look. It took me by surprise.

"The nature of achieving extreme and heightened physical pleasure and awareness requires an understanding of each student and their reactions to stimuli – external stimuli. So, in order to facilitate this understanding so that the training can keep proceeding successfully, as it's not simply one session, in regard to the sexual component, the student is blindfolded and cannot see, when appropriate, who may be *touching* at any point. It will vary and usually is multiple trainers as the student reacts to their own individual sensations. It may be no guy at all but you'll never know. As far as you are concerned, we always say to picture it with whom you feel most comfortable with, though it may not be that person. It honestly makes no difference. It's solely how you react and how fast you learn. We always take the best approach. Success is the goal."

I felt like she was reading a textbook by heart. I paused to let it all sink in and they waited patiently. So, I wouldn't know. Mmmmm I thought. Did I care? I knew my next question.

"OK, I'm fine with that," not being completely sure I was but for now, okay I told myself. My wanting all of this was slightly superseding my fear. Slightly. Somehow though, I felt I could trust these folks. Didn't know exactly why, but I did. "Follow-up question..."

Zach interrupted me.

"You just passed gate number two. Funny, because we were going to bring exactly that up. But you asked on your own." Everyone applauded.

"What?"

"You are willing to trust us and willing to open yourself up to the possibility of a guy touching you intimately. But it is solely *training*, to know *yourself*. And depending on the individual, different methods may be taken. Guys know guys better at times to get results. That simple. Or maybe a girl seeing that she should take over. That's why you'll never know. It doesn't matter except results. It has absolutely *nothing* to do with orientation. It solely means you are openminded enough about yourself, trust your own instincts, ...and you hold enough of your own self esteem. And you trust us. Some guys pack it in at this point. Not many, though. And that is totally okay. It shows whether you are serious or not, about learning yourself at the expense of your own fears. Remember that 'wall' we discussed? You are starting to bring it down. Congrats!"

Congrats came from around the circle. I felt like I won a medal.

"I thought you had said no one ever bailed..." I posed sincerely.

"I had said once accepted and they start, no one ever bails. It's getting to that point. It takes a lot of courage to let down our guards that have been built up for a long time. And to trust us and most importantly, trust yourself. Do you still wish to continue?"

Without hesitation, I answered.

"Absolutely."

I caught Teri's smile.

Episode 27 ~

Wow was all I could think. I definitely knew a lot of guys that would have bolted straight out that door. Then it occurred to me. Did I? Did I really know which of my friends would have bolted and which would have stayed? Remembering the game, I honestly didn't know. Damn.

"Yeah, well I figured if I can't see who, what the hell! I want this." I sounded to me a bit unsure but the room was nodding in agreement. Then it occurred to me, what if I wasn't blindfolded.

"Wait, what if I choose not to be blindfolded during?" I wasn't sure even myself if I had wanted to ask that.

"Not allowed," Denise chimed in. "You must be. The trainers may keep switching and if you can see them, it will cause constant flux in your mind."

"For instance," Josh broke in with his boyish tone. It put me at ease and I didn't know why. "If one trainer is working and it appears to them to have to switch for whatever reason, they will switch so *perfectly*, you will not know it happened at all. It'll all be the same to you. If you could see, it would upset the flow. It's very unique training."

I actually understood the reasoning and still couldn't believe any one of these folks could be touching me at any given moment or some others or… It finally hit me that I was going to dive into this training willingly and I felt my crotch tighten (and not in the way that you think. Dirty minds!)

Oh boy, was all I could think. I surely didn't want my friends knowing that anybody could, would be… My mind stopped in its tracks. And what makes it so 'unique?'

I then also knew why Zach pressed so much about finding your inner secrets and conquering your fears. I *did* fear my friends knowing. And knowing and fearing anything else that may come out of all of this both sexually and emotionally. Would I appear different if I embraced some deep intimacy I was hiding as a guy, as a person? Or anything else I may be hiding? Suddenly, the non-sexual part of the training seemed very attractive, too. Zach and his people were good. My next questions came out naturally.

"Who pays for all of this? Who owns this mansion? Where does all the training take place? How many people are being trained at once? How do I dress?"

My last question took me by surprise. I'm sure it didn't matter.

Zach answered. "I pay for everything. I and my silent partner own this place and all the facilities. These folks are paid trainers, yes. All the training takes place on the premises. There are many rooms on different levels depending on the training part, including the dungeon."

'WHAT?!' didn't come out of my mouth but was definitely on my face. Then I knew I was taken when I heard the light laughter.

"Sorry, that was too easy!" He continued. "We have a vast network of rooms below and stretching out under the grounds to accommodate our client students and where they are at in the training. We fondly call it 'the dungeon.'"

"OK, you got me. Good one." I continued, "this has got to cost a fortune. Do you honestly pay for it all?" I wanted to ask about the 'silent partner' but knew not to ask.

"Yep. And think about it. What's the overhead? This was my family's home for generations. I am one of the remaining survivors and converted a lot of it to this purpose, while keeping the main décor and feel. The rest of the overhead is materials and trainers. And as I mentioned before, I don't need any money. I am very well off. My sole goal is to help guys, and girls, achieve their full potential in their lives, and experience the highest heights in *every aspect* of their lives they just never dreamed of, and finally, really know themselves. For what in return? Two things: the spreading of a new generation of human self-knowing, acceptance, and respect for each other and secondly, as I said, it's a nice repayment for someone very special. It's better than money."

His sincerity was amazing.

"So," he continued, "let's eat something and can chat individually as you will — OK?"

I took a deep breath and agreed. I was eyeing the chilled raw oysters.

We all got up at once. They all came to me and shook my hand, saying welcome, giving well wishes, and patting me on the back. Somehow, two of them really caught my attention now and also from the start, and I didn't know why — Teri and Josh. They were almost like brother and sister. And I had that same feeling. Weird but I let it go and was willing to see how everything went. One step at a time.

I looked over at Zach as everyone went to the small feast.

I could see and knew he read my mind.

Episode 28 ~

We socialized and ate very well. I continued asking my questions as we all stood around mingling. I began to feel a growing camaraderie that comes from everyone being at ease with a strong sense of real honesty from everyone. There was a surrealness about it all and Melissa's warnings still hung in the back of my mind.

I was going to receive a folder with all information within it and a starting schedule. The training timetable was completely variable, with classroom and lab sessions, but no minimum or maximum. All depended on the speed and responsiveness of the student, as well as how long they personally wished. It was the benefit of no costs involved. Some finished the intimate part sooner than the class part and vice versus.

The training was for guys and girls but I was told was very different. Men tended to be so resistant that the training was geared towards aiding them to release it all and learn to break down their 'guy-walls.' And was also told honestly that the few guys that bolt before starting, even though they initially wanted to come, said they saw nothing for them to learn nor did they have any hidden desires or fantasies – which is literally impossible not to, which in all fairness, they may not recognize these are in them. And some weren't accepted because of general closemindedness of their inability in accepting the differences and diversity between people, which is seen in society a lot.

In the end, their analysis is that most really just have such a fear inside of opening up, a perceived view of possibly losing their masculinity, nothing to gain, and finally, the fear of peer, family, and social repercussions of what they may *discover* about themselves – or already know and are unwilling at this point in their lives to share anything openly. It was all good as it is a difficult journey, they kept repeating. And that it only proves how innately we have been conditioned to only see sometimes a perceived world by all the external stimuli thrown at us constantly from birth.

All girls were different. No one every left, nor were any never accepted. I wondered why such a difference existed.

Suddenly I thought of a question for all of them.

"I got a final question. Well maybe 'final,'" I posed.

"Shoot," replied Jason.

"Looking at me, hearing me, and just everything you know so far, what's my sexual orientation?" I smiled waiting to hear their evaluation. It was immediate.

Laughing, Don answered with, "have absolutely no idea!"

"Could be anything," Denise added.

"Can't tell," Maxie joined in.

I was taken back. Surely these folks, these trainers can see into someone's orientation or at least an educated guess. "Seriously?" I replied.

"Seriously," answered Teri. She then put her hand on my shoulder. "There's no real indicator of anything with anyone. We are all complicated and each has their own way of being. You could be any orientation. How would anyone know?"

I saw her and their points. The recent game came back to me. The thought of now really not knowing any of my friend's *real* orientations flooded my thoughts for a moment. And what about Melissa? Was she hiding some secret way about her that she fears letting me know? For some sake of justification, I blurted out, "I'm straight."

"You sure?" Zach added.

I looked at him and all of them, then back at him. "Um, yeah, I'm sure."

He just smiled at me his crafty 'I can see through you' smile. I wanted to then ask his orientation but felt not the time. "Do you have any more questions or can we wrap this up?" Zach asked me directly, following up with, "and there will be time during training to ask more or just call me."

"Honestly, I do not right now. I somehow am sure I will have more."

"Great! Good to have you onboard and remember about looking into yourself – No Fear, Only Courage!"

The most interesting conversation ending up being with Josh and Teri together as they both lingered behind when the rest graciously said their goodbyes, congratulations on my new journey, and their well wishes of my fast success. As Denise was passing by Teri, she placed a long full mouth kiss on Teri's lips, hugged her, and left. Teri saw me and winked. Trying not to stare, I wasn't ready for such openness and wondered if everyone was this intimately carefree with each other. Another part of me strangely welcomed it. I needed to know more.

Even Zach left after saying his thanks and left the folder on my chair. I wondered how many of these initial group sessions occurred in a day.

The three of us just naturally hit it off and simply continued the conversation alone. I couldn't help feel extremely at ease and relaxed with all of them but especially these two. I couldn't pinpoint it.

"We need to move to another room if you wish to continue, which is fine with us to continue," Teri noted. I figured there was another interview group session and probably with other trainers if Josh and Teri were staying with me. It made me wonder how many trainers there are and how many people 'graduated' from here. Who knows, I may know some and don't even know it. Fred came to mind and I was meaning to drill him to find out.

I followed them through a side door and found ourselves in a beautifully crafted Victorian room with a completely different feel and visual. Man, Zach has exquisite taste for sure, I mused. I also remembered him saying he was one of the remaining survivors, which I logged for later, too.

Then it occurred to me, now that the main encounter was over, and I had survived – was I going to be able to survive the rest of whatever was to come – or be the very first guy to bolt *after* acceptance. I thought, Melissa is so not going to like any of this, especially the physical part. She warned me of the consequences. But it was too late for me to turn back, especially meeting this out-of-the-ordinary unique group of humans.

I knew I had to hide it all and somehow get through it without her ever knowing. I felt bad about the hiding and surely the subsequent lying, but she gave me no choice. I wasn't just going to blurt out, "Hey honey! I'm going to find my inner intimate self, break down my guy walls of fear and peer reprimands, and find exciting new things about my personality and total self! Yippee! Oh, and by the way, many people are going to be touching me sexually. No big deal, honey."

Right.

Episode 29 ~

"Why do you think a lot of men would never take this dive?"

"Good question, Darian," Josh replied as he sat in a huge kingly throne-chair.

"Excellent one," Teri agreed. She halfway reclined on a Roman-style sofa. I forced my eyes from her partially bare crotch under the miniskirt. Somehow, I knew she fully intended her look at that moment for me. Was it a test? Am I supposed to look or not look?

"Why do *you* think?" she asked.

"A question answering a question. I like it," I grinned. She smiled back.

"Seriously, we'll let you know our thoughts. But is it okay if you go first?" Josh asked. I nodded.

"It's perceived unmanly. No need. Why bother."

"But it's not. It's actually *more manly*," Josh replied leaning forward. "See the image we guys, well, a lot of guys, have of ourselves is so imbedded, with intense and implied peer pressure added all the time, that any thought of any of these things that can truly open us all up is forcibly cast aside as *unmanly*, as you so nicely put."

"And even if we or you can get inside some brains and logically convince, right away the 'wall' comes up..." she added.

I cut her off.

"The 'wall of fear.'"

"...exactly," she finished. "Finding your intimate self, your deeply emotional self where you are completely vulnerable, *completely vulnerable*, to outside criticism is simply taboo in this current male world. Again, not all, but many. While some guys are very open, we believe it's the vast minority."

"But we all get emotional," I countered. "Look at say a football game or even a championship game, you can't tell me there's no emotion with both guys and girls. What about a funeral? Some guys *will* cry." I felt I found a loophole.

"You are absolutely right!" Teri answered. I was shocked. I was right?

"Then what's the point?" I pressed.

"You may not like what I'm going to say," Teri continued.

"Try me," which came out too competitive. She looked at Josh and he nodded. She turned back to me.

"We are all human. We all have deep emotions. *Very* deep emotions whether we believe it or not. It's part of our evolution, our species. How those emotions allow themselves to be *expressed* is the discussion here. And beyond even expression, many completely deny they even have such emotions. It's too powerless to admit, nevertheless even look at. And yes, on certain occasions, like funerals, the emotions bubble up so strong that they can't be held back. Which proves they are there. But that is not the norm, the everyday norm." She stopped, obviously wanting it to sink in.

Josh continued.

"Picture a balloon inside every person. Inside that balloon are all that person's deep emotions – from the easily obvious ones that float at the top to the ones deeply hidden that are pressed down to the bottom, where no one can see them. There are many ways a person can choose to release these emotions, for they cannot be couped up forever. They always come out or we suffer psychological and even physical damage to ourselves. They are so powerful and we can't get around that. But here's the thing. It's *how* they come out or better yet, it's *how we decide* they come out. Because they *are coming out.*"

Teri picked up. "Because these are coming out anyway, as you see, this balloon will keep growing until some release. We humans make decisions we don't even know we're making most of the time and then 'channel' the forced release in different ways at different times." She paused and cocked her head seemingly asking if I was getting all this. She continued, "ya know something, this is actually part of your initial training! Well done asking and bringing this out now!"

Josh followed with a light applause. I felt honored but still was trying to comprehend though the mist was clearing.

"Every day," Josh then continued, "we knowingly or unknowingly seek to release, and a better word would be 'express,' our emotions. But we are so conditioned to hold them in, ignore them. Think about road rage. Something is built up inside someone so badly, something that has nothing at all to do with driving, and then emotions are triggered and explode in a channel they may not have wanted to use, such as road rage, and ta da! The emotion is released. And again, it may have absolutely nothing to do with a traffic occurrence. That was just the trigger and the channel."

I interrupted. "So, getting back to a championship game, our emotional outbursts in support of our team is just that? Built up, kept inside emotions?"

"Exactly. It's a wonderful channel, too. And there's absolutely *nothing wrong* with it. Competition is always an emotional release. We crave it. Even when we lose, there's an emotional release. We feel love of our teams, our cities, and that emotion of love is very powerful and releases very easily. One channel for release is just such a championship game. It's a wonderful thing but remember the point is that there's an emotional need for 'love' in *a lot of things.*"

"Love equals connection, *requires* a connection. We connect when we love. Whether a sports game or a loving partner in life or a child. We *connect* when we love. And that love MUST come out. Because love is *love*, extremely powerful, no matter the connection that is made. It's still always our human emotion of love. We have an innate need to love. Do you see?"

I actually did. Amazing. I then continued.

"But what you are also implying is that we may channel certain emotions in say surrogate ways?"

"Exactly," they both said in unison. Teri continued, "we definitely can use certain channels to release emotions that have nothing to do with *that channel*. It can be times that our emotional release at say a championship game is partly or wholly pent up from another reason. Some may use sports and competition for that sole reason of release and they don't even know it or would ever admit it. Again, nothing wrong at all with it. It's just learning and realizing more about your own self."

"Remember, the bottom line is that emotions WANT to come out. To be expressed. But many times, say a very deep emotion we don't know we're hiding, comes out of the balloon *looking like another emotion*. It just needed to be released for the balloon was overloaded. Bit complicated. The key to learn, and accept, is to start seeing our own emotions for what they really are and what they really mean, to us."

"No, I get it," and realized something about myself just then and there, but was unwilling to speak it – at least not now. "So, then, it follows that at the deepest bottom of the balloon, are the emotions and feelings we keep very hidden, may not even know, and their energy still needs releasing and may come out as a different expression, or a different emotion. And we are unaware of the actual source. Like say taking the anger and frustrations of a bad work incident out on your partner or children at home, using a completely innocent happening as the reason."

"I think he's passed the first course!" Josh exclaimed.

"Damn right!" Teri agreed. "But sorry, you still have to go to that course."

"No problem. So, then, it also follows that both guys *and* girls have the same type of makeup."

"Correct. And there's more about the juxtaposition of the sexes but that's for later," Teri replied confidently.

"Then, it also follows that based on our conditioning, the way we're brought up both socially and by our parents' influence, and peer influence, school influence, and everything influence, we are each trained to not allow the deep and especially deepest emotions from ever coming out as themselves, and we therefore hide a lot of our true selves behind the 'wall' that can be and needs to be extremely strong."

"Correct again," Teri added.

I felt my love of psychology coming through.

"And…" it immediately dawned on me, "that includes sex."

"Bingo!" Josh exclaimed, pointing at me.

He continued.

"Because sex is one of the *most* suppressed, primal feelings both physically and emotionally we have. Look at human history. And now back to guys of today. The majority do not even know what they are capable of except wham bam. Oh, yeah it's great to have an orgasm," he said it like it was a mere thing, "but it's another thing to experience male 'shock waves' and beyond."

"And female," Teri added, looking slyly at Josh.

"Sorry, I stand fully corrected," he lightly bowed to her. She nodded back and I found myself loving these dynamics.

"You see," Josh added, "when needed, if we can break down a guy's intimate fear of his own sexuality, even his own possible sexual orientation or curiosity, completely bare him wide open to take the *vulnerability plunge*, only then will he see and find his true inner intimate self and in turn, such a breakdown of *that* 'wall of fear' inevitably breaks down other 'walls of fear' *nonsexual*. And the journey of self-enlightenment is well on its way. With the added bonus of 'shock waves.'"

"So, now knowing that first, *there is a wall* or *walls*, and second, that you *can* break them down with courage and help of others, and *third*, how unbelievable you will feel in the end both sexually and emotionally, a whole new world opens up and that whole new world *is the true you*. Being deeply intimate will be normal. Expressing deep emotions amongst guys will be normal. Peer pressure will be irrelevant. Society's random rules and taboos ignored. You will breathe differently."

That last comment took me by surprise but I understood.

"And you may find things about yourself that you really know but just won't look at," Teri added.

I nodded tentatively at Teri's remark, wondering what was really in me though I was starting to see at least a bit over my 'wall.' Just a bit.

I felt daring, so I asked, "when do I get to have 'shock waves?'" sounding like 'when do I get my ice cream, mommy?'

Episode 30 ~

"Soon enough, if you're open to it," Teri answered smiling. I knew she was partially kidding and partially warning me to keep going, with opening up my true sensitive maleness, *whatever* that was, and not some imaginary person.

"I think we're good here. You?" Josh asked me.

"Yeah, yeah, good. How do I get home?"

They both stood up and looked at each other, questioning who would take me home. "I got it," answered Terri. Part of me wanted to jump for joy knowing to see her bare legs next to me in a car… I told myself to calm the fuck down and don't fuck anything up. I agreed with myself.

"OK, great and how to I find my way back?"

"All in the folder," Josh replied, holding out his hand. I shook it and felt the unusually strong grip I wouldn't have expected for his demeanor and build. I was learning a lot of not judging people, ever. I smiled both at him and myself.

"Ready?" Teri asked as she again put her hand on my shoulder and was up a bit closer than I expected. I wondered if orgies really happened here, or maybe just as a side perk, or even a graduation ceremony orgy. Damn, this place and people made me really start thinking a bit over the top but I did enjoy the openness and friendliness, and the growing imaginative ideas (I think). My little red flags were still somewhat up from my natural warning system, but they were slowly coming down. Regardless, I was still pretty apprehensive about the touching thing. Wouldn't you be?

I picked up my folder and followed her out into the main corridor I had recently come down with Maxie. I noticed the group session door was closed and wondered.

As we strolled out, I glance at the folder.

The title on the outside read: 'Welcome to Shock Cum!' and below said: 'Your Journey Awaits You...'

I still loved the title. I smiled at the possibilities and was glad I had followed through...so far...

With deep apprehension still there and...

Terror.

Episode 31 ~

I was still amazed at the mansion, being outside to again see its expanse and beauty.

"Gorgeous, isn't it," Teri said with her attractive husky voice. She sounded female and male at the same time.

"Yes, it is. It certainly is," I replied looking over at her as we walked to her car.

I was a bit surprised that she drove a Toyota Corolla, thinking that everyone here was into high-class autos and homes. It was a bit refreshing.

"So, I assume you know where we're going?" I asked knowing the answer.

"Yep, to your home." I almost asked if she knew how to get there but again, knew she knew. I sat back thinking being chauffeured back and forth was kind of nice. And at the same time doing my best not to stare over at her beautifully sculptured legs while she drove.

"You can look. It's ok," she glanced over and smiled. Fuck, she's good, I thought.

"I wasn't..."

I was cut off.

"Sure you were. I love the compliment." She beamed another smile at me forcing me to admit it by my own smile back. "It's okay to be yourself and to express yourself. No need to hide you adore my legs!" She laughed out loud. I shook my head chuckling.

"May I ask you a personal question, then?" I posed.

"Anything!"

"It seems you and Josh are good friends."

"Yep! And the answer to the correct question is, yes, we are lovers. Not monogamous, just good friendly lovers."

It took a moment to digest 'good friendly lovers' and realized I liked it. The sincerity of these folks was amazing. No games. It wasn't exactly easy to adjust to it but I knew she was patient as were all the others. So much more than sex this is, but I did understand how important that was too in the whole new way of being. I wondered the possibilities. Definitely a *Brave New World*, like the novel, I mused. She continued.

"We're always open for a threesome," she said not looking away from the road. Was surely an invitation, as my mind reeled though at the sudden out of the blue statement, even while getting more adjusted to the carefreeness. I was beginning to also realize there were different kinds of 'shock waves' to be shocked by.

"Um, what? With me? You mean me and..."

Again cut off, but nicely.

"Yeah Darian. With you. Who else do you think I meant?" she grinned a slight reprimand smirk that could have been simply summed up with as 'duh!'

I was taken aback as you might guess with such a sudden, direct proposal of people I just met. Where does it all lead to? What other unexpected 'things' may be down the road? Again, another conflicting feeling consumed me, this time embarrassment and intrigue.

I was silent for a moment as the heated memories of how I lost my virginity was actually in a threesome after playing strip poker with my friend and his wanna-be-girlfriend. I always felt like I had tagged along for the ride but it was my first. And for the record I reminded myself, he and I never touched each other. Only her, though we did it together.

Suddenly, I felt awkward knowing that this invitation meant *all touching all*. I couldn't answer. It wasn't my intent to do so, being straight, but at the same time the charm of it all was making me think how this could work and should I... Then it dawned on me that I may be looking over another 'wall' I didn't know about until someone like Teri pulls me up to glance over it. But still, naw! As if reading my mind, she broke the silence.

114

"I know you're straight from what you stated earlier. It's just that we're both attracted to you. No, worries. Just wanted to put it out there. Never know. Could be fun!" she finished with an uplifted tone. I knew I couldn't, though I was flattered in a very strange way. And being with her was in a way teasing me into it. I pushed that aside. A lot of things at once were hitting me, yet I was intrigued by the adventure of it all.

And when did they have time to discuss it? Or was it body language or some secret way to communicate, 'hey, he's hot! Wanna do him?!' I just couldn't shake the eerie and constant underlying feeling of mystery surrounding everything they all do. I pushed 'cult' back out of my mind...for now.

"Yeah, I don't think that that's for me, right now." I don't know why I added 'right now' and wanted to take back those two words but I let them stay out there in the open air. Did I subconsciously want to leave that door open? I then realized I may have also added them so as not to insult her with her generous sudden offer, giving hope of something I had no intention of doing. While, it was still strange how the proposal caused my mind to picture it.

"OK, suit yourself," she beamed another smile and flipped her bob hair. Her sudden hippie flower-child image struck me.

I wanted to ask if she would like to just with me but since it seemed so inappropriate, I let it go. For now. Then I heard her say, "you'll never know unless you try," in such a nonchalant, confident, sweet feminine/masculine tone, I knew she was setting a 'seed' of a forbidden fruit for me. Not having any idea of how to react or answer, I remained silent.

She knew exactly where to take me. The rest of the ride was in a pleasant silence. I still hid my admiration of her legs as best I could but knew she always knew. My thoughts went to how nice it was there was no game playing, no inhibitions, intimacy out in the clear open, just being their real selves with complete confidence and no malice or desire to hurt. And complete acceptance.

I thought how wonderful it would be if everyone... and another dawning occurred to me. What if the whole world was like this suddenly. No inhibitions at all, not hurting feelings, complete accepting, and apparently, no rules – except respect. My mind went to Zach. Was this the end-goal? A *New Garden*? If it was, I may be very interested, regardless how scary and intimidating it all seemed. Give it time, I told myself. And give *myself* time. It was a lot all at once.

She pulled up slowly to my place and stopped in front.

After a brief awkward silence, she looked at me and said, "come here," in that deep raspy yet feminine commanding voice I couldn't deny. I knew what she wanted.

I came face to face with her as she slowly pressed her lips onto mine, slowly slipping her tongue in. It was such a completely smooth motion that I was mesmerized and then followed, too, controlling myself not to overdo it and lose the moment. Maybe it was all the day's uncertainty, excitement, surprises, and final crazy openness that this simple kiss meant more to me than any other kiss I ever had, and it was over in a few seconds. I felt my heart rise, if that was possible.

With her face still close to mine, and our eyes glued to each other's, and feeling her soft warm breath, she simply said, "welcome aboard, Darian."

Episode 32 ~

No matter how much I was trying to get used to all of this, I knew I was nowhere near where they all were. And even though, bit by bit, I was understanding and getting the feel of it all, so many more questions kept popping up in my confused but happy brain after she left.

Somehow, I felt I was going to wake up from this dream and laugh at how silly I was to dream such a thing, to believe such a thing, such a mini-world where everyone was happy and seemingly carefree. I thought, maybe it was some kind of drug like Soma from the story *Brave New World* where everyone takes it and everyone is always happy. And then on top of it, it was like a revitalization of hippiedom. Free Love is back! I smiled at the possibilities albeit questioning the realities.

OK, Darian, I told myself, it's seriously time to regroup. And seriously time to drag Fred by his heels to the bar and then grill the shit out of him. He owes me an explanation – not in a bad way – but deep inside I know he is involved more than he made out to be. I just know it.

It was still early so Melissa wasn't home just yet but would be soon. I did a quick glance through the documents in the folder – a schedule of classes was one document, and interesting enough, half of them said: 'Lab Work.' Guess I could figure that one out, I tentatively mused. The rest were directions, attire, expectations, conditions, etc that I wasn't ready to dive into and wanted a clear mind before doing so. But a pamphlet stood out dramatically.

It was headed: 'Achievable Male Orgasmic Scintillations Handbook'

What?! Scintillations?! OK, need to look at this right now. It read like a textbook but the underlying message was purely sexual. Purely *male* sexual to be exact, with short descriptions next to each. It was listed as:

117

Gabryel Kevyn

Shudders

Spasms

Shock Waves

The Strokeless Orgasm

The last one really made me wonder...

The Cumless Cum Effect

What the hell was that? And the others? Were these really feelings and sensations I could achieve (still not knowing what they fucking were!) That guys can achieve? Well, whatever they really were, I was beyond intrigued. And how the hell does a guy learn all of these? Do guys actually achieve these or are they theoretical? Where did they come from – and please *don't* pardon my pun, I told myself.

The short descriptions were exactly that, short. Each described a level of extreme pleasure by the physical *reaction* associated. One 'experience' led to the next 'experience,' then to the next 'experience,' with The Strokeless Orgasm being an endless effect of pleasure that was difficult to control. It sounded like controlling wild horses, which fascinated me even more while at the same time made me wonder: was I able to achieve any or even all of this? What the hell did it feel like?!

And 'The Cumless Cum Effect' just was a weird contradiction but I knew a person like Zach wouldn't claim something if it wasn't true. Would he? Why would he? He's making no money out of all of this. I took a deep breath and again felt swimming in the unknown and thinking to keep taking the steps, keep taking the steps, until either all of it was just a shit game, maybe a type of blackmail, or maybe, maybe just real.

I read the final note at the bottom of the page. It read: 'You have a Power you don't even know about – both physically, intimately, mentally, and

118

emotionally you will now begin tapping into. Keep your Courage up!'

I swore to myself that without a doubt, Zach had to have been a motivational speaker. But his fellow trainers were all such nice people, open and kind, supportive and understanding, with absolutely no judgment. Why fake all of this?

I knew I just needed to talk with Fred. Don't you? I was about to call him when I realized the time. Melissa would be arriving soon. Like a boy hiding pornography from his mother, I quickly gathered everything back into the colorful folder and scrambled to find a place to hide it. I found a perfect place.

I went and made a drink and called my dear friend Fred.

"Yo Darian!" he answered with his usual happy confident voice.

"Hey good buddy," I replied dryly.

"Uh, oh. What's up?" He sounded genuine.

"You! That's what's up!"

"Me? Little 'ole me?" I heard his sarcastic, playful tone and it annoyed me.

"Come on! Game is up!" I tried to sound calm but what the fuck.

"What game? ... oh, wait, you met with Zach. I can tell by your tone."

"Yes, I did and at his place and with his... what you call... his *trainers*."

"Mmmm... well hope it was good." I could see through the phone his grinning face toying with me.

"Get off it Fred! What do you know? Really know?"

After a dramatic and I knew intentional pause, "Why, are you accusing me of hiding something from you?" I thought I heard a chuckle but wasn't sure. Again, this was Fred, the master of disguise and intrigue. I knew he was having fun.

"Yes, I *am* accusing you. To Danny's!" I demanded.

"You want to meet at the bar? And now?"

"Stop playing. I'm serious. Yes, and now. I can't here."

"Well, I think I can get free..."

"NOW!" I heard myself scream, my tone reminding me of *Ralph Kramden* from the old sitcom *The Honeymooners* yelling at *Norton*.

"See ya there!" he exclaimed in a sing-sounding tone.

I hung up, hearing that 'I got over on you' tone. I knew he'd be there, so I left in pursuit of the truth. The whole truth. And nothing but the truth!

Well, also more in pursuit of all this... 'scintillating stuff,' but let's just leave it at that. You all know what I mean. Don't you? At least I think I do. I think.

What the fuck.

Episode 33 ~

As I was getting into my car, Melissa pulled up, looking at me with the 'where are you going' look. I walked over.

"Hey, going to meet Fred for a few. Got some work stuff to talk about that happened today. Real shit day," I lied through my teeth with a sense of urgency to avoid any prolonged querying. It worked and I felt bad but had no choice. Time to pay the piper Fred my man was all I could think about. I just didn't like being set up. If that really is what happened. Or a huge hoax at my expense. Fuck! I was questioning everything now.

"Do you want dinner?" she asked in a pleasant tone as I walked to my car.

"Naw, I'll eat there. See ya in a bit."

"OK, bye," she said strolling over, giving me a kiss, and striding into the house.

I felt relieved and horrible at the same time and then realized, shit, I had actually cheated on her with Teri's kiss. Was that cheating? A simple, friendly, sensually crazy, wet, tongue kiss from a hot, horny, cute bisexual girl? The lines are open! Please press '1' for Yes, '2' for No, or '3' for who friggin' cares! It was great! I pressed '3'.

I sucked in a deep breath and drove away, avoiding not to drive at 110 miles per hour.

Fred was ahead of me as usual, already sipping on his drink, gabbing with the cute redhead bartender half his age. She glanced up at my arrival, causing Fred to turn.

"Yo, buddy! You made it!"

"I made it? I asked you here — more demanded," I replied trying to be dead serious but with Fred, I smiled. Damn.

121

"So? How did it go? Nice place, huh?" He spoke like we were talking about a football stadium.

"Yeah, nice place. YOU KNEW! You knew all along! Fucking set up!" I was speaking loudly but lowly, but couldn't help my smile. Bartender stared at me and I smiled at her too, putting my arm around Fred to calm her down.

"What'll you have? On me," Fred offered, completely ignoring my mild outburst.

"You know."

"Done!" He ordered my drink and motioned for me to take up a stool. I did.

We waited in silence until she placed it down and left. I really didn't want the bartender hearing our conversation. I thought of the *Cone of Silence* from the sitcom *Get Smart!* Anyone remember? OK, sorry, back to Fred...

"OK, OK, yeah I knew and know all about the training and all." He was looking forward and then cocked his head towards me with a smug smile. "Thought it be best if you experienced everything by yourself without any prejudice." I looked glaringly at him. He continued rolling his eyes at my stare. "Dude, you would have asked me a million questions and I could never have given justice to it all – and Zach asked for it that way, too. I'm sorry. I was thinking of you."

Damn it, I thought. How does he do it. He just put me at ease with his sell, which made perfect sense. I took a deep breath and was getting seriously tired of taking deep breaths all the time. I gave him a leering 'fuck you' look and then smiled at his pleading, acting-innocent, pouting face. A smile grew on his face. I knew he felt relieved, at least I felt he did. All I could think was: 'so, a setup after all.' I wasn't sure to be angry or glad.

"So, what *do* you know?" I finally asked, getting to the point.

"Everything."

His matter-of-fact tone took me by surprise and at the same time didn't.

"Everything," I repeated. "Everything. Like the blindfold drive, the group session, the tests, the interviewing..." He was nodding each time I stated something.

"…and the food," he added. "Pretty nice, huh?"

I stared at him.

"Come, on," he continued, "was it that bad? Would you have gone if I told you any of that – except the food?"

I still stared.

"No, probably not. You would have had to sell me on it – AND I know that would not have had the same effect, even if it had worked."

"Which it wouldn't have," he added. "You needed to have your own curiosity drive you into the unknown. You showed courage. So, can we get past this shit now. I want to know what you think."

"No, no way. I'm asking the questions." I felt the warrior in me rise up. Needed it sometimes with Fred. But I did like the courage part. "First, have you gone through all of this? Don't lie."

"Yes."

"Yes? Really?"

"Yes."

"Really."

"Yes, dufus, really."

"Huh," was all I could muster as my mind swirled picturing him in classes, in those labs whatever they were, and wait… "did you graduate?"

"Yes. Of course."

"Whoa, my dear sir. You mean…"

He nicely cut me off.

"Yes, I experience all of it. Amazing actually." The matter-of-fact constant tone was pissing me off but not as much as my sheer intrigue was driving me forward. But here was living proof, a real person, a close friend I trusted, providing validation to everything I so far have been told and read. (We guys may have hope as long as we don't have to get a clitoris!)

Was he now my sponsor like joining a fraternity lodge? It didn't matter. I felt a lot better while at the same time a bit uneasy now with Fred. Was he now a 'different' person than I had known before? What secrets did he know? Did he expose all his inner desires? And to whom? Did guy trainers touch him? Was he…? Question upon question upon question until…

"Does Katie know?" jumped out of my mouth.

He paused. "Yes, she does and is a female grad." That took me by surprise. But anymore, I was getting used to surprises, I think. "And pretty good acting at the party, huh? Can't just blurt out all this stuff and then expect not a million questions. People interested have to just go through it naturally, themselves, and we all join together after!" He raised his eyebrows and his drink and grinned that Fred-grin.

"Seriously? Damn, she was good," I reacted quickly. "I have so many questions…"

Cut off again – nicely.

"No way, dude. Like I just said, I'm not. No insider information for you or anyone. Not how it works. You must go in blind and trusting – or any predisposition will compromise it all. It's simply set up that way. The whole reason I introduced you to Zach the way I did. I'm only discussing this, this far, as a friend. Honestly, trust me, it's really worth it. I just wish there was a way to get a ton of guys to break down their walls and take the same plunge."

There was that word again… their 'walls.' And what the hell was 'the plunge' and why won't guys take it? He did.

"OK, I won't press… a lot. Tell me this, if you will," giving him a contemptuous look, meaning you need to answer, "were you doubtful at first? I mean this whole weird orgasmic male thing…"

"…abilities."

"Yes, abilities. Were you doubtful? And if so, why did *you* take the plunge? Doesn't seem like you. Whoever you are now."

He grinned with a pretend crazed look, playing on my words. "Come on," I pressed trying not to sound pleading but did.

"Zach. He's so convincing, so alive, and I was at a point in my life where I felt…" he stopped, thinking, calculating his next words, "…blah. Same o, same o. Work, wife, sex, golf, bars, everything. I mean, don't get me wrong, but it was like…" he went back to thinking, and I could see he found the words he wanted, "…it was like every time a team would lose say a championship or a playoff or whatever, I would get so down and out and took time to recover and then right back into it with the next team or season. And that's just one example." He took a long sip of his drink.

"But more than that. Everything was always up and down, up and down. Even sex. And marriage. And work. Everything in my life. And the funny thing is, I really didn't even notice until I met and spoke with Zach. Didn't even notice. Somehow, he could see through me and understood more about me than I did. Which isn't my style at all, you know. But the openness and sincerity were contagious."

"I didn't know it, but looking back, I was inside wondering if there was more to my life than what I was doing. I loved everything I did and do, don't get me wrong, but it all in the end seemed to have some kind of drab covering over it, muffling out my inner screaming, and everything just repeating over and over and over again. Endless. Never any real satisfaction. But then you keep diving into the same things again and again. As if I was searching for 'myself' in all my own activities – which never, EVER would have occurred to me. Not me. No way me. Like someone turned on a lightbulb. Better yet, a blinding spotlight. Then I started to really evaluate *everything*. Not to change anything. Just, was there more? Was there *a lot* more? Was this all I had in life and all I was going to be? Do you know what I mean?"

I now just stared at him speechless. Yeah, I did.

"I felt my sense of worth was outside of me, not in me. As if I was constantly *seeking* my sense of worth. In marriage, in sex, in golf, in sports, in work, in any competition. Especially competition."

I nodded seeing a Fred I never saw before. He was really opening up to me and kind of blowing me away a bit. There was sensitivity, not weakness, and a feeling of camaraderie at that moment. A side of Fred I never knew before. Was it a new side of Fred or just one hidden?

And it hit me that it was the same feeling of camaraderie I felt earlier in the day with the group and Zach. *And* a guy talking openly with another guy about his inner feelings and doubts. 'Wow,' was all I could think of. I looked at him with a look of sincere: 'please go on.'

"Well, maybe Zach could read me better than I could. And I only met him through playing golf with buddies – you know, people get invited in and you meet different people now and then. Well, he just was different. Really different. But I couldn't pinpoint how or why. Like a feeling of being drawn in. Magnetic. And so we just got talking here and there and I guess he saw somehow a ...*need*? Maybe *my* need. Or my... shit, I don't know. Something. He definitely has a knack."

"Yes, he does," I interjected. "I felt the same thing. It's like he sees through you, knows you."

"Yeah, exactly. But in a good way. Like a brother would. And it's like this amazing street smartness he possesses, like someone who's been through hell and back and actually made it. And now wants to impart it, a new way to be."

"Good way of putting it," I lifted my glass toasting to the point. He joined. I now was wondering where it would all take me. Again, excitement and fear at the same time.

"So, back to the story," he continued in stride, "he simply asked me if I would be willing to try something new in life, something new also sexually. Well! What the fuck! I thought he was coming on to me. He noticed immediately and reassured me it wasn't the case. Then he went through all you already know. And I just went. Simply went, like you did. Just to see. And I'm sure with all the questions and worries you had and have. It just draws you in." I nodded but let him finish.

"Honestly, at the time I thought it was one of my golf buddies putting him onto me, kind of like I did to you," he smiled genuinely, "and after graduating, it *was* one of my buddies. It's like a secret society, building member by member, but always going in blindly, with blind trust. A brotherhood and sisterhood of guys and girls who honestly are more powerful and strong inside and outside than they ever were before. Kind of like we all achieved together another level of living and only we know. This stuff brings out of you *intense* emotion, personally and intimately, and how do I put it... a maleness we never knew was in us. We are stronger and without facades. We're free to express our emotions, our previously hidden..." he paused, "...*desires*, and then naturally are open to everyone else's. You'll see more about conditioning, repression, and especially, resistance. It's a bit scary at first. But once you're one of us, you're one of us."

He smiled a grin reminding me of the *Cheshire Cat* from *Alice's Adventures In Wonderland*, though Fred didn't disappear. But I got that eerie feeling again...

Anyway, it still sounded like a cult and maybe it was, but with a possibly new meaning of 'cult?' Was this how you felt when being inducted or better yet seduced into a cult? Was Fred and Katie brainwashed and didn't know it? No. I can believe Katie but no way Fred. Then, maybe, just maybe, it was really a new 'society,' an underground new hidden *culture*. A real-life *Utopia*. I actually liked the sound of that.

And I was still pondering the word 'powerful.' Are we really that conditioned? That repressed? Resistance to what? And we don't even know it? Nor do our spouses and partners? Going through the same motions as our parents, our fathers, our friends, our families – expectations over expectations ...centuries over centuries? Was war just an explosion of our inner male emotion that are so deep, they are forced out of our internal protected balloons? Did we *need* to fight, to *conquer*, to express our real selves, but not in a constructive way, but in destructive ways. Was any form of modern competition, whether organized or personal, just a replacement for war without destruction? Did we therefore *need* to compete all the time, to win all the time, or experience it in others' competitions and wins? Was this need hiding other needs deep in us? That would be scary. My thoughts were airborne.

I may need a parachute.

I ordered two more drinks.

Episode 34 ~

We toasted our shots with Fred saying, "to new beginnings!" I nodded, still swirling a bit and not from any alcohol. I told myself to slow down because I still had to drive. I told him, too.

"You mentioned a 'secret society,' is there really some society like the Elks Lodge or Knights of Columbus?"

He looked at me with a slightly piercing gaze that I took as, 'dude, way more!' He took a sip and fully faced me.

"I really shouldn't go this far, again because you need to do the journey as planned, but since you seem highly motivated, I don't think letting a tad bit out will hurt. If so, don't blame me – OK?"

I nodded.

"It doesn't end when you graduate – unless you wish it to end – but no one ever wishes it to end. Reason? Because it's like making hundreds of new friends and now getting to thousands of new friends. This is not small, dude. But it is amazingly secret, I guess for now. Zach's wish to keep everything as he puts it: 'pure,' without infiltration of bad seed. Reason for such screening and the screening continues as you go through this." He paused to let that sink in and somehow, I knew that would be true.

"It's so hard to explain. It's such a feeling of…the only thing I can think of would be a strong feeling of connection with everyone who passes through it – a brotherhood and sisterhood that is now so natural, you see it in each other's eyes immediately. You know them when you meet them. And it's more than a 'brotherhood' or 'sisterhood' which implies separateness. It's like a 'humanhood.' And you never lose anything. You only gain. It's a continuing happiness. Like someone handed you a billion dollars with no conditions.

Better yet, someone handing you the keys to your personal Heaven and everyone has theirs – and we share as we will. Even if it's just a friendly chat. You will know them."

"So, it *is* a sort of lodge thing like that. Or a cult?" I threw it out there.

"Not a cult. Seriously. You think I would be conned into a cult? And it's not something you join nor something you need a charter member to sponsor you. Doesn't work like that. You immediately are a part, an individual who is also one with everyone. It's a *sense*, not a literal membership per se. And nothing binds you, either. That's why it's called a society, not a lodge thing. Or a cult," he mimicked me a bit which was fine. I think I got his point. Next question and hoped he'd continue.

"Is there a name? I mean other than 'Shock Cum!'

He laughed. "I so love that name! *Shock Cum*! Like Shot Gun!" I looked at him to get on with it and answer my question.

"OK, OK, yes, and it may sound a little corny but it's really serious. It's simply called '*The Society of Oneness and Ultimate Love.*' We call it our '*SOUL.*'"

It sounded really weird to me at first, again very cultish and even corny. But when broken down, word by word, it made sense. And I assumed somewhere in there was the 'physical' stuff. You know…'o' 'r' 'g' 'a' 's' 'm' lol. Back to our show…

I whispered it slowly back at him. After a quick pause, I followed with, "I like it. I actually like it."

"Really? I was sure you'd think it was weird or corny. …*of Oneness and Ultimate Love?*" Wow, he read my mind but I still liked it. I knew Fred was being honest, too. Still sounded a bit cultish but I didn't care at that point. A lingering question was waiting on my lips but I waited.

"No, no, it's totally appropriate," I replied, thinking of that magical kiss from Teri. That kiss was more than sexual. I knew now it was a sort of love, a gesture of offering a kind of *oneness* and by someone I just met. How could she be so open? Most people would never.

"Zach loves it too because the oneness means we are all in this life together and accept each other unconditionally, without prejudice. And as he puts it, which you will see, *love* means every part of love – love of life, love of each other – friendly and/or intimately, and especially as he always says is the most important and the basis of everything: love of yourself – both personally *and* sexually. You will learn to really love yourself – with no fear. That's what you will experience and learn if you follow through. Plus the cosmic cumming!" *Cheshire Cat* grin again. "Hey, it's *all* amazing. Never thought I'd ever be part of something like this."

I was listening but looking down. *If?* He doubts I'll follow through? He read my face.

"Dude, love you like a brother. But 'male resistance' is so strong in us, each step you will take will be a breakdown of that resistance and it may not be easy. You may wish to just leave."

He made me feel weak, that I couldn't handle it. I felt a bit of anger at somehow being called a coward. But what if he was right. What if it ended up being too much for me. No! I was dedicated and would fight my way through this resistance thing no matter what. I wanted that gold at the end of the rainbow …and more!

"Tell me more about the society."

He took a deep breath and I could tell he was debating whether to or not. He sighed and continued.

"*The Society of Oneness and Ultimate Love* meets monthly if you wish to go and the group gets larger and larger each time. We now have video conferencing for folks unable to attend for any reason, but mostly out of state and some out of country."

Wow, I didn't realize it was that big. He continued.

"It's literally amazing. And the camaraderie when we meet will blow your mind. Strangers hug and kiss. No stress, no fear of rejection for any reason, or how you are, or want to be. Folks will ask you if you need anything, any help, a nice talk, and yes, sex. It's completely natural and goes against almost all of society's rules and expectations. That's why it's a private society."

"People will offer you gifts, their time, offer you intimacy, anything, freely, and you can accept or not, no repercussions, no jealousy, no hurt feelings. If you have a sole partner, it's respected – but they will still ask! It's so honest, people just naturally accept you. There's no judgment of sexual orientation either. And if you're curious, like bi-curious, there's always someone who will listen. And, if anyone is in financial distress, it's solved. Period. All chip in without being asked. Really weird at first but once in, you breathe differently when together. And you miss it when gone."

I was taking it all in. Sounded like a new world to me. I again thought of *Brave New World* but without the Soma drug. It intrigued me about the partner part, thinking about Melissa. "Tell me more about when you have a partner."

"Again, the societal rules of 'partner' change. Well, basically no rules, only your own wishes and how you want to truly be. But in the end, the definition of a 'partner' changes where the ownership idea simply goes away. No one feels that way. 'Partner' then becomes the one you like being most with."

I thought of Teri again and Josh.

"In the end, having a 'partner' more becomes a 'favorite' and again it eliminates ownership, eliminates jealousy, eliminates cheating, eliminates divorce. No one thinks that way anymore. The new inner feeling molds and gels more completely every time, for yourself and with everyone else. It's like a growing ...Nirvana."

I thought of Sir Thomas More's *Utopia* and wondered if this was the realization of it in modern times.

He paused, contemplating, then smiled broadly, "and the sex play! The creative ways and wonderful set ups! Expecting the *unexpected* is so much fun and people get really creative. Or can be a simple candlelight dinner and soft romance. But destroying all the 'false boundaries,' while keeping respect, we all gain everything. And it's not a big orgy, unless you organize one," he grinned again, "it's complete and honest freedom. Free to be you. Free to experiment with no judgment. And back in the world, you see everything differently, and so easily see the societal made-up boundaries, limitations, and criticisms. It's a 'not going back' kind of thing, in fact an unwillingness to go back, because it doesn't make any sense anymore. Taking this plunge, full board, simply creates a fearless, respected, accepting world. One you don't want to ever leave."

"Whew, OK," I chimed in, "well you probably went further than you were allowed." I was glad though. I thought of Melissa again and logged in my mind to think how to bring her in – and into something I wasn't even into yet myself, or completely sure of. But the feeling of adventure was amazing.

Then again, what if it didn't work for me? Whatever 'worked' meant. But, I was psyched more than before. And that kiss I could taste, and if she and Josh were examples of such openness, I wanted in – both sexually and personally. And it all started with 'hadn't noticed.'

"Not for everyone – at least not everyone is ready," Fred added. "That's why it's by invitation only and referral only. Zach is very careful and protective of all of us, and us of him. We're a human free family. I always told him that we could make millions from this and he just laughs me off. Not his goal at all as you know."

Did I know? For sure, *know*? Again, overloaded. But 'shock waves' kept coming back to me. And that *kiss*. I can't get over it. And a knowing I was beginning to really *feel* more, *want* more. It was intoxicating and magnetic at the same time. I wondered if this whole conversation was another setup. If it was, I was OK with it.

"Well then!" I exclaimed facing full forward to him, going for the jugular. "Answer this! Have you had the pleasure of '*shock waves?*'" A very slow grin grew on his mouth. And he waited, just looking at me. To me, this was one of the main points, main achievements I wanted (almost to prove a point), as well as the whole picture painted. And I wanted *male* 'shock waves' – *whatever* they were – and I was going to get the info from him. Period.

"Well, my man, I see no reason at all to disclose whether I have or have not."

"You said openness."

"Yes, openness to how open you wish to be. Doesn't mean I or anyone has to answer anything. And remember, you must accept that."

"Fuck you."

"You wish."

I thought, did he mean that?

"Not."

"I mean *you* wished, not me," he laughed. I gave him the finger and he laughed more.

"Come on!"

"All I can say is, it is totally worth it and you will be very, *very* happy," he claimed confidently. Damn him. I somehow knew there was no way he would disclose any more and I knew it wasn't that he was scared or anything. He just wanted me to experience it in the right way, in the right path per the program. I guess also, in *my* way.

"OK, you win," I conceded, "*but*, if I am not VERY happy or made a fool of, I'm coming after you!" I grinned but it was a serious grin. He got it.

All he said finally was: "trust me. Welcome aboard!"

I sighed and resigned myself to my own destiny. We finished our drinks and as I walked out, all I could think about was my guy-horny-crotch exploding in shudders, in spasms, *and* the ultimate, and fabled experience of! That's right Johnny! These damn here *fucking* 'shock waves!' And another kiss...

This all better be fucking true.

Anyone know the Vegas odds?

Episode 35 ~

I drove home feeling somehow uplifted like I never was before. I felt inspired by everything while at the same time feeling very horny. Strange combination.

I knew I was going to get to the first thing on that schedule as soon as possible. The lab time scared the hell out of me. What was going to happen? I told myself to shut the fuck up, man-up, and get a'movin! I chuckled at my 'man-up' reference. Such a cliché! Can someone 'woman-up?'

In the end, my only real debate, and I think my only real fear, was Melissa. My debate was to just let her know, keep it open, no secrets. And I honestly wanted to convince her to go also – though I had no idea what the program was for girls. But if Teri, Sam, Maxie, and Denise were any indication of intimate and personal (and sexual) freedom and happiness, it's gotta be worth it for her to just check it out. And I knew I'd be a completely willing partner to be taught the ways of ultimate clitoral power! I shook my head at my so recently new crazy thoughts and metaphors. Who am I becoming?

Then again, arguing with myself as I drove, she may completely blow up on me and follow through with her threat to leave. The word 'threat' hung on my tongue. When did we end up with a 'threat' before? Never. Is this how relationships evolve? Is this...*acceptance*? Threats?

I just knew that my heart was wanting her to join me on this venture, the two of us, together journeying into the unknown, finding and discovering things together as one. Obviously, her first instincts were highly negative and defensive. Zach warned of this. But still. I knew I had to do this and couldn't let her or anyone interrupt this voyage, this path I was on, this crossing over into the fathoms yet unseen. But somehow, seen. Weird. But I needed it. I needed more. And even though I needed her, I needed me more, I was finding out. Know what I mean?

My mind paused. Does anyone really need another? Or was it in the end just fulfilling a need of their own, inside. Fuck. I was thinking like Zach and now Fred. Was this brainwashing or them helping me evolve into a new evolution of me? I had to find out. Never saw *so much* centered on the male of the species and *his* needs, his powers, his sexuality, his conditioned inhibitions, and anxieties of discoveries. My mind was crisscrossing randomly but onward I told myself. Too far already.

I pulled in and walked to the door. It was slightly ajar. I thought, this is unusual. Felt like it was beckoning me to enter. I had a sense of danger, of not entering. I stopped at the door for a second and then just entered.

Walking through the foyer, I turned into the living room finding Melissa sitting on the couch looking up at me with a strange look. I paused and realized it was a combination of anger and betrayal. It took another second for my eyes to disengage and look down at the coffee table. Strewn all over the table was my folder and all its contents in an almost wild disparage manner, as if each paper and document was examined and tossed anywhere on the table. My heart sank both from embarrassment and that feeling of being 'caught.'

"Are you fucking serious?!" came out of her mouth with such force I could almost feel her hot breath from where I stood, with her eyes piercing with anger. Normally, I would struggle to reply back to her when she got this way, even though this time it was the most I ever encountered from her when she was seriously pissed – which was actually very rare.

But for some reason I didn't this time. Something in me stood up inside. I knew what it was. It was courage.

"First of all, who said you could go through my private stuff?"

"Private? When did we have '*private* stuff?'"

"Come on!" the anger was building in me and my mental flags sought to control it. I did. "Not everything can be shared, even with couples. And this is private to me and we agreed that if I wanted to, to just keep it secret away from you." My calmness surprised me after that.

"I don't remember it that way," she hissed.

"Well, it really doesn't matter…"

She cut me off.

"It *does* matter, Darian! Did you read this? Are you planning on having sex with like …multiple people?" she paused waiting for an answer that didn't come. "Seriously? You are!"

"I have no idea how it works but there's a process," I was making up what I could, not really knowing the exact facts.

"Even better! You have no idea! Do you hear yourself!"

Of course I did and I continued. "I hear myself loud and clear. This is my business, my need, my path, and my life."

Who the fuck was talking? Me?

My matter-of-fact calmness I saw took her by surprise – and me, too. But the torrent revived.

Looking up at me and then down at the document right in front of her and then back at me, "this 'STEPS TO TRUE MALE FULFILLMENT' states it recommends to then 'teach your partner.' Teach me what?! I am not getting involved in any freaky sex act no matter what you *neeeed!*"

"It's just saying that partners should help each other find their fulfillment…"

Cut off again.

"No! I don't care. This whole thing has gotten to you. Why? Because I said something after sex that one time? Are you that shallow?"

Shallow?

That was it!

"Shallow?! Is that what you think I am…"

Cut off again.

"I think all men are shallow. Your fragile fucking egos are sometimes too much to deal with. Goddamn male ego falsely trying to believe you're something you're not and always compensating… most probably because of small dicks. Very tiring." She forcibly sat back on the couch with a finality.

I didn't think my dick was small but I let that one go. I just paused, letting all that sink in. Whether it was the recent talks or just a newfound psyche, I let loose.

"You know what? That's all complete bullshit. All the fucking shit about fragile male egos is such fucking bullshit! It's a put down honey. It's gaslighting. Don't you see. If you say it enough, we all end up believing it or worse, pushing it deep down inside where it festers."

I felt like Zach for some reason. But the words just kept coming out. And I remembered reading somewhere about gaslighting technique. Her face was simply 'amazement.' But I let it out – more than I wanted but I couldn't stop myself.

"Ever since your fucking sexual revolution you women gained such confidence it's been an endless foray of put downs to us in order to build and keep that confidence. You won! Bravo!"

I was seriously wondering who was actually talking. And I honestly had no problem with that sexual revolution. It was right. I was talking about us guys and the effect long-term on us! It was like I was watching myself from the outside.

"Yes, we have dicks, cocks, peeeeeeeeeeenises! Why the fuck is that a crime all the time, why are we blamed for it all the time, why is it a… *fault*?! Is it because you don't?!"

I knew I was heading down the path of pure hell but couldn't stop.

"And if we're not around, here comes the dildo! Maybe it's you that have the obsession with our cocks and you hide it. And then blame us for having one. Pathetic! Then put us down and we start believing all this shit."

My tirade kept exploding out as if bottled up for centuries… Battlelines were drawn! Protect the flanks! All reserves in now!

"I really believe it now because you and every other female may *lose control*. You dress up extraordinarily sexy, half-naked, and then blame us if we look!" My mind flew to Teri and how she thanked me for my complimentary watch of her beauty and her show of her sex. I finished with words I never thought would come out of my mouth. "You play with our minds to boost your own egos... *your own fragile egos!*"

Gloves were off! She pounded back.

"You're fucking crazy and you know it. This is a game from Fred and obviously Zach too, all of you completely consumed by your own egos. Especially that Zach!"

I felt myself strangely wanting to defend Zach, wanting to say, 'he's just extremely confident in himself,' I said nothing because I knew at this point it was going to go nowhere. This wasn't an argument either would win. Always down to a battle of the sexes. I hated it. But I resigned myself to it.

And the strange thing was I was helping it along. I wanted it all out. I thought suddenly, how would I have actually reacted if I was fully trained? It was regrettable. At least hopefully not the irrational tirade I just performed. She continued after taking a deep breath.

Here came the 155mm howitzers full blast.

"You're on your own with this. Join that shit...fine! Perverted to me. Or go to a sex therapist. You're being brainwashed." I heard doubt in her voice. "I'm done with this bullshit and your middle-age crisis." Then in a final volley of anger and exasperation, "and *FUCK* your ego! Fragile *shit!*"

She stood abruptly. Glared at me and I saw both hurt and confusion. She stormed upstairs to the bedroom. I knew there was no recourse nor did I want any recourse. I didn't like what just happened but everything in me felt relieved for some reason. My pent-up emotions, my balloon, had exploded wildly. They were right. And it dawned on me. Even in my haphazard amateur way, I felt my own confidence. And it was real. I knew it.

And I had no intention of hurting Melissa but there comes a time when things go awry uncontrollably, especially when a partner exhibits a newfound freedom they didn't know existed before. Maybe that's a threatening thing. And inside I knew it wasn't her fault, or my fault, or anyone's fault. Change is difficult, it's always said. And now I really knew it. What was going to happen next I truly wasn't sure but I knew without doubt I was going to follow through. Nothing was going to stop me now. Half of it was sheer curiosity of what and how I can become so much more in every way, including intimately. I was completely addicted now.

My last thought before going into the den to watch TV and eventually go to sleep on the recliner...

Will the battle between the sexes ever end?

Episode 36 ~

I awoke with a start not realizing I was still in the recliner. It's that strange feeling when you think you are somewhere else but you are not. It was already light out and I glanced at my watch for the time. Shit. 8:25 and I had a call at 9:00. I jumped up off the chair and hurried upstairs. Melissa wasn't there getting ready and I assumed had already left for work though it struck me that it was earlier than normal. I couldn't process that at the moment. I shaved and cleaned up myself for the teleconference.

Since I worked remote, there was no need to change into anything except my shirt which I did quickly, grabbed a fast cup of coffee, and sat at my desk in my home office.

With five minutes still to go before the call, I fingered through my emails and texts on my phone. Nothing new of any importance. I half expected something from Melissa after yesterday but there was nothing. I put down my phone and got on the call.

I kept trying to put all the recent happenings out of my brain as I was a major contributor of the call that had at least 20 colleagues listening and speaking. I kept my focus as best as I could but still found myself wandering to different thoughts in between conversations. The conversation came back to me on the call and I proceeded to discuss what I needed to discuss when my phone buzzed. As I was speaking, I propped my phone against my laptop's screen so I could see the text while still looking forward into the camera. I almost laughed thinking like when driving, I shouldn't text and teleconference at the same time.

It was Melissa. I opened the full text and waited to read it, though I was itching terribly to know. I so wanted her onboard with this as Fred said Katie was and we could all commiserate on our adventures. Definitely would be both fun and strange at the same time.

The call went a direction away from me, so I chatted 'brb' and turned off my camera and mike. I read the text.

'hi. I didn't want to leave a txt but didn't want to discuss this anymore at least not right now. going to spend some time at my sis and took an overnight bag. hope you understand I just need to sort this through. love M.'

That was it. A quick 'I'm outta here.' I read it again and then again. I had no idea how to reply. An 'overnight bag?' Does that mean one night, two? A week? Forever?

I could tell the conference was coming to a close so I decided to bail. I chatted I had to go and dropped. My fingers just started typing.

'hey. you don't have to go. can we just talk again? can I call you now?' I didn't expect an answer but one came immediately. She must have been waiting.

'k'

I called and it took a moment for her to pick up. I got the strange feeling she might not have answered.

"Hey," she said quietly.

"Hey," I replied similarly.

Awkward silence. I went on.

"You don't have to leave. Seriously. We can talk this out." I was afraid if I didn't do something now, it may be forever. "Melissa?"

She cleared her throat. "Look, I know you have to do what you have to do and I know you well enough you are going to no matter what," she started, in now a firmer tone. "It's just like all of a sudden. I don't even know you anymore."

I let that sink in and it came to me that she was right. Maybe better stated was 'not know all of me.' Maybe this was true with all partners, married, living together, whatever. Maybe we all need to open up our insides and conquer the fear with courage and self-power and maybe there'd be so much less stress in relationships, in marriages, and less divorces. Do we always enter into relationships half-knowing everything at best, and the remaining underlying things become natural landmines we never see coming? I focused back.

"I know this is a lot…"

She interjected, "weird."

"That's your opinion. I just want to see. I want to take the plunge into whatever it is that will," I paused not wanting to say the rest but I did, "…help me find the real me."

"The real you? So, you have to have sex with a bunch of people like an orgy or whatever to *find the real you?*" The rising vindictiveness was irritatingly apparent. I accepted it. Who was I becoming?

"Yeah. I may have to if that's what it takes."

"So, you mean the real you…sexually?"

"That's part of it. And my inner self behind the 'wall.'" I regretted what I said and at the same time, felt good having said it. I was in a contradictory world. What was I going to lose? I tried not to think about my dick but I did.

"What wall?"

I knew it was going to get too deep and tried to get away from a long dissertation of at least what I knew at that point. I felt like I was on a highwire strung across a windy desert, a thousand billion feet up, and any false move I would drop to my untimely bloody, bludgeoned death.

"It's just a phrase they use…about…whatever is keeping my true emotions in…it's complicated."

"So, you're not sure? Not sure what you are getting into? Seriously? More than fucking with others — which by the way is not acceptable to me. But my feelings aren't important because you *are* saying fucking others is mandatory to find your newfound… identity. So, how I feel doesn't matter in this equation?"

So that was it. It had to do solely with the physical part. She didn't really want to hear about the whole experience and that sex is an integral primeval need we can all struggle with along with our emotions, fears, and everything else that embodies each one of us. I heard my own thoughts as if a preacher was inside my brain. And I realized the preacher was me.

"Yes, not a newfound identity… a fuller, complete identity."

"And you need to fuck for this?"

She wouldn't let it go and just wouldn't understand, nor wanted to. She was fixated. Inside I could understand her point but it was a jealousy point not an understanding point. I didn't answer for I didn't know what to answer anymore. It seemed moot.

"Maybe it's good we take time apart," I heard myself say.

Silence.

I continued, "it may be for the best until I get through what I need to get through, as the more I learn, the more I may want to know. And it's not brainwashing. It's logical actually."

Silence.

Finally, she spoke. "I completely agree. Let's leave it at that."

I paused at her finality. "OK, let's leave it at that. But we are not breaking up."

She paused and I knew she was processing my firm statement.

"OK, let's just see what metamorphosis the new Darian appears to be in the end. But it's also the sex thing. I gotta go. See ya." She waited.

All I could say was, "see ya," because I knew she was done talking. And she had added that final knife wound of 'but's it's also the sex thing,' into my side letting me know for sure in her mind that it really wasn't about any metamorphosis at all. It was about having intimacy with others and the strong probability of that continuing afterwards. Which, I knew, was a sure possibility though I also was really beginning to understand that it was ok even with having a 'partner.' Even healthy for the relationship. Pure openness and acceptance. Could it really be possible? Could people actually be that way?

I didn't have to press the end-call button as she already did.

Episode 37 ~

We knew each other well enough not to get really angry with each other. It wasn't our style. We made a joint decision (though I wasn't totally onboard with it but didn't see any other way), and that was that... for now. I actually felt relieved in a way that I didn't have to hide anything anymore and took it as if a vacation to a secluded spa. A potentially insane spa, but I desperately wanted to go. My heart was completely into it. And to see Teri again, if that was possible. Not as a new partner, but ... I really didn't know why. Something about her. And even Josh. They both exuded a kind of pure sensuality with complete confidence in themselves. Plus, they were both attractive.

I paused. Did I just think, say to myself, that a guy was *attractive*?

Paused again. Yes, I did. And why can't a guy see another guy as attractive without sexual desire? Girls do it all the time with other girls. I could feel a strange mindset rolling over me. I was thinking differently. It was creeping in. And was creepy, really creepy. But I wanted this weird freedom to think, say, feel, even touch any way I wished. And without judgment.

I smiled a half smile. I believe most of us guys are so behind girls in expressing ourselves. And as I was learning, it is no longer some manly thing to repress. It was *there* to *be* expressed. And many a guy never will. But it's literally impossible to be human and not have deep feelings. And even hidden feelings. We ignore them and therefore are contradicting ourselves. I needed to find out more and vowed in the end, I was going to convince Melissa of the same.

I knew what was going to happen next. She came back that evening and packed her things. Not for an overnight but for a while, probably a long while.

145

We were both amicable though there was naturally an underlying tension. I could also feel that she was confused that I wasn't putting up a big fight to win her and convince her not to leave. And the fact was that I wasn't going to do that. I actually wanted her to leave, on top of all the feelings that I wanted her to stay. I just knew I couldn't have both. So, leaving was the right thing to do... right now. At least that's what I told myself.

I helped her take her things downstairs and to her car. After placing them in her trunk, she turned to me, face to face. I felt her soft breath. And saw watery eyes.

"See ya," she whispered, gave me a soft, touching quick kiss, turned, sat in her seat, closed the door, and drove off.

I whispered, "see ya," to the evening air.

Episode 38 ~

Next couple of days were routine, albeit no Melissa. But the quiet solitude worked well for me. I needed to rest, unwind everything, and then put it all back together, like a new puzzle.

I did my normal stuff: work calls, routine masturbation, bars with friends, burgers, some lamb chops, TV sports and action movies, reading, sleep, work calls, routine masturbation, bars with friends...

I realized suddenly but not unexpectedly that I was truly in a routine, a constant round-robin of the same stuff, with my general excitement being bars, burgers, and TV. Oh, and masturbation. I thought to go to some singles bars or try dating sites but I was still hooked on Melissa and pushed those temptations away, for now.

As each day went by, I felt like some typical male 'image' playing out the roles – with absolutely nothing wrong with it as I did enjoy everything as guys and I guess girls do too but there was also an increasing awareness of an emptiness. I didn't know at the time but I had actually stepped back away from myself and was looking back in – something I had never done before. It was surreal.

I was the actor in my own play and the audience at the same time – or maybe the accused and the jury. For me at least, that vantage, day after day, brought out a weird hollowness as if there has to be something else, that there *was* something else – and the feeling crept deeper and deeper and I felt the 'wall' more and more – somehow in my way. My own personal hidden 'wall.' I couldn't get away from it.

The following week I scheduled my first classroom session. I chose all of them in the evening. My first lab I scheduled for the weekend as that's when they were only available, which struck me as odd. There was no explanation for the weekend timing. I assumed maybe needed more time, more energy. More energy? Was I fit enough for whatever this was? And of all of this, it was the 'lab' time that still had me crazily puzzled with that dreaded feeling of anticipation – and fear. I kept thinking this is where the pedal meets the metal (pardon the cliché but fuck it!)

The rollercoaster ride intensified as the days drew near. I felt my normal, how can I put it now, my normal maleness? ...my normal masculinity? ...my normal guy-ness? ...my normal macho Italian-ness ...all kind of grinding down with an increasing sensitivity, a vulnerability that I couldn't shake. Like a doomsday looming. I knew it was coming, and fast. All by my own doing. Well, I can blame Fred, too.

Can we just continue to hide our deepest feelings, our hidden ones we don't even look at or even know, but somehow do know there's something there, behind the 'dude-veil,' behind the 'cocky-show,' until some catalyst tears at it and pushes us to look inside. With each day the unnerving feeling grew more and more like a growing storm approaching as I somehow knew that not turning back at the last minute would forever seal my destiny. But my destiny of *what*?

I kept thinking of Teri, Josh, Zach, and even Fred and all their confidence yet complete frankness of their feelings and their acceptance of themselves and each other. It was that experience with them that kept me moving forward to my day of decision. My D-Day. Hitting the beaches. Blind. The struggle was a struggle I never had before. Was I going to bare my complete soul and then breakdown in front of everyone? Or look into the abyss and scream running? Or stand strong and weather the onslaught? But onslaught of what? 'Our intelligence network has broken down, sir!' I just didn't know, and that's the fucking frightening part.

In a way I blamed them for pulling at me but knew full well it was my own decision to take those initial steps. And for what? 'Shock waves?' Yes. 'Shock waves' and every other power I had inside I didn't and never knew.

The others I have not known long but Fred, Fred I have known long and trusted.

And maybe finding more of yourself *is the want* – actually finding there *is* a want. I found myself just wanting everything – the sex power and excitement, the openness, the clawing and ripping down of my 'wall' or 'walls' until I lay bare, and knowingly and acceptingly being vulnerable, and then to know if I really had the courage to do all this, the courage to see my sensitive, emotional, sensual, intimate, elusively subtle part of me side by side with my masculinity. It finally hit me. Femininity and masculinity side by side. Or maybe, maybe not side by side, but as one, married in me, one human, not defined by a fixed gender image that has existed since the dawn of human civilization, since the *Garden*.

Was I ready for any of this? Are any of us ever ready? And was I willing to see and accept something of me, a part of me that I just couldn't see right now, and allow it to be, knowing it was irreversible? Allow it to be courageously. To lose my 'control' virginity forever?

Episode 39 ~

I thought to discontinue all my activities other than work during my 'training' time and then thought otherwise. I agreed with myself to keep the same routine and see how it may be affected. I felt suddenly like I was in some kind of movie or experiment about a mad scientist subjecting me to his (or her) evil potions and spells. Let's see, if we do this, what will Darian do now? And if we do this, then what does he do? Ad Infiniti until he becomes a mush of destroyed human psyche ready for the looney farm.

I was letting my imagination run wild and did nothing to corral it in. Let it. Let it find its way into reality and let's fucking see. The strong urge of adventure was growing to a frenzy peak and I let it. At the same time wanting to get the hell out of the landing craft. I can hear the machinegun fire hitting the sides. Please! Don't let the ramp down!

The night before D-Day, I did want to get out and went to the bar and found some friends hanging out watching the baseball game as well as other sports showing on the many TVs. I felt at home and relaxed. We were a good group of guys and girls and we were jabbing back and forth about the game and any topic that anyone wanted to bring up. I decided a round of shots was in order. Didn't have to ask anyone as all usually accepted them. I took a car service so I didn't care how much I drank and did it intentionally.

"Ladies and gentlemen! And I use that lightly! Here's to being friends forever!' I exclaimed above the mild bar noise. Sounded a bit lame to me.

A bit?! I know... let it go...

I raised mine and all followed. Bam. Done. Good.

After another round, and feeling pretty at ease and daring, I decided to broach a subject that had me curious – and not for any deep reason, just seemed appropriate at the time — at least for me. How it will go, I wasn't sure but knew I (and you) will find out. Yes, ladies and gentlemen, I was going in! I had to see…

"OK, listen up. I got a question for everyone." No one was really listening. "YO! LISTEN UP!" I yelled louder than I had intended but it worked. All turned to me, guys and girls. Suddenly, I thought 'don't do it!' but I also thought right after, 'fuck it!' (the pedal to the metal thing).

I was surrounded by looks of 'if you don't hurry up, we don't care.' I continued.

"Question! What's the best sex you ever had!?"

The looks broke into laughter and they started turning away.

"No! No! Seriously! Anyone?" I pleaded my best 'come on, play the game,' and the answers came in.

"With a hooker I knew!" Followed by Joe's girlfriend playfully slapping his arm.

"In a threesome!" Johnny yelled.

"By myself!" Karen exclaimed as all turned to her. "Yep! By myself!" she reiterated.

"No, no. Not what I meant," I tried to clarify. "I mean what act, what action, what blew your mind!?" The looks changed to 'what the fuck' and to 'why do you want to know?'

"Blowjob!" Sean burst out.

"Licking my clit!" Karen exclaimed confidently again. Then the conversation focused on her about how do you play with yourself and lick your own clit, with the ensuring laughter and joking. It wasn't going where I wanted it to go.

I interrupted. "Sean, why blowjob? What made it special? What was the feeling that you loved?" I seriously at that moment wanted to pull back every fucking one of those words! His face contorted a bit and I knew he either didn't process my ask or more likely, was no way he was going to discuss this — either with a guy or in this crowd or with anyone.

151

"Are you fucking serious?" was all that came out of his mouth first, then followed by "I ain't answering that!"

"Dude, why the fuck do you want to know?" Joe asked the question I knew all were probably thinking. I froze.

"Honey, what was yours?" Sally asked in a sultry voice as she came up close to me, playfully fingering my shirt. I retreated.

"Forget it! Let's do another shot!" All seemed to relax and I ordered another shot, turning towards the bar relieved. I huffed a long sigh of thankfulness that that was over. What the fuck was I thinking?

"Hey Darian, maybe you need a sex therapist. They can tell ya what you want to know!"

I returned a weak smile and proceeded to ignore the comment.

I knew I had no right to bring up such a topic. It was completely not me nor my image, but something in me wanted to just see the reactions. And I exposed myself and fled in the flurry of resistance, of huge embarrassment. Great courage my man, I told myself. At the same time, was trying to get back into the conversations as if nothing had happened. And no one seemed to care either and we went on as usual as if nothing had happened. I thought maybe it was because it was a bar and maybe one-on-one would be better. I shrunk from that thought like a dick after a cold shower.

And I couldn't blame anyone for my insanity. After a while, I looked around and realized that a part of me wasn't there. A part of me was there and a part wasn't. And there was nothing wrong with it. It was just an interesting viewpoint I never had before. I realized I was in the process of a paradigm shift, when the norms are not the norms anymore or have shifted to a morphed norm. I suddenly wanted to talk with... Josh.

That surprised me. I really thought my mind would have said Teri but it didn't. It wasn't a sexual thing but I wanted to then and now talk with another *guy* from the other side, whatever that means. And Josh popped into my head.

As I waited outside for my ride, I tried to resolve my conflict with everything I loved to do and those I loved to be with, and still did, with a new viewpoint that I at this time couldn't fit them together. And I felt like I was slamming the hammer wildly to make them fit together.

As I got into my ride, the thought came to me. If 'shock waves' were not a normal sexual occurrence with guys today, nor was an unabashed openness of feeling, and with it, open discussions, maybe a new sexual revolution and societal shift may really be in order, already in the works, and may be really dawning with Zach and the 'Society.' That's a pretty damned big lift.

I knew right then and there, and with no bad feelings with my friends or Melissa, I was taking this solo plunge head first and see where I end up. If I ended up looking like some weird, strange, ridiculous person, then you know what? Fuck it! I owe it solely to me and if ridicule or repression or condemnation ensues? Again, *fuck it*! And if no one gives a shit about it all? Then a *BIG fuck it*! I'm going on this journey alone if need be. And if it's new friends and/or partner at the end of the rainbow, then so be it! You're welcome to still come along and find out together! Let our adventure begin!

Without speaking out loud to the driver, I whispered firmly to myself, "*onward!*"

Episode 40 ~

The day had come. My D-Day. I was finally hitting the damn beaches! Somehow I felt naked, versus having a machine gun, a bazooka, and a couple grenades. And some tanks...

My class was at 7:00 p.m. so I had all day to mull over everything and even talked with Fred briefly. He wished me well, and made a note to maybe go after Melissa now. I thought it over after we talked and decided to text her to see how she was doing. I had refrained from contacting her out of respect for her requested distance but more so not wanting to rehash again and again our current differing points of views.

And I was also afraid at this late junction that any conversation may sway me to bail on the first class and possibly the whole thing and drop it all. Inside, I knew I wouldn't but didn't want to take the chance. I texted her anyway.

'hi wanted to see how you are'

'i'm good you?' came back faster than I thought would.

'good too. how's sis?'

'all good. how's the training?'

'oh, starts tonight, a class'

After a pause, 'a class?'

'yeah not sex, I mean not sexual. I mean...like a normal classroom'

'what for?' I could hear the undertone of the real question not asked, being 'class about sex?'

'not sure exactly. i think about opening up feelings that kind of thing'

'oh k'

A pause ensued. She then continued.

'had a convo with annie about all of this'

I paused. Why would she discuss this with her best friend? I took the bait.

'oh yea what did she say'

'well billy was there too'

'oh in person. and?'

'to my surprise she was intrigued'

'and billy?'

'he thinks you're gay or bi or will become'

I thought, who *becomes* gay or bi? But more pressing, I wanted to know why.

'become gay? that is so insulting to the LGBTQ community. why would he say that?'

'all your talk and wanting more sex and all'

'first of all, that is even more insulting to the gay and bi community. and that makes me gay or bi? wanting something more?'

'does it?'

'you think that?'

'you tell me'

'i don't know how to answer this'

'well he said if I couldn't please you enough, and i'm a girl, maybe you feel you want a guy instead'

The sheer absurdity of the texting was sinking in. I only wanted to learn what more there could be, and not somehow just switch my orientation, and at the same time I wanted to defend anybody and everybody's orientation. The idea of unfounded prejudices was sinking in from this disturbing reality. Who the fuck thinks like this?

I was pausing and knew it wasn't helping my case, whatever my case actually was, which at that point, I had no idea.

'first you please me enough'

'doesn't seem like that'

'i just want to know if there is more to a guy, *not* if you please me'

'so you want to be with a guy'

155

'NO! that's not what I meant or said'

'what did you mean'

'to every guy, is there more we don't know about *ourselves*!'

'i see'

I was now getting exasperated. I knew she wasn't buying any of this but I was being completely honest. The word 'conditioning' popped into my head and I was in the real midst of its effect. I refused to continue as it was leading nowhere, a nowhere I wanted to head off.

'we discussed this already. if they or anyone wants to judge me offhand like that without speaking with me, then nothing i can do. and the prejudice is fucked up'

'you didn't say you weren't gay or bi yet'

The cut was deep. She completely ignored me. I knew I hadn't answered because no matter what, it was my business, and she, like a politician in a heated debate, struck low. And I also knew she was seeking justification of my actions in a weird sort of way.

'i don't feel I need to. let them and you think what you want. i'm not going to answer it and you can keep wondering. and it's so *not* the point'

'oh come on lighten up. i still love you even if you are'

ARGH! Was all I could think.

'you play dirty'

'yes I do'

'well played but not playing'

'thanks anyway'

'maybe you should go to a class, to the training. may learn something about yourself and maybe more about me.'

Gauntlet thrown!

'maybe'

That threw me completely off. Maybe? Would she actually...

I ignored it and finished with...

'the door's always open'

'gotta go'

'me too'

'bye'

'bye'

I put the phone down. What the fuck? Was she playing with me or was she serious? It dawned on me that maybe the whole gay/bi thing was her wanting to know her *own* adequacy and this line of questioning would somehow justify it. I wondered if she was ok if I was or maybe she wanted me to be — at least bi. Was *she* actually bi and I didn't know? Again the whirlwind whips up.

"Wait!" I told myself out loud. "She must have talked with Katie!" was all I could deduce that made any sense. Who knew how that convo may have gone! I chalked it up to a 'find out later' and got on another work call.

During the call, there grew the creeping feeling that maybe everything may work out in the end. I pictured she and I and Teri and Josh tearing each other's clothes off and diving into a foursome fling. Would I do that if Melissa wanted to? Would you? Sorry, had to ask (…I can't hear you!)

Too much to digest and I pushed it all back as I engaged on the conference call.

I looked forward to the class with newfound zeal.

Episode 41 ~

On my way to the mansion, I had time to mull over our texting. And I couldn't make anything out of it except confusing. She's against it. She's for it. She's 'maybe' it. What the fuck. She should talk about gameplaying. But inside, something conflicted with my mild anger. It was that maybe she's trying to honestly figure it out, my need for more (because how many men actually recognize that *need*), and maybe getting away from guilt feelings that it isn't her. And it *isn't* her.

I let it all settle into the back of my thoughts as I pulled into the parking area. I was still enthralled by the beautiful estate and the grounds. Had to be one of the most exquisite training places in the world. It had majestic awe to it. And maybe that was intentional to not be some sterile environment or therapy office. Helluva an accomplished intent, I thought pleasantly.

I arrived pretty much on time and with my folder in hand, attempted to stroll casually to the door, but feeling like a high school freshman. I was nervous. Very nervous. Extremely nervous. This was it. H-Hour as they say in the military. The threshold was right in front of me. I could leave with no problem – except my own regret. Why the fuck was this so difficult?

I knew the answer. It was because crossing that opening meant I was going to bare my soul, bare my sensitivity, probably bare my skin, bare my feelings, bare my manhood, bare my vulnerabilities, and the worst part was I somehow knew there was no return to the way I was – not losing anything, but gaining and being different forever. Gaining new perspective that once gained, is impossible to be rid of. Did I really want that? A 'perspective virginity' gone. Once not a virgin, never a virgin again. Once eat from the *Tree of Knowledge of Good and Evil*, you're never going back. The gate to the *Garden* locked forever. Innocence gone forever. I sighed, took a deep breath, and opened the door. One door closed leads to another door open. I was so hoping.

I was greeted with smiles. To my right was a beautiful ornate table with name tags, where to go, and greeters helping everyone. Seemed almost festive, with light music playing in the background. So not what I expected.

Past the table into the large foyer, was a very relaxed and large group of guys and girls of seemingly all adult ages mingling, each with a name tag. There were refreshments and folks were simply chatting and seemingly getting to know each other. Had to give Zach and team credit, they knew how to relax people who were embarking or had already embarked on a special journey of their lives – and willingly.

I put my name tag on, took the where-to-go information, and proceeded to the edge of the group, not exactly sure what I was going to say to anybody. Then I felt the tap on my shoulder.

I turned and there was Teri smiling.

"You made it!"

"Did you think I wasn't going to? Did you think I was going to bail?" I returned the smile with a smirk.

"Some do bail right at this point. Few, but some. And that's OK. It's just not their time. None bail after the first session, though," she finished with an evil grin and a wink. Did she mean first session classroom or lab? Plus she never answered my question.

"I see. Did you think I will bail?" I asked again with a tilt of my head.

"You? Never. You're dedicated."

Somehow that made me feel comfortably confident. If she had faith in me, I sure should, too.

"Thanks. Not my intention to bail…yet."

She looked at me with a questioningly cute leer. I couldn't stop looking at her short bob haircut. I looked into her eyes. "Just kidding. I'm in for the gold."

159

"Good." She kissed me on the lips and bounced away. I thought she's gotta stop doing *that* or I will...I didn't know what I will do. So, I accepted it as it was so endearing and personal at the same time. What a way to start the training.

"Darian!" I knew Zach's voice.

"Hey Zach," I replied as he stepped towards me gracefully but with strength. I had the image of my new personal *Sex-Demon* greeting me to my own private hedonism (or possible hell). Isn't a *sex* demon a good demon? *Good* demon? Why not?! Something in my heart said a good demon is actually an angel in disguise...

"Well, you ready?"

"I think so. No, I know so."

"Great. Love the attitude. And if ever, during anything or after, you feel uncomfortable enough to want to leave, you see me first. Promise?"

"Promise." Again, the support was amazing. And his demeanor was magnetic, almost diabolically alluring (that *Sex-Demon* thing).

He smiled and walked over to a microphone.

"Hello everyone!" His voice bellowed with the echo of the room and immediately drew everyone's attention. The room fell silent.

"Just wanted to welcome all you newcomers to your first step on a beautiful and exciting journey that hopefully will change your viewpoints and your life!"

I was still amazed at his power of persuasion and motivation. The room hung on his every word and his penetrating eyes.

"And I wanted to say one thing before we break to our respective rooms. You are all extremely brave people. This is not an easy thing to do and go through. It's unbelievably unique. But you will feel vulnerable until you conquer it. Fear is your enemy. Courage is your sword. Faith in yourself is your shield. Use them. Use each other. Talk freely. Help each other. Because that, in the end, is the ultimate goal. Sure the sex will blow you away, and do not pardon my pun."

The room broke into laughter.

"And I want to make one thing perfectly clear. The intimate part of this training is to once and for all force you, *force you*, to eliminate *ALL of your inhibitions*. You will be strung out more vulnerable as you never have before! Don't underestimate this! You will need to reach deep down to do this. I promise, it's all training. But being able to be open to a new *intimate* experience, which again is *solely* geared towards breaking down ALL your inhibitions *in life*, you will find you can be open to anything and anyone. This applies to both guys and girls here."

My thoughts went to Teri and Josh.

"And you get the added bonus of getting to know your own true individual power and prowess. We are here not only to train, but to help. Because each and every one of you are worth it!" He paused.

A round of applause instantly erupted.

Above the applause, he continued. "We will break down your walls! We will incite you to see your selves as you really are! And yes, we *will* take you to heights of sensuality, but more importantly, the heights of your emotions! I know you will find it utterly amazing! Scary?! ABSOLUTELY! Taking a risk, and you will be taking *risks*, is what life and learning are all about! Without taking risks, you will remain stagnant. It's why you chose to be here and face the unknowns, your unknowns. So, embrace it all and embrace each other! I mean NOW!"

We all stared at him and realized what he meant. Suddenly, everyone was embracing each other with vigor and emotion, as I was too. It was an amazing spontaneous moment I never had before. I could hear my breathing and my heart pumping. I felt like we just won the Super Bowl!

Finally, everyone turned back to a waiting Zach who had also embraced, as did all the trainers, with everyone.

"Now you're getting the feeling!" Applause and shouts. I felt a lot of pent-up energy was being beautifully released. I thought of the inner balloon of emotions.

Gabryel Kevyn

"OK, time to get this show going. Please break to your rooms. There are signs guiding you. I'll see you all soon!" He applauded us and you could hear folks voicing approvals and thanks.

I felt so invigorated as I followed my signs to my room as did others, still feeling like a freshman.

I walked in and eventually I was among nine guys in a room with chairs facing forward to a portable whiteboard that had a cover over it. We were a very diverse group which was appealing. And the feeling of being back in a common schoolroom was somehow relaxing, though the room was amazingly exquisite and the chairs looked like mini-thrones.

We all said hi and naturally then sat. I then noticed an empty chair.

Through the open door came our trainer. It was Jason from my first encounter. He closed the door behind him and proceeded to the front of the room. The side of my eye caught someone entering from a side door who then sat in the lone empty chair.

It was Teri dressed in a different miniskirt.

But it was a miniskirt. Does she wear anything else! (I'm not complaining)

I forced myself to look forward but somehow knew she knew my thoughts.

I felt her eyes.

Episode 42 ~

Every guy eventually, glancingly, noticed her, too. I did another quick glance anyway. She looked studious, looking forward at Jason. I think we all had the same thought reaction. Why ten guys, and one girl who was a trainer? But our moment of reflection suddenly burst. Jason commanded the room.

"Welcome fellow warriors! I am Jason, your trainer for today. You may see me again or another, as we vary the mix so as many points of view and expressions can be given to you. But today you have me!"

His stocky stature, fatigue pants, black tight t-shirt that showed his toned muscular build, all reminded me of a boot camp. He had ten guys' undivided attention.

"I'm sure you have taken in information from your first meeting and possibly talking with some of our trainers on the side," he said as I thought of Teri and Josh, "but today, *today* we get into the nuts and bolts. Are you fucking ready!!" We were all taken off guard by his instant change of behavior and tone.

"YEAH!" we all joined in together.

"OK! First, let me introduce our lovely moderator Teri," he motioned towards her, she stood and lightly bowed, and sat back down. "She's here to make you nervous! She's here to see if you can drop any bullshit facades you bring here and let loose in front of her. And she will fucking challenge you, poking at your walls, playing with your egos, with your minds, and don't take me wrong here recruits! She *will* tear you down!"

We all glanced her way and saw the small grin. Suddenly, a bit of fear rose in me. And the aura of a dedicated Dominatrix. I was intrigued by the imagery.

"So! Let's get some ground rules down. And these are absolutes! No exceptions!"

I thought, here it comes, whatever that was.

Jason strolled back and forth as he spoke. He stopped at the whiteboard and tore off the cover. He proceeded to read each line without looking at them.

"ONE! Complete *Honesty* or OUT OF HERE!"

"TWO! Complete *Acceptance* or OUT OF HERE!"

"THREE! Complete *Engagement* or OUT OF HERE!"

He paused to let it sink in. His face showed extreme seriousness. He continued.

"Let me explain," he said in a softer but firm voice. "You must be honest. This will be your biggest challenge. Honest with everyone but most importantly, honest with yourself. Your walls are deep and strong. You've been so fucking conditioned," as he spoke his voice got louder and firmer, "you've been taught to hide your deepest feelings. You've been taught your dick is a detriment to you. Yes, that's right! Ever hear 'you think with your dick?' Huh?! That's total bullshit! Your masculinity, *and* your femininity, is your power! Yes, recruits, your femininity! Better get used to that now! But it's your *honesty* that rules in the end. And *can* you deal with all of this?! I promise, you *will* learn to embrace all of this, every part of you!"

"Next! Acceptance. You must accept everyone regardless of anything. Who the fuck do you think you are to judge anyone? What do you know of anyone really? Until your walls and facades and everyone else's are crumbled, we really do not know the other person. If you are a homophobe, change or get the fuck out! If you hate women, change or get the fuck out! If you hate your neighbor, change or get the fuck out! If you hate YOURSELF, change or get the fuck out!"

He paused dramatically, knowing it was sinking in.

"Next! You MUST engage! In conversation, in openly letting your feelings out, in challenging the guy next to you to do the same. You must dig deep inside yourself and find those fears you hide so well. And find maybe things about yourself you don't consciously know yet and repress constantly for fear of ridicule and fear of your own self false image. And you must engage in *any* sexual activity we say and train."

He stopped cold. I could tell he knew that was going to be a tough one for a bunch of guys who had just previously entered a room, not knowing each other, and especially not knowing what the fuck he meant. We all stared at him.

A mischievous smile grew on his face.

"Now that I got your attention and, I see you are all still here."

Still silence. I believe we all were waiting for the explanation and the bombshell. I noticed some guys slightly fidget in their chairs. He didn't let it go too long but made sure it had its effect.

"I do not mean what you are thinking. This room has a combination of orientations that we derived from your first visit."

I realized then that the whole game from the first visit had a lot more to do with than simple perceptions.

"We have a cross section of you guys from each sexual orientation and trust me, we would never try to make you do anything against that. But you all will be expected to accept anything else we deem part of your sexual *power* training. And your *emotional* power training. And your *mental* power training. It's all *one* training. Isn't that one of the main reasons you are here?!"

If he expected an answer, he got none. He put his hands on his hips, looked down, and then back up directly at us.

"I FUCKING ASKED: ISN'T THAT ONE OF THE MAIN REASONS YOU ARE HERE?! ENGAGE!!"

"YES! and "YEAH!" came out of all our mouths. I swore someone would have bailed at this point but no one did. Maybe out of embarrassment and would bail later, or maybe no one wanted to bail. I didn't know. But the atmosphere was unnerving.

"GOOD!" he bellowed. He looked over at Teri and nodded. She stood, took the floor while he sat in a chair next to the whiteboard.

"Hey guys!"

"Hey!" we replied. Her husky sweet voice had a calming effect after our emotional and craze-driven drill sergeant.

"I have a question for you," she said as she proceeded to stroll around us, touching and stroking some with her finger. "Are you all men? Huh?"

We nodded and some in an almost whisper said "yeah." It was amazing this sweet girl could command a room of ten guys so easily, I thought. Wait. Am I so conditioned to think she couldn't?

"So, tell me boys. What is a 'man?'" she asked coyly and continued to stroll among us.

No one answered. I thought no one wanted to be first. Looking around, we were a mixed group of guys in age, physique, ethnicity, look, dress, and apparent attitude. But no one answered.

"Really?" she playfully asked. "You just said you were 'men.' And you can't explain it?"

I couldn't stop myself. It just came out. "We all have equipment." I heard chuckles.

"Why are you chuckling?" she asked around. "He's absolutely right!" Her voice rose. "And I am a woman because I have a pussy, tits, and clit!" No one chuckled because her tone was suddenly commanding. "Plus I have two X chromosomes and you have an X and a Y. That's it boys. That's what make you men and me woman. Don't you see?"

We all looked at each other confused. Of course, we saw, knew that.

"Well that's fucking obvious!" one guy spoke out. She smiled. Other guys nodded. I felt the challenging, almost macho attitude grow in the room. She never broke stride though.

"It is, isn't it," she said matter-of-factly and waited a moment and continued. "OK, each one of you, chime in. Do you agree with Mark here that it's 'fucking obvious?'" she mimicked his tone, smiling at him. She pointed down the line to each of us and everyone said "yes," even me. I could now feel an underlying growing antagonism. Was it intentional?

"That's it then?" she posed. "So, our genitals make us men and women? You're absolutely right! OK, now that we have that settled. So, then why the FUCK do we dress different? Why do we use makeup and you do not? Why is it wrong for a girl to go topless on a beach when men are accepted topless? Why are kid toys designed for girls and some for boys? Why are commercials targeting us as separate entities? Don't you think it's a lot more than your cocks and balls, my pussy, tits, and clit, that *society* defines *men* and defines *women*? And listen guys, EVERYONE just follows that! Accepts that. Fucking *blindly!*"

Silence.

"Let's talk about dress, what we wear that makes us so-called 'men' and 'women.' Years ago, it was wrong for a woman to wear pants! Did any of you know that? They would actually get arrested! Or to go braless! It was laughed at when men wore the shorts you mostly wear today. Back then, they were called 'Bermuda Shorts' down over the knee because it was a law in Bermuda – and if you wore them here, you were laughed out. Yes, laughed at. When did we decide that all men's thighs and knees needed to be hidden? Why? They are sexy. And there's that feeling of freedom when bared if you wish it. A man today now is laughed at if he wears a bikini bathing suit. That was the norm before! So, which *way* is the *real* men-way?

What the fuck then makes us, *defines us*, as 'men' and makes us, and *defines* us as 'women?' I dare every one of you to put on makeup, eyeliner, and mascara and go to your favorite bar or hangout. None of you would, except maybe a few that have already accepted more of themselves than most of us do today. Get my point?"

Silence. I knew she was right but it was very, very difficult to digest. I felt the same around the room. She was tearing at us, ripping at our own false egos.

"And how many of you, no need to answer right now, would love to wear a bikini bathing suit on the beach or at a pool? Show off yourself. Bare yourself. Or have say nipple piercings? Worse, how many of you seeing a guy wearing one or with nips ring-pierced or both would immediately think he's probably *gay*?"

She waited. Then she pulled the trigger none of us wanted.

"See number one up there? *Honesty*? And number three? *Engagement*? You're all on! Raise your hand if that would be your first impression seeing a guy on a beach in a tight skimpy bikini bottom and nips pierced as probably *gay*!" It was more of a demand than a question. "NOW!"

Everyone raised their hand. I did too and felt embarrassed in admitting my stereotyping. But it was true. I would think that.

"May I ask who is gay or bi here? Please raise your hand." Her sweet tone was back. Four guys raised their hands. "Tell, me, honestly, you raised your hand to admitting you would think he was probably gay – but you are, too. Why?"

One guy spoke right up, "because that's what we are inherently taught to believe."

"Exactly," she replied.

Another spoke up, "and people, guys *and* girls, would laugh among themselves pointing it out. Which is really wrong."

"Exactly!" she replied again but with intense fervor. "And damn right it's fucking wrong! To literally *laugh* at another fellow human being for their freedom of expression because it's not fucking yours?! Just for being different than *you!*" She paused a second, eyes piercing us, and continued. "You see, we are so conditioned to believe *as a group*, to defend those beliefs *as a group*, and *validate* those beliefs *as a group*. We then think it's natural to *act* as the group believes and behaves, to ridicule *as a group* a fellow person for simply something different, and as we have been told, taught, shown, beat into us, these false beliefs about each of us we all hold. The 'group' is safe, it's a hideaway *to unfairly and cowardly judge*, and we absolutely fear going *against* the group. And guess what, when the 'group' then accepts a *different* thing or mode, like Bermuda shorts, *that* becomes the new *group* rule. What the fuck!

Thinks about it! It's all pure *bullshit*! It's pure *cowardice!*"

"Who has *the right* to judge like that? Fucking who?! Think of a world where a guy could stroll a beach in a string bikini bottom and no one even notices. Or me going topless on a public beach. Or bottomless? Of it being *completely* accepted. Tough, isn't it? The current societal rules would simply and immediately condemn. And I say 'current' because guys, societal rules *always* change! Throughout history, and with every example I gave. And you know there's more examples! Just think about it."

"And that's just one example of the walls and fears we *all* have been given. It would take a very brave guy to wear that knowing the ridicule occurring and *be able* to confidently not care. Even flaunt it to the group-*face*. Very brave. If one of our requirements in training was that each of you must wear a bikini or thong on the beach for a day, or put on makeup and go to a bar, right now — how many would do it and how many would bail?"

Silence.

"Well, no worries. We're not going to ask you to do that — at least not now. And it doesn't mean we all have to go do these things. These are just examples. But if someone does, why the judgment? Better yet, why the prejudice? *Individuality is squashed for safety of the group*! Cowardice is covered up by the group! The group generates *fear*! It's so easy to ridicule than to be different. The group actually *wants* things to ridicule. It's childish. And yet we call ourselves adults. Yet deep inside every individual in the group lies their own wants and desires…and *fears*. Don't you see the insane contradiction? The pure cowardice? The absolute wrong to another fellow human?"

She paused and took a slow breath.

"Here, we believe in individuality *first*! Individuality *above the group*. And then acceptance — fucking unconditionally! Now you know us! Think *deeply* if you really wish to join us and change!" she finished with a commanding smile, nodded to Jason, and returned to her seat.

Complete silence and awe.

Jason rose and moved to the center.

"Guys, this is where the pedal meets the metal. Do you have *it* to be able to crush those walls, crush those fears, crush those false judgments, crush those inhibitions, crush those stereotyping, crush those beliefs, crush those prejudices, and stand up to the group confidently and be your true self – once you find it, whatever it may be? Or will you cower *in fear of the group*? Will you be a *coward* for the group?"

"See, we can only become our true selves, personally, intimately, sexually, and expressively, when we *no longer* fear the group. And then we become the beautiful, absolutely unique *individual* each of us really are. With innate courage and camaraderie. And the wonderful mosaic of humanity shines through. And truly love each other as we are."

He continued, "and these honestly are just examples for illustration. There are so many books on this exact topic but only read by a few, and regardless of the logic behind it, they still do not have the courage to truly let themselves be their true selves. Take time on your own, alone, at home, wherever, and think about it. Think of how different it was 50 years ago and how different it will be 50 years from now. So, what then is the *norm*? Think about all the rules we have and taboos we falsely believe in but *strenuously* uphold. It's all bullshit and even if you bail, I am completely sure, this class will remain in you, no matter how hard you hide it. I beg you stay and learn more about each other and yourself and about each of us." He pointed to himself and to Teri. "We don't live 50 years ago, nor 50 years from now. We live solely today! Seize it all before you end up regretting it!"

"You have successfully begun your journey today by being honest, being accepting, and being engaged. Much more to come!" He and Teri stood there applauding us. By some natural force, we applauded ourselves, too – and them. We then shook each other's hands and theirs. There was a strange immediate feeling of a new friendship among us. I liked it.

Though I was still fucking scared. Yes, a scared *guy*.

Episode 43 ~

The next couple of days felt like a fairytale. I felt disengaged from my normal world, being that my new world, in its infancy, was...the only word I can describe it was 'blossoming.' I knew to myself that sounded unusual in my normal vocabulary but I conceded that it was the feeling, and the word.

And it was more. More and more, little by little, I felt somehow bigger. Not in stature, but somehow personally, emotionally. Not that I lost anything, it's just that I guess more of me was peeking through. They had a way of bringing it out, making you look at it, look for it, little by little, and not only by words but by their very presence. It was addictive. Wanting more, and the more wanted, the more both scary and exhilarating it became. Like traveling through a dark tunnel to an unknown light ahead of you.

But I knew the real day was coming. Saturday. Tomorrow. Was I going through with whatever sex 'activities' they had planned and/or were part of the course curriculum? It seemed weird to say 'curriculum' when it came to sex. I won't even say pardon the pun. I smiled at it though. I just wanted to know and experience 'shock waves' and 'spasms' and all of it. And how do you *do* a strokeless orgasm if there's no touching? What the fuck.

I'm your regular guy (I think) and I'm talking and thinking these things? And what 'regular guys' want to look deep inside themselves and possibly see things they don't want to see or even know? And maybe the problem came down to the term 'regular.' My mind went then to the word 'mediocre.' Shit! Was I just mediocre? And I really wasn't judging any other guy either, which isn't fair. I knew I was really just judging me. So, my apologies.

I guess being told by your partner she 'hadn't noticed' meant mediocre enough, to not being noticed. Well, one thing was for sure. I was going to find out. It's just that I didn't want to be 'regular' anymore. I didn't want to get really old and look back with regrets when I now know there's potentially so much more to be me, and to the experience *of me* – as I *really* am. I was now on the hunt. Bring it on! Fuck it!

I was to arrive at the appointed time in the morning, no alcohol, no drug use, completely straight, and only one cup of coffee. I kind of get that. Most drugs skew the feelings though some to me enhanced it but I was going to follow the rules. Just had no idea what to expect and again, was wildly intimidating and surreally exciting. And maybe that was intended.

And there was no sex or masturbating for a minimum of three days. I guess a full load was required. I couldn't hold back the laugh. OK then! But since Melissa left, I had been wanting to try to experiment with myself. Try to see if I could elicit some of the sensations they claim. I could get myself pretty excited but in the end, I knew I'd finish it off as normal. Couldn't help it. How do you stop mid-stroke after reaching the summit of climax? Seemed counterproductive. And I was actually *analyzing* all of this… Any guys out there wanna pitch in? Need a go/no go decision dudes!

But maybe I and most guys are just so inexperienced in our own arsenal that the awesome demanding feeling just drives us to finish, cleanup, dress, and grab a beer (or rum and coke). Done. Thanks. See ya next time. So, what has Zach and team figured out that is beyond what sex therapists know and prescribe? And beyond what the average young male has learned from *girlie* magazines and their own clumsy hand.

I finally told myself to shut the fuck up and get on with it. I knew well enough that I'd know very soon if this was a sham or not – or maybe works with just 1% of the male population and this whole thing was some kind of psychological, biological experiment paid for by some university grant.

The last thought I had was I hoped I was in that 1% if that was true. But somehow, I felt that it was more than 1% - and the reason why was them. Unless they were the greatest actors in the universe, it was extremely difficult to believe they didn't believe and know all these things and possibilities.

Shudders! Spasms! and Shock Waves! The Strokeless Orgasm

Onward, once again!
To all units! The Go Code was giving!
Shit.

Episode 44 ~

The morning had arrived. I was having my sole cup of coffee waiting for the time to leave. My thoughts just kept wandering. I sincerely hoped that after this 'lab' session, these thoughts and concerns would dissipate forever.

I thought of growing up and learning sex. No one taught you. You just found it, found the dick. I think I found mine in the crib (I did, seriously). I guess girls found their clits at some point (duh). Wasn't fair, I thought. We're left to our own devices at an early age. Maybe that's part of what Zach and team are trying to reverse with us.

OK, bear with me. Need to divulge some things before I take that leap into the dark side. Let's call the following: *History of Darian – Part IV – He Was Fucking Innocent*!

OK, after fumbling in the crib with probably simple primordial actions (does that make sense?), I remember rubbing down there in the bottom bunk of our bunkbed as a child (I actually do!), just doing what felt good. There was no real embarrassment when you're innocent. Guys find it eventually. And you don't even know what it is you're doing anyway. Just felt good doing it. Girls? Same?

Then one time, it got all wet. Shocked me. Whoa, what the fuck! I thought I peed! Wasn't until later, I don't know when, when I found out it was cum. Again, nobody tells you this, you poor ignorant child (that's me). And then it would keep coming every time (...and we will ignore that pun). Now we had to always clean up...ok don't need those details (but girls, we had to! Just saying...)

But then we get good at it – at least the normal basic hand technique, up and down (you know). And then the fantasies. Hey now! Girls in miniskirts, bikinis, fascinating every boy-child with such interests with images of what was under there, what did it look like, feel and smell like, how did breasts actually feel, why was all this in front of us, in the neighborhood, in classrooms, in the schoolyard, and seemingly unavailable? It wasn't really appropriate at recess to say, "hey, um, pardon my curiosity, but can you pull down your panties and let me see and maybe touch…" But these were the puberty thoughts and wants (at least mine at the time). And I'm sure if you knew you were gay at an early age, I'm sure you still had puberty thoughts and wants of guys. Girls to girls, too. All awesome. Not meaning to exclude at all. Just relating what happened initially to me as a young curious boy (and there's more aspects to cum…I mean come, about me throughout this whole tale that I discovered – so hang in there!)

So, I had a seemingly insurmountable wall at that age. Ah, but then my *girlie* magazines (and not demeaning any of the models, just a societal cliché). If we couldn't actually touch, we now could see! I loved them!

The *Tale of Girlie Magazines*:

I had initially found my father's *Playboy*'s, making sure to carefully put them back exactly how they were after my use. But then, in drugstores (back in the day), there was *Penthouse* now! Seemed more sensual than *Playboy*, more intimate, more stuff to see. I liked (loved) the covers. Maybe it was such an inner drive to have, to see, more that drove my courage, as a horny discovering teenager, to for the first time, go to the shelf as if looking for a crossword puzzle book, pick up the newest copy of *Penthouse*, get excited about the girl on the cover, try not to take an inside glance (somehow that felt taboo), nonchalantly as best as I could, walk over to the counter, face the druggist, place the *Penthouse* on the counter face up with the *Pet* girl showing right there (figured be brave about it), and look him straight in the eyes with the look of 'yeah, I'm buying this' when inside I felt 'please, please let me buy this!'

And to my extraordinary delight, he did! There was no age limit then and my courage, probably driven by my own increasing self-pleasure appetite, paid off. I became a regular customer every month waiting for the next issue, creating my personal collection. With each issue, these were my girlfriends, my lovers. They were always so willing, too. And it only increased the infatuation of actually doing it. And of course, that time eventually came and the rest is standard male (and female) sexual history. And we (us guys – well, at least me) were clumsy oxen at first but got better. We started figuring it out.

And girls knew what they wanted (we thought) and we, or at least me, followed, wanting it. Fingering pussy, feeling wetness we didn't expect, the warmth we didn't expect, finally eating pussy (what a new weird taste), caressing tits (didn't expect them to be that soft), and finally, the ultimate experience of engulfing entry, yeah, yeah, yeah. Worth every moment. I, for one, was definitely out to please girls I had sex with and *wanted* to please them. And I would get *my* rocks off, too but somehow I was always focused on them. The power of Eve, I thought, had me smitten.

Now, I will continue some additional divulging that actually occurred to me much later. Like most humans, even after actual physical contact with a partner, we still masturbated (don't lie). And I still had my *girlie* magazines, my private lovers – a widening collection. Yes, I was truly infatuated. But there was something that (now is occurring to me) was going on during such acts. I promise will get more into later, but a small mention here seems appropriate. Looking back, I remember not only gazing at the beautiful naked, sexy girls on the pages, but also, maybe as equally, was gazing at my own self, too. I guess you girls needed a mirror? OK, more to come on that...back to *History Part IV...*

But now... after many years... even today... I was doubting everything about the act of sex. Did I just say '*act* of sex?' An *act*? Maybe in my mind that's all there was – acting it out to please girls. I needed to be reassured I'd get back in there again, plus the honor of pleasing. Damn right. Or was there power in it? The power, the right, the ticket, to get back in. (Please!)

Yeah, we'd cum sooner or later, usually sooner, but who noticed. Was it just a payback for our pleasure service? Or later if not with our partner, then by ourselves, to complete the final act, alone. Not that I blame the girls, as they are surely worth it, but in the end, was I just acting for no one, or for her, and all girls, the same role over and over and over again. A slight change here, there, and same, same, SAME! The Adam-syndrome. Thanks for another bite honey.

Like an ego-sucking dawning, I simply realized: boring...lame...pathetic...was my sex life, my ya know...cumming, to be specific. 'OH GOD! Bam. Done!' But it *was* good. And then it hit me. I really believed it was *great*! Fantastic! Unbelievable! But they were actually as I just admitted, in the end, compared to a girl ...just *good*. If a band on stage is just 'good,' not many in the audience really notice them anymore. And did Melissa think I was sexually boring? Just 'good?' Sexually lame? Sexually pathetic? No. She didn't think anything because she 'hadn't noticed.'

I shook myself out of my self-imposed false-ego lamenting. I told you I was somewhat obsessive. Somewhat? But constantly reliving wasn't helping anything. I remembered a plaque I had and decided once and for all, I was going to follow its advice: 'Don't Look Back. You Are Not Going That Way.'

End of *History of Darian – Part IV*. Thanks for listening!

I finished up, locked the door, got in my car, and drove off to my destiny. With all pun intended this time, let it come! I truly needed it, something...

Episode 45 ~

The day was sunny and brilliant, a beautiful summer day, for a beautiful unknown, possible insane, fearful, tension-ridden moment I was committing myself to where I probably should be committing myself to the insane asylum. I couldn't shake the anticipating tightness in my chest of the unknown. What the fuck was I doing.

And maybe this was the whole point. Could I face this unknown and live through it sane. Or end up going running, screaming out the door into the woods, never to be seen again, and happily play with squirrels the rest of my cowardly existence.

"OK, shut the fuck up," I spoke to myself as I drove. "Fucking coward."

If my mind and fear wanted to turn around and never look back, my pure curiosity countered it and won. I reminded myself of the saying, 'if you don't take a risk, you will never know, ever.' Yeah, that helped! I hesitantly mocked a chuckle and kept driving.

I arrived, parked, noticed other cars in the lot, wondered why, knew it didn't matter, got out, took a deep breath, closed the door, looked at the mansion door and deserted flowered pathway, and walked steadily to the entrance. I saw no one else around which irked me a little. Was this the moment in the horror movie when the audience screams 'Are you *that* stupid! Don't go in there!' I opened the large door and went in there. I thought I heard the audience whisper, 'oh no!' but they didn't. It was me.

To my surprise, I was alone in the big foyer. No table, no greeters, no fellow students, just me and my equipment ready to go. I suppressed a smile.

I didn't know what else to do, so I took a seat and waited. Then I wondered if I was at the wrong time and looked at my watch. It turned exactly

9:00 and bouncing down the large hallway was a young girl I'd say about age 25 with extremely short hot cut-off jeans and a practically open blouse, waist-tied. Reminded me of my farm-girl fantasy. I could tell no bra and I noticed she was barefoot. The cutesy smile and confident big eyes were looking right at and possible through me. Was this my trainer? Mmmmm.

"Darian!" she exclaimed as she came close. I stood naturally. "Glad you made it! I'm Lisa! Are you excited?!" She, as with all the others, had that commanding, confident, sensual, endearing tone all at once that relaxed and mesmerized at the same moment. I was excited, yeah, but I didn't know for what.

"Uh, yeah, I believe so," came out so lamely and with a bit of wavering that I wanted to take it back.

"Great!"

"Where is everyone else?" I suddenly asked the question I really wanted to ask.

"Who else?"

Then it dawned on me. "Oh, it's just me?"

"Of course silly it's just you. Did you want a group session?" She said the word 'group' with an adorable sarcastic tone.

"No, no, not what I meant. Aren't other guys, girls, supposed to come to this on the weekends? I don't see anyone else." There, I finally made some sense, not a lot, which instilled my confidence back, a little.

"Oh, yeah, sure, but we never have anyone show up at the same time. We feel this must be a completely private adventure for you and for each person. No distractions. Kind of think of it as you are the star." She cocked her head and beamed that girl doll smile. It all felt surreal.

And my mind was still reeling with 'what the fuck am I doing! Run you bastard!'

"Ah, OK, I kind of like that and I'm glad. Will it hurt?"

She gave me a quick not-understanding look and then widely grinned. "Silly boy. Unless you like that kind of thing."

I gave the same questioning look back and then realized she got me back. 'Silly boy' stuck with me. *Boy?* Somehow, everything here, regardless of age, had a youthful energy. Again, addicting.

"Come on, let's go and have some fun! OK?!" She came close, clasped my shirt, and lightly pulled me and then released once we were walking – to where, I had no idea but had no issue following our girl Lisa.

Episode 46 ~

We went a different path than before for the classroom. I followed her down a curving hall that was adorned with a more modern style than the baroque of the other hall and rooms. Now we turned left and went down a short corridor that led straight to a closed door. It looked like any other door in any other house, nothing special about it. The short corridor had no adornments or paintings. Was just a white painted pathway to a white painted door. (The audience stirs.)

She stopped at the door, turned, and gave me what I could only deduce as an anticipation smile meaning 'here we go, are you ready?' without saying a word. I could only smile back in some kind of agreement to proceed. I felt my heart start to beat a bit faster and harder. They had a unique way of suspense which only drew me in more, while at the same time wanting to bolt.

Lisa gently clasped the knob and opened the door. I half expected either a killer monster to come crashing out slitting my throat or a group of ladies in lingerie coming to greet me. Neither. It was just a staircase going downward like to any basement. But this was more than that. The steps were a plush red carpet, the walls leading down were painted with exquisite colorful murals, definitely hand painted and portrayed wonderfully half-naked and naked figures lounging around, some next to each other, some alone, and even with the nudity, I could only think how tastefully arrayed the imagery was and how much it drew my eyes from one scene to the next, almost like a story being told. I could only think how idyllic and romantic it all felt. Like entering the *Garden of Eden* where no one knew they were naked, nor cared, and all was blissful.

Lisa turned and motioned me to follow. So, down we went.

181

I couldn't help to continue to look at the endless murals on both sides of the stairwell and then continued down a wide corridor with unusually high ceilings for a basement, which I came to know was much more than any ordinary basement. More of a sublevel continuation of the upper floors but with much more interesting visuals.

As we slowly walked, I continued to gaze and realized that some of the male figures actually had erections and some did not. I wondered why and at the same time found myself suddenly seeing them in an almost feminine way. And the female figures had an almost masculine tone to them, though both males and females surely maintained their genital difference. My thought went to Josh and how he may look like one of these. I quickly caught myself and pushed the thought away. I knew it was just curiosity and started to believe that all of this was to stoke exactly such curiosity, such openness.

I knew I wasn't homophobic, at least I hoped I wasn't when I pushed such thoughts out, but the thought of maybe we're all the same inside and our outward manifestations, our outward expressions of our bodies were just that – simply expressions. A growing realization started in me.

And even more interesting to my sight was finally actual beautiful sex scenes. Guys with girls, guys with guys, girls with girls, trios, foursomes, and more, all combined various sexes, and transgender. It was like the murals exploded (pun intended) into a fantasy world of every possible sexual preference imaginable, and none of it phased me. In fact, I was completely intrigued. I was inside a pure fantasy, but also inside a real experience in my mind that just made me want to see more. I wanted to stop to examine it all deeply.

But I didn't. Instead, I almost walked into Lisa, not realizing she had stopped. She was facing a white door to the right which stood out starkly against the vibrant, colorful murals. It was the first of many white doors lining the rest of the hallway on both sides. I could only assume each was a 'lab' room or torture chamber. I held back the chuckle of pleasurable torture. I liked the idea. Who is this guy?

"Well, here we are, or should I say, here you are!" she beamed as she held her upward palm towards that first white door. She bounced away back the way we had come and disappeared up the stairs. I heard the top door close quietly. I stood alone with only one option. Well, I guess two options, one of which would have been just following Lisa back up the stairs and leaving forever.

The other option was to face whatever was behind the door in front of me as I could almost feel it beckoning me. Somehow, I knew it was myself beckoning myself to take the plunge and face probably the most life changing, or at least the most sensual changing moment I may ever face. I was facing myself. The weirdness and scintillation was overwhelming.

Deep breath.

I glanced at the murals.

I so felt like a virgin.

I slowly opened the door.

Episode 47 ~

"I thought you'd never come in," grinned Teri, standing there in front of me with her gorgeous legs and waist bare from the skimpy outfits she always wore. I wondered how many she had. "Took you awhile."

"Um, yeah, sorry," I stuttered trying not to stare and at the same time wondering how long I had actually stood outside the door after Lisa left. Somehow, I had expected Josh to be here too but only Teri. My mind was a bit jumbled and I wasn't sure what to think, and my expectations had been really running wild back and forth as to what to expect or what they had in mind, because it was still a mystery even at this point, standing on the verge of an infinity of hidden possibilities that just never ended. My *mind* was about to climax.

"Your face shows everything," Teri smiled a wonderful disarming smile. "Trust me, it's all part of the experience – the anticipation, the mystery, and even the fear."

Fear? Yeah, she was right. I was in fear. Almost panic. What was I doing! And another realization. It was not just the fear of what these folks are planning but my own fear of how I was going to react. All for 'shock wave' *ultimate* male decadence? I may even be terrified. Could this be worth it for any guy?

"Hey, relax, you're in good hands, literally," she grinned a pretty sinister fun grin (the Dominatrix again) and gave me a hug. I completely didn't expect that and hugged her back. Somehow it made me relax. She released me and looked at me with a curiosity look. "Are you ready to have your first lab session? You can always leave." She point to the door.

Her last sentence, that last moment of decision, she laid out there for me to grab and run away. Run away from my fears. Run away from not trusting everyone there and their pure confidence and desire to help me, help all of us. I wasn't going to let fear stop me. Period.

And I wanted this! I could tell my grandchildren someday how Caesar Darian changed the male libido world and how guys look at themselves forever more! I tried not to laugh but was sure my face gave my thoughts away.

"I'm here, I'm staying, and show me the way!" I replied with a mild exuberance I didn't expect from myself. Suddenly, the courage swelled up in me.

"Great! OK, now you trust me, right?"

"Absolutely!" And another thing hit me. Teri was here because she had taken me under her wing from the start, my personal mentor. And she was continuing to guide me, which struck a touching empathy in me.

"Good. Now comes a bit of the hard part and no pardon the pun," she laughed. Then she became serious. "Everything, *everything*, from this point forward, is *solely* to break down *all* your inhibitions by making you completely *helpless* and absolutely *vulnerable* with absolutely no possible recourse. Do not be concerned," she again grinned that evil playful grin. "It's all part of the first time and necessary." Now she had me scared again and she saw it. "You'll be fine. Relax and seriously, enjoy it! It's *your* power, it's your moment of *discovery*! Be your own exhibitionist! Be your own craving voyeur! Let loose!"

I nodded, holding firm my courage. "Now, I'm going in there," she pointed to a door, "and you are going in there," she pointed to another door. "When you get in there, again don't fear, I want you to disrobe completely, put on what's on the table and simply lay on the table. And then relax and trust. Breathe. Do you trust me?"

"Yes, I trust you." I heard myself and knew I meant it. The adventure was truly beginning and I suddenly hoped I wouldn't fail. What if I failed? And I didn't even know what 'failed' meant.

She crept back up to me, kissed me gently on the lips, held the kiss for a moment that seemed an eternity, and whisked away through her door. She successfully got me primed.

    My door awaited me.

    (…a hush fell over the audience…)

    I knew now, I was crossing the Rubicon…

    …Hail Caesar! To Roma …march with me my fellow warriors!

Episode 48 ~

I crept open the door, visualizing some fiend or the real *Satan* ready to drag me to my eternal inferno. When none attacked me, I knew inside, the fiend was my fear. And *I* was now *The Sex-Demon,* the seducer, begging me on to my forbidden fruit. I was so excited and so scared and ...*so alive!*

First impression was the dim lighting. Not dim as shadowy but more surreal, and was multi-colored, though there was no blaring glare. The rug was plush and somewhat padded and made no noise as I stepped in. I sensed a fragrance that was alluring yet very subtle as if not even there. But it was there. But that wasn't what caught me.

Directly in front of me was a table, like a gurney but definitely wasn't sterile-looking. More like a massage table. It appeared to have a very thick mattress with an almost hallucinogenic tone of various blending mosaic colors. Kind of witchy. Again, extremely subtle as seemingly intended not to draw too much attention, but to be... *inviting*. And none of this caused, in the end, to draw attention away from something else. For I finally saw the things that truly drew my instant and absolutely amazed awareness to them.

In the middle of the 'bed' lay a silken purple I assumed 'underwear' waiting for me. The femininity of it was at first disturbing for me, a guy, but I let that go, knowing I was following through no matter what now. But that wasn't the real two main interests. There was more to this growing realization of what laid ahead.

On both sides of the table were padded handcuffs, the kind that had a strap like a belt that could be adjusted. But they were extremely padded obviously to cause no discomfort but to definitely without doubt constraint the victim's hands. Whoa. My mind used the word 'victim.' I corrected myself to myself and thought 'trainee' but 'victim' hovered nearby. But nothing stopped me from thinking that some mad scientist was going to walk in, forcibly strap me down, and start laughing like a wild hyena as he prepared his vile experiment on my exposed body, freaking out my horrified soul. And I'd be at his mercy versus at, hopefully, Teri's mercy. But that imagery faded (a bit dramatic I admit lol) when I saw the last two things.

At the apparent head of the 'bed' was a padded fire-red blindfold just lying there seemingly beckoning me. It spoke definitively that it was for me, wanted me. I began to feel the creeps stir in me. Was sadomasochism the means to achieve these 'shock waves?' I may have engaged in many different types of mild fetish activities (don't tell anyone) since my early years but never sadomasochism. Yeah, I played with handcuffs and blindfolds as mild sex toys with girls, each playing the role of master and slave. But this just looked more ominous, much more serious. More torturous.

The final coup d'état of my brain and soul was hanging on the wall. The phrasing seemed out of a Shakesperean tragedy. A fluorescent sign of many vibrant colors spoke the words:

Vulnerable Be You Now!
Inhibitions Be Gone!

I remembered Zach's opening words before class. They were fucking serious. I quickly looked around and confirmed again there was no one in the room. For a second I sensed someone was, but there wasn't anyone. I knew though sooner or later there would be or what was the whole point. Fuck. When Zach says courage and trust are needed, he meant it. Fuck (again). Argh! What do I do?! It was my life's biggest moment of no return.

I sighed deeply and slowly. Eager exhilaration and dreaded fear were fused together in my tightened chest. The wild plunge was here, in front of me. Staring at me. Staring through me.

I reminded myself of my quest, of Teri's protectiveness, of my sincere want to know, and I knew right then and there, I wasn't going to skirt this now. My want to know greatly outweighed the *extreme* weirdness of the situation I found myself in — actually, the situation I *allowed* myself in. I thought of Melissa and smiled. She'd flip seeing this. But my adventure-drive and a hidden, kinky part of me were triggering all at once. Kinky? Me?

Darian Dracco and My Quest for Eternal Ejaculations! Darian at your service! What the fuck, get on with it! I groaned a surrendering "shit." Game on…

I stripped completely, placed my clothes on a small table which appeared to me to be for that purpose. I picked up the silk panties, looked closely at them, examined them, felt the insane smoothness, shook my head, and slipped them on. Definitely not normal guy-stuff! But I couldn't believe the immediate reaction from my crotch. I was getting hard. Shit. I wasn't ready. I asked myself, 'ready for what?' Wasn't this the intent? Damn the suspense! And damn the torpedoes!

But I found myself beginning to like it, to even love it. It was like a new sex game. Gotta be a first for everything. At that exact point, I just didn't care anymore. Especially standing there naked with girlie silk purple panties on! A definite first…

I assumed I was to lay on the bed so I did. I didn't touch the handcuffs. Seemed it wasn't my role or place to handle them. I took the blindfold and slowly put them on and then laid my head back on the firm but soft small pillow. The pillow was just enough to not make me feel I was falling backwards. I forced myself to relax with the still growing sensation in my crotch, the silkiness, the tingling sensations, and my otherwise nakedness, and the now darkness on my eyes.

And I surely felt eyes on me.

The unbelievable, overpowering exhibitionist, voyeur feeling only made me harder. I couldn't stop it. I was completely exposed. Naked on a stage. My nudity. My stage. The breathless drama was *me*.

I found myself loving it even more. Loving every searing, scintillating moment.

Gabryel Kevyn

Then the soft music began.

Episode 49 ~

<u>WARNING</u>: The following is Rated **XXX** *(...for explicitly excruciatingly exciting!)*
(For the shy, queasy, puritanical, prudish, squeamish, or fainthearted, please skip the next four Episodes!)

(The Management)

Crazed anticipation is an understatement. I lay motionless, afraid to even move a tiny bit and wasn't sure why. There was nothing, no sound except the soft ethereal music, nothing else — just my deep breathing. The silky underwear was doing its job. As well as being completely exposed. I couldn't help the bulging hard-on under it and figured that was on purpose. My thoughts gave way to why don't guys wear more like this, as the feeling was amazing! Another taboo for most guys and a 'wall' most of us never get through...until someone advances us past our predetermined social and peer pressure conditioning. I told myself to stop the fucking psychoanalysis and smiled. Couldn't help it. I was soon captivated otherwise.

Out of nowhere I heard a voice right next to my right ear and felt its breath. It was sultry and deep, masculine and feminine at the same time, and I couldn't figure which, and was in no position to keep trying as the surprise of someone entering the room and moving towards me this close without any sound at all was enough to shock me. I froze even more if that was possible.

"Relax. Relax. Relax," was all it said. The tone was so amazingly sexy and strong I had to obey as best I could, laying there naked except for a purple silky underwear and now a rock hard-on under it. Nothing was going to quell that thing. My desire suddenly became that I wanted this phantom to touch me

191

there. Do anything there. Get on with it! Or I will.

But that didn't happen, to my increasingly hot-blooded, feverish angst as I was there now wide open with someone else in the room viewing me, readying me. Felt like the beginning of a massage time, but more. I then felt soft hands gently lifting my wrists into the handcuffs that were attached to the table. One side, then the other side. It was almost lovingly done, with a slight caress of my hand each time almost as if to say 'good boy.' I couldn't hear any footsteps as this person moved about.

It was amazing and eerie at the same time for I could not pinpoint where they were or going. A feeling of scintillating helplessness started to overwhelm me, of being dominated, of just letting go, an experience I never had before. The vulnerability was *insane* yet …ridiculously *bewitching*. I was utterly powerless, completely visible, no control at all, and lay embarrassingly bare both body and mind.

My waist shifted with the pressure of my hardness against the silk. The slightest touch, movement was starting to drive me a bit crazy and a lot craving. I felt my hands instinctively try to move towards my crotch but there was no way they could. All I sensed was blissful *panic* and growing ecstasy at the same time.

I heard then something behind my head move and suddenly any sifting light that was around my blindfold disappeared. I was now in complete darkness. Edgar Allan Poe came to mind and a sudden heavy anxiety took me over. I couldn't control it.

I never felt so exposed in my entire life. I finally knew what exhibitionism truly felt like. Scary. Yet, I wanted it. I craved it. It was a growing addiction. Being a guy at this point didn't matter. All resistance fell away. I felt completely under a force I couldn't understand and knew at this point any resistance was futile – yet I *didn't want* to resist – that's what was driving me crazy with an emotional and crazed sensual longing I never felt before. And then the next words made it worse.

"We are just beginning. Remain still. Say absolutely nothing. Ask for absolutely nothing." The soft breath now in my left ear made me want to kiss something, some lips, something. My mouth felt a want that was amazingly unfulfilled and needful. But the one thing that captivated me was the word 'we.' Who else was in the room?! What were their sexes?! What was I in for?! Then came the immediate panic …fear …wanting out! But the pure excitement was blinding. The anticipation literally made me crazy. What was going to happen…

Then it began. Out of nowhere and random. I felt ever so soft fingers start touching me lightly anywhere and everywhere. Then hands, many hands. Everywhere was being ever so lightly stimulated and then gone, and then another part of my body, caressing my skin, coming close to my hardness but never touching it, which was driving me wild with want. And I couldn't anticipate it. 'Touch it! Caress it! Do something!' were my quiet demanding thoughts! I couldn't speak.

Then very light caressing started on my hardness. My whole waist instantly stiffened and rose. It was frozen in the air as I sorely wanted more and more but it was random! A touch here, a light motion there. I wanted that hand to just fucking grab it and stroke, stroke, *stroke!* I knew I couldn't speak and ask for it, so I worked my waist to try to force it. The hand immediately left. I felt my waist drop but I was throbbingly so hard, it felt like it was still there! After a moment, I felt an ever so slight finger caress downward my length, then it stopped and was gone. I gasped. Then under and around and gone again. Insanity. My breath left me. Then up and across the head which sent a shudder throughout my whole body. I couldn't predict anything! I was at the mercy of that caressing hand and finger. And all the caressing hands and fingers. They were slowly inciting sensations all over I never knew or ever felt before. My whole body, my whole spirit, was under a spell I can't describe, as if floating on a bed of everlasting open joy.

Then everything stopped. I craved more than I ever craved before. I couldn't believe the feeling, as a guy who never, would never believe this was possible. I mentally demanded it start again. Slowly, it did, teasingly, and dare

I say, lovingly. I felt a strange oneness with my tormentors.

And all of it was on top of the silk which caused a soft gliding feel every torturous time, adding a strange feminine sensation beyond any sensation I ever had as a guy. My body begged furiously for every tingling touch, every brief stroke, demanding satisfaction to just fucking finish! Then the lone loving touch was gone again and again the unbelievable feeling of it *still* being there was overwhelming. I could still feel the fondling that wasn't there anymore. I realized in my ecstatic frenzy that I had just been primed!

All the time, other hands and fingers continued to excite every nerve ending of my entire naked body. I lost the care of who were doing this to me and started to only want more and more. I became one with them. My defenses were completely down. Touch harder, finger harder, touch longer, caress longer, but to no avail. The intense teasing of my *entire aroused body* was driving my crotch and mouth into a frenzy. I wanted to kiss! I wanted to cum! I couldn't stop my hips from rocking, now causing the silk to rub even more against my ready-to-explode cock, which felt like it filled the whole room! And I felt I was going to cum so crazily right then when it all again suddenly stopped! Fuck!

I finally actually heard my heaving breathing and realized how hard my heart was pounding, ready to shatter into the air. I had no idea how long it all happened. There was now no sound except the music, no touching. I found myself wanting it all back. Start again! Please! Touch it! Hold it! Kiss me, please! I felt myself fight the cuffs. My entire body was excited beyond comprehension. I felt every part of me was pure pleasure, pure sensation, pure scintillation. Words cannot describe. I had lost all control and succumbed to this incredible bliss. It literally commanded me on its own.

As if known to be ready to speak, a light touching hand covered my mouth indicating to shush. All the while, the non-stop passionate pleasure of the experience still had my hips slightly and rhythmically rocking and I concentrated on that, knowing if I continued, it would cause the silk to finally make me...

Shudders! Spasms! and Shock Waves! The Strokeless Orgasm

Hands on both sides tenderly stopped my rocking hips. I had to obey. I was their tormented, helpless prisoner. It was insanely wonderful. I felt my wrists involuntarily try to move again but the cuffs held them back. I was in forced motionlessness and couldn't take it. I needed, wanted, craved, demanded fucking satisfaction. They couldn't just leave me like this. It was pure *pleasure-persecution* I never known before, ever. Nor ever knew I could actually feel and experience such an eternal insanity. I wanted to break loose and just finish it. But I did as I was commanded. And it didn't matter because I surrendered and they were in total control.

Just before I went limp in complete submission, I felt a tugging of the silk on both sides, apparently separating the sides, and suddenly it was gone. I was completely naked and my crotch was completely exposed to multiple unrestrained cruel phantoms in the room. The room where I was the victim, *their* victim...

Unbelievable embarrassment and pure excitement overwhelmed me and my hard-on was so intense, so out of control, I felt again it was larger than my whole body, filling the whole room, throbbing uncontrollably in front of them. My complete attention was solely there and my balls felt like pleasure giants. Everything below my waist was larger than life, larger than possible. But it was sensually beautiful, both masculine and feminine, and I completely and eagerly succumbed to their will. I finally knew what passion meant. Beyond anxious, I waited for what was next.

My 'wall' was completely down.

Episode 50 ~

My erotic tormentors knew their skill. Extremely well. I think they loved it. The pausing not only slowed me down (which I never *ever* would do – when I had to, I finished – period) but also increased tremendously the anticipating next ecstasies planned. Regardless, my uncontrollable writhing waist demanded more – continue damn it, do something! My nakedness didn't matter anymore. I was naked and fully exposed. I accepted that and liked it... really fucking *loved it*. I never felt so *me* before.

Suddenly, all at once, many hands were all over me, all over my sensitive, teased body, sending unbelievable sensations everywhere and anywhere. My tactile feelings were being overwhelmed, overloaded, and some hands and fingers would start lightly and then disappear only to be followed by a more pressing caress of different hands and fingers, continually teasing, focusing, defocusing, forcing me to completely let go all care. I became a complete bodily sensual, sexual organ being caressed by angels, building, heightening, then dropping, then again, then there, there, everywhere. Delirious sensations thrilled everywhere, each touch a pleasure-bomb exploding from the slightest, slightest contact, sending exhilarating, insane blasts of ecstatic ecstasy throughout my entire being. I couldn't take it. I started to pull at my imprisoned wrists to free myself so I could finish it!

In between it all I felt the distinctly noticeable feel of kisses start, faint at first and then increasing, all over, with the touching, craziness spiraling. I bit my tongue so hard as I felt the warmth of breath with each tender kiss, as if intended to be felt. It made it wickedly worse! How could a breath make me cum! But I didn't cum! My body was moving, flowing with every sensation, as if in a forever dazzling sexual, sensual dance, complete blissful bodily joy beyond fantasy, that not only didn't end but somehow kept increasing, more and more, higher and higher, my own breath panting loudly, my hips and thighs throbbing out of control. I was struggling like an insane person in an asylum. I was in the hell of pleasure.

And never had one touch, one kiss ever touch my now bare crotch, which was so sensitive, felt unbelievable enormous, and I felt a climatic explosion any second. But somehow they controlled me, these tyrants of desire, under their complete spell. They wouldn't let me go!!

In my delirious daze, out of nowhere, a single finger I felt under my crotch, stopped waiting there, while all else continued in the frenzy of eternal overwhelming madness. I wanted that finger, wanted it to move, wanting it more than anything, mentally begging it to move, for it focused all else *right* to it. I moved the best I could to get it to go on its journey. Finally, it slowly was moving, not caressing but just moving, creeping. It was the most sensual thing I have ever, ever felt, this one tender finger.

It seemed the hands, fingers, kissing, breaths were now all focused on that one point, each ever coming close to it, then moving away, as the gentle tip of the finger slowly made its way pressing so lightly between my balls and when it reached the base of my crazed hardness, I let out a gasp, as it suddenly, lightly shook my whole body uncontrollably, and as it then moved upward, my body shuddered lightly again, then again, then again. I was out of control.

I felt my precum dripping and out of nowhere I felt a tongue lightly lick it up. I had no idea male or female and didn't fucking care. Because right then and there, a spasm of please whooshed through me that I had never experienced before. It was amazing! As the finger reached right below my head, a second ecstatic spasm lifted my body off the bed and rushed through every limb. The finger crossed onto my head and rolled over the tip and was gone. And then returned a moment later on the uppermost part of my cock below the head and so delicately caressed, sending blinding pleasure throughout me to the point of cumming so hard and right before that, it was gone but the feeling of ongoing, non-stop explosions continued amazingly somehow. And all the hands and fingers and kisses were gone too! But I was experiencing as if they were all still there!! I was in a never ending climax.

My body was now dancing to a pleasure rhythm I was generating all by myself by my slow motions, by lightly tensing and releasing, and the movement of my waist and crotch. Instead of the heightened titillation subsiding, to my absolute amazement, it was increasing, by my own will! With absolutely no touching, I felt as if *there was touching*! Every nerve ending was sparkling, was shooting out, and back in, and I felt an endless orgasm growing deep inside that I was actually controlling by my slight movements, by my mind! I was in an orgasmic trance of *ultimate* pleasure. Male ecstasy! Pure male mindless endless ecstasy!

I could increase it, decrease it, build it, focus it, and then I felt the cuffs release on both sides and a hand clasp gently each of my wrists and without resistance from me, I let them guide my own fingers to lightly caress my thighs, only my thighs, ever so lightly. And it felt as if my fingers were directly caressing my crazed hard-on but only my thighs were being touched. The hands let go and I continued it and found that I could guide my coming orgasm by a light finger thigh touch or many fingers, each sensation causing more ecstatic spasms, and then I felt a light touch where I never would have allowed. I instinctively lightly spread my legs as my fingers played with my thighs. And a hand and fingers unbelievably tenderly caressed my ass cheeks and lightly touching occasionally my anus driving sensations I never knew I could achieve, as if everything was bursting everywhere, the pleasure was so intense, and then light fingers caressed each nipple, sending more spasms through me.

Then it started…

Episode 51 ~

I could feel nothing but ecstasy, pure fucking ecstasy, as my hips rose and fell, and reached a climatic build that I felt would never end. Instinctively, I stopped touching and all other touches were gone right when I stopped touching. It was purely uncontrollable now. My insanely intimate cravings and sensations overwhelmed me as I began the final skyrocketing build that kept going and going and going, more intense, more intense, but *still* had not reached the point of explosion. Everything was alive. I was in orgasmic heaven and time seemed to stop as my entire body engulfed into a climax that was eternal. And I felt the final tumultuous moment with nothing touching me and I knew I was cumming unbelievably and felt the warmth of my endless semen everywhere and the whole time my body convulsed in enormous unstoppable ecstatic body-pulsing waves, pounding one after the other, again and again, my body shaking each time, during the whole endless explosion of my spectacular, infinite climax. I wanted to grab myself so badly but didn't as the final blinding wave shot through me as I heard myself cry out. The climax didn't just end abruptly as normally would but seemed to slowly dissipate with the same exciting convulsing waves, continuing less and less, and my hips started to relax as the climax soothingly, slowly subsided.

I finally actually also heard my panting deep breaths and found it hard to control my breathing until light touching hands ran slowly over my whole physique causing me to slow my breathing by the sheer focus they caused. My breathing returned to moderately fast and then under control finally. My mind was in a complete daze. I took two deep breaths and felt the limpness. But for some reason, I still felt very aroused. For some reason, I felt I could go again. I laid there amazed at the whole experience and that I let who knows how many people see me naked, see me sexually aroused, and then crazily crazed, and allowed them all to touch me, everywhere, and they all witnessed my insane...and then it hit me...my insane *strokeless orgasm* and deeply personal 'shock waves,' that lasted for eternities. *My 'shock waves!'*

And my mind somehow quickly assessed that I had actually experienced the sensually real ...shudders, ...spasms, and finally, '...shock waves!' It was possible! And I now instinctively knew that it could also be repeated, increased, tailored, joined with other people, and yes, taught. And it was hilariously fun! Then it came.

Still blindfolded, the room erupted in an exuberant applause and cheers! I couldn't tell if the voices were male or female or both and I just didn't care. That 'wall' was so forever broken, torn down, and gone. I had personally conquered vulnerability! And so was the 'wall' of fear and resistance of my own male intimacy and male experience. I was now open to anything because I deserved anything I wanted, and no person, rule, perception, whatever, was going to either bother me ever again, bind me ever again, nor stop me ever again. And it was the amazing open, uninhibited, *sexual* experience that sealed it! What power! Fascinating!

I felt a swelling pride as the applause subsided. I waited, exhausted, not knowing what to do but figured, hey, at this point, they were in control and I was happy for it. I felt completely relaxed, at ease, naked, in their presence. I never felt like this before as a guy, but I felt giddy, childlike. I loved it. Loved it all.

I heard whatever it was that had added to my complete darkness of sight be moved back behind my head. Then, the sultry voice was near my ear again.

"Well done," it whispered. "When the music finishes, you may take the blindfold off, get changed, and someone will get you. OK?"

I nodded and then the breath went away. I craved for it to return. For all of them to return.

Episode 52 ~

Not sure exactly how long I laid there motionless, almost afraid to move. I finally decided to remove the blindfold. The room was exactly the same as when I had entered. I peered to my left and then to my right. No one was there, just me, naked, and then I realized all my wetness was still on me, in fact all over me! A growing laughter started in me. It was actually beautiful, a part of me. I never thought this way before. For some reason, I had expected someone to clean me up! My uncontrolled laughter continued with the thought of 'they *already* did enough!'

I propped myself on my elbows and looked down. To my surprise not only was there cum everywhere but I still had a fair hard-on. "Fucking amazing," came out of my mouth.

At the foot of the bed was a purple towel. Well, at least they left something for me to use! I leaned forward to grab it and then felt the extreme tiredness of my waist muscles and thighs. Sore was probably the better word. What a fucking workout.

I cleaned up and moved my legs over the side to stand up. I stood and grabbed the bed. "Whoa," I uttered. I was wobbly, I mean completely unsteady, almost trembling. Felt more weak than after a long deep tissue hot stone massage. I re-sat a bit onto the bed to gain my composure. "What the fuck" and "Damn" were my next words. I smiled outwardly and inwardly. In their world, I was friggin' sexually out of shape! They surely taught me a lesson on the power of the amazing male orgasm, an understatement to say the least. And I felt the want to learn more, not only sexual but everything, to feel free to express everything that is me. Could the freedom of sex ignite the freedom of everything else? I now understood their technique in how to create

201

a totally uninhibited, free spirit. Well, if crazed, uninhibited pleasure was needed, then so be it!

I finally got back to my feet, still a bit wobbly, and went to my clothes. Took a bit to put them back on and afterwards, I realized I still had the remains of 'masculine wetness' on me. And for some reason, I didn't care at all. It was a special trophy of my adventure.

I looked at my watch and was shocked. Almost 90 minutes had passed since I had taken off my clothes! Holy shit! I had completely lost track of time and how in the fuck could all of that lasted so long. Amazing. Then the thought came to me, could I actually do this on my own, for that long? And can someone else also 'assist' if agreeable? And could I experience 'shock waves' with *actual stroking*? Many ideas kept popping in my head and I could see my quest was going to continue, with myself, and with others, and also non-sexually. Freedom derived from freedom. I felt a completely different world in and around me. Weird.

Then another thought hit me. I have no idea of the sexes that were 'assisting' me. Could have been all female, all male, or a combination. No idea. What if it was all male? Or even one male and all female? Would I now let another male touch me? I couldn't answer that question so I let it float away, not to ruin the wondrous aura. But the sensations were so amazing, did it really matter the sex partner? Was this part of the lesson? To bring out the conditioning that may be planted so deep inside over so many years, that even the mere thought of a male touch was abhorrent to some, to many? Was it to me? I knew I was accepting of any orientation but was that accepting just a mental decision? Now it came down to *me*. Was I now accepting to me, myself, as a *complete* sensual being, without any inhibitions, to experiment *anything*? It was a very challenging but intensely alluring 'wall.'

I went to the door I had come into and opened it.

Lisa was standing there.

Episode 53 ~

"Hey!" she exclaimed happily. "Amazing, isn't it?"

I hesitated, thinking, was she involved, too?

"I would say so," which came out so lame I felt the need to recover. "I mean, yes, it was beyond amazing." I smiled tiredly back at her beaming, knowing, childlike yet adult eyes.

"Well, you are definitely one of the few," she said as she turned away, obviously for me to follow her through the utopian murals we passed through before. I followed.

"What do you mean, one of the few," I asked to her walking back.

"Oh," she answered still walking in front of me, not turning, "not many get to 'shock waves' the first time." She giggled sweetly.

"Really? Uh... Really?"

"Really! Very impressive!" Then I heard it. It was *her* sultry voice in that room! I smiled.

"OK. Wow. So, how many times, sessions, does it take to..."

She cut me off.

"Usually two. Sometimes three. No more."

"I see." I didn't know what else to say as we walked back up the stairs. Would I get a trophy?

We made our way back to the main part of the mansion and she guided me through to a room I hadn't been in before. It had all the wonderful trappings of the rest of the mansion: paintings, sculptures, plushness, yet still subtle.

"Have a seat," she offered to one of the throne-type chairs. I obeyed happily, happy to sit back down as my legs were still somewhat weak. "See you around!" she blurted with enthusiasm and bounced out of the room, leaving me sitting there alone. OK, now what? What was next? Some kind of inquisition?

Anyway, I found out.

In came Zach, Teri, and Josh, all smiling. I weakly stood.

"Well, well, my boy! Aren't you the sensitive sexy one!" Zach exuded playfully.

"You are!" Teri followed with.

"You da' man!" Josh followed with a big smile.

It occurred to me again that specific trainers must be assigned right from the start to help, guide, and motivate. I was happy with mine

"Come on, it was merely just sex," I replied playfully, too. They all laughed and each hugged me. I didn't expect that but it felt good, like family. The openness of our talk and behavior was always intoxicating.

"Well, you were amazing from what I was told," Zach claimed.

So, he wasn't there.

"Thanks but I didn't plan...I mean it wasn't my..." I had no idea how to answer him without sounding victorious and ego-filled, and even macho. Yeah, macho-naked-guy-blindfolded-vulnerable-loving-exhibitionist-touched-by-both-sexes-until-climatic 'shock waves' rocking-his-known-world − right in front of all of them! Me? That was me all right. Did I actually do that?! I knew I did and had zero regrets.

In fact, I just wanted so much to explore more and more and with others who know, too. It was suddenly experimentally a really fun thought. The freedom I felt was astounding. And the possibilities were amazing and this newfound liberty from the experience was mind-blowing. There had to be a way to make millions from this.

"Damn it man, give yourself some fucking credit," Josh pushed back grinning, interrupting my internal self-analysis. "You will never be the same now."

That I knew very well. And all from sex? Yes! From absolutely amazing *sex!* My expectations will now be at a bar, at a level of achievement that even at that moment, I knew there were even higher heights of loving to playfully achieve. A ton of 'what if's' was filling my mind.

"How do you feel?" Teri finally asked almost singing it.

"Tired. A bit weak, in the legs. But beyond satisfied. I mean it was blinding."

"Oh, I know. It'll happen more and more," she grinned. "That's not though what I meant."

"Um," was all that came out until I realized the real question. Before I could answer, still not sure how I was going to answer, Zach and Josh took their leave and both said they would catch up with me another time. I was kind of disappointed they left but my focus went back to Teri and her question.

"I feel really wonderful. I mean, I feel lightheaded, and not from the physical exertion. I feel...happy!" I said with enthusiasm I meant and felt. She sat down across from me, smiling and waiting.

"To tell you the truth, the whole experience, and not knowing who was there – and not caring anymore – and the naked exposure, the willingness to submit and be vulnerable, somehow...set me free." I wasn't sure where those words came from.

"Yes, that will and was intended to let, and even force, your 'walls' down and even destroy them once and for all. And not just sexual 'walls' but *every* human-made 'wall.'"

"I know that now."

"It will still be sinking in for days, trust me. We all went through it in varying ways. More and more you will see a new you, especially back in the world." Her 'back in the world' went deep inside me. I knew I wouldn't be the same ever again, as a person, and after just one classroom and one 'lab,' if you could call it that.

She stood, came over to me, and sat right next to me on the arm rest, her bare legs laying across mine. I felt suddenly like we were little children. A day ago, this would have shocked me, made me uncomfortable, but now it seemed completely natural and welcome. "Sex is powerful. It is the most powerful need after the need to eat. And being that, it is the most repressed, from our own fears and our conditioning. Freeing sex and its damn walls have the crazy effect of freeing lesser conditionings and walls. That's why it's such a powerful major part of our training. Plus it's really fun!" She laughed at herself. I couldn't help but laugh, too.

"So, may I ask something?" I posed looking up into her gorgeous childlike eyes.

"Sure!"

"What was the mix? I mean…"

She cut me off.

"Do you really want to know? Does it really matter? Or would you like to keep it unknown to stir the fantasies more? Let your imagination run wild!"

I knew she would answer me if I really wanted to know. I wasn't sure I wanted to know and not because of anything wrong, but exactly to her point, I was seriously beginning to enjoy the mystery, the unknown fantasy of it all. It was mine to own.

"OK, yea, not now. Maybe another time."

"Good! Whenever you wish. It's amazing though, isn't it?"

"Amazing yes!"

"Not what I meant."

"Oh, what did you mean?" I knew she meant something else than an overall amazing experience.

"Answer me honestly, OK?" she almost whispered, with a glowing sincerity in her expression and eyes.

"Will do. Ask."

"You found your female side, didn't you." She said more of a statement than question. I had no choice but to answer her gentle piercing eyes.

"Yes. Yes, I did." I paused, thinking and feeling at the same time. The honesty swelled in me and I realized again how I would have lied before, hid before. "It was as you said, amazing. I felt both as a guy and as a…" I hesitated and then continued as she waited, "…as a girl, a female. The sexiness was all male and female at the same time. You're right. I had insane images of being a girl laying on that bed. It's really hard to explain. But I would never give it up either. I'm greater now."

She leaned down and kissed me lightly and then said, "it's in all of us. We are all both. In fact, in the womb, we all start out as females. Now, and as you go forward, you will see more and more, feel more and more, both the power of the male, as you are finding out, and the power of the female. You will always connect them. Marry them as one. It will become one inside you. Trust me. It's so wonderful to be, see, and feel both!"

I knew she was right. Not because she said it. But because I truly, really felt it. A hidden part of me was exposed, brought out, and I was forced to look at it. And I freely accepted it. And I could see the male in her now. Amazing. I knew now I could and would accept everything and everyone.

"You are so right and I am so thankful. I really want to keep going and find more about myself and honestly, more about others. More about you. More about Josh…I mean how he feels and sees." I recovered from the notion of saying something I didn't mean to imply. She cocked her head at me almost in reprimand. I knew what she meant by it but I didn't say any more. She pursed her lips and suddenly stood up and moved right in front of me. She put her hands on the arm rests and next, her face was right up against mine.

"Keep going," she whispered as I felt and smelled her warm breath. "You will find more and more about you and everyone. For now, be amazed with what you have found. And the offer from me and Josh still stands – anytime. We would love to be part of your next discoveries and add to them as you can also do for us. Maybe dinner some time? Or we just pop over?"

After she cutely giggled, she kissed me full on the lips, slipped her tongue in, and I was again enthralled. She pulled away, touched my nose with her finger, and turning away, walked out of the room. My eyes were planted on her bare legs and waist and felt my hard-on return. And I also just wanted to simply get together and talk, have fun together. And also experiment, too. I actually *want* to challenge myself! Push my limits. Amazing the power that comes being completely without inhibition. Was so new to me.

I took a deep breath when she was gone. I found myself again alone in the room and knew I could stay or leave. I was now part of the family, trusted, and it felt really nice and exciting. I got up, made sure I had my balance, and proceeded through the mansion to the front door. I felt at home.

As I closed the door behind me, the thought wouldn't leave me.

Her and Josh.

Would I?

Could I?

Dare I?

Mmmmmm...

Darian Dracco, that hot-blooded Italian-American guy?

I smiled at that image and went to my car.

Episode 54 ~

I couldn't believe only a week had gone by with only one awesome enlightening class and well, you know the other portion of the fantasy-like tale. Exhilarating power. I felt more alive than ever before. I tried to pinpoint the exact reason but it wasn't one reason.

I spent a couple of days pondering and absorbing it all in, from the classroom to the lab, and getting personally close to amazing magnetic people I never encountered the like of which before. The word 'awakening' kept appearing in my mind. It wasn't that I lost anything at all. I had literally gained, gained so much. It was as if so many doors inside me were so locked and now they were swung open, and even doors I didn't know existed. The feeling of freedom was just ...beautiful. Like the first gorgeous Spring-like warm day after a cold, dark Winter.

I had experienced through thought and feeling a heightened intense awareness of my complete *self*-intimacy, sensual prowess, and *sexual power*... yet there was an amazing female feeling in me. I can only explain it as a birthing of a hidden new power that was blossoming out of control, and with all my prior male intention to *not* let this happen, I couldn't stop it. I just couldn't stop it.

And I found I didn't want to stop it, and found even more so, that I wanted more of it. I now knew that *complete sex* was being *both* male and female, a union, an inner marriage, all at the same time – and both guys and girls can experience it. It was exhilarating, the complete feeling of independence to be and do as I wish, as I am, as I am more finding out about myself, and not fearing any of it, or anything, nor fearing *anyone*. Complete abandon to be *me*.

I knew I could even now speak freely of my feelings, my desires, my understandings, to anyone, even at the bar or at parties or one-on-one. And it wasn't just the wide landscape of *intense* masculine pleasure. Yes, I have firsthand experience of what a guy can intimately achieve beyond anything we ever knew. And no sex therapist I believe could have provided this acute awareness and power. It had to be experienced, to know it was true. Otherwise, it was just words — as they had only been just words to me before.

The naked vulnerability though was an enormous trigger setting off all other observations of what I held in, what I believe guys hold in, each individually having their own personal 'walls.' And girls, too. Everyone. I'm not judging anyone specifically, just my sincere general beliefs from my experience. I know all are different and have to look into ourselves each individually.

And I also fully understood why this all was so selective. Zach was building a community of free-thinkers of any and every possible thing any of us wanted, and wanted to express. I suddenly thought of putting on makeup and laughed. If I wanted to, I would. Period. Well, doesn't Captain Jack Sparrow? Maybe…eyeliner? Seems like it. It's cool and dramatic. Anyone know?

And if I wanted to wear a bikini bathing suit, I would. Period. Or get piercings, I would. Period. Piercings? Interesting…

If I wanted to tenderly express my love for someone without fear of repercussion, I would. Period. If I wanted to dance down the street in happiness for whatever reason, in broad daylight, I would. Period. And if I wanted to give, perform, accept *any* type of intimate sexual action, I would. Period. It didn't matter what. It only matters that I can be me regardless of what I had been taught, learned, told, pushed, reprimanded, repressed, resisted, and conditioned. Just one week. I smiled and planned my next classroom time. I needed to get back to hear more and contribute more.

And I felt bigger than I was before (maybe in many ways…I'll have to measure and let you know). I actually and strangely felt more of a man than before, more masculine and knew most guys I knew would never understand that — but I didn't care at all. I wanted to express it all, and to every guy and girl.

And most importantly, I not only knew what I was taught by words, and by actions, but mostly, by *example*. It was how everyone *was*, how all were so unconditionally *accepting* of each other, no fear, no judgment, we all can say and do *anything*. A unique, new *Utopia*.

I also wondered what the next lab would bring!

As I sat back pondering and letting everything flow freely, I thought of Melissa. I actually didn't feel bad not really thinking of her through this, as I felt no fault in it. We each, guy and girl, have to find our own way and each person is different, yet now I see so many commonalities between the sexes I never saw before. I thought to text her and wondered how I would be, how I would now perceive her and our relationship. Then my thoughts went to Teri and Josh. And I saw two different worlds.

I wanted them to be one world.

Episode 55 ~

I decided to call her instead. Texting a lot of times loses meaning and intention as there's really no tone or expressiveness. I waited to see if she would answer. She did.

"Hi Darian," I heard her familiar voice. It was pleasant and calm which I had not expected but was grateful.

"Hey. Just wanted to call and see how things are," I replied, leaving out 'and I miss you.'

"Thanks. All good. How are you doing?"

Loaded question I knew, and knew I would have lied before.

"I am doing really well. A lot has happened in a short time. Would love to talk with you about it." I felt the enthusiasm swell in me.

"OK, shoot."

"Oh, no, if I may, I'd rather in person, if okay with you. Just talk."

"Um, is this going to be about Zach and about... about things you have engaged in?" I heard the tentativeness in her voice, and even a touch of fear?

"Well, first I'd like to just see you. I miss you," came out of my mouth and I knew it was true, just not missing the recent bad discussions.

"I miss you, too." Pause. She was waiting for my real answer.

"Yes, of course it's about that but it's amazing and want to share with you all of it. Maybe afterwards you may wish to check it out yourself. It's not just for guys," I replied with all honesty and thought of Teri and Lisa. She'd probably really like them.

"Like, I mean, are you going to talk about the sex you had? Is that it?"

I knew that may be a game changer so I tried to express it as not just 'sex.'

"Honey, it's everything. Mostly what I've been taught, like in a classroom and yes of course there's a sexual, I would even say sensual element but it's all part of a new awareness I never felt before. I firmly believe more than any standard therapy, though there's nothing wrong with that either. It's just so powerful. I'm being positive here." I suddenly felt proud to be part of their community and almost felt like a teacher myself now.

"I don't know."

Silence.

"Trust me. I am not going to talk about sex the way I think you're seeing it. Just trust me, and if you feel uncomfortable with our talk, we can end it and move on."

Silence. I knew the 'uncomfortable' and 'move on' were being digested. I also just realized how much different I was feeling towards her. I no longer had a feeling of ownership or she was 'mine.' I felt a feeling of one human to another. It kind of caught me by surprise but made it easier to express myself. Fascinating. Another 'wall' fallen.

"OK, we can try. I have been curious of it all anyway, maybe. Especially knowing you, and that you would not engage in anything bizarre or illegal."

Bizarre? Mmmm I thought. I guess that's up to interpretation. I smiled and replied.

"No not illegal." I ignored the bizarre only because it could be taken different ways by different people, and especially a person's current individual conditioning. Suddenly, I felt like Zach talking. "If you are curious, that's a first step. I really want to be open with you. It's such a better, even wonderful place. Think of it as an experiment."

Did I just use the word 'wonderful?'

"All this? All this in what has it been, how long?" she challenged but I knew it wasn't a mean challenge.

"Uh, yeah, a week," I replied, "but it's still going on." I wanted to tell her about Fred but held back. Wanted this discussion just her and I.

"A week." Her flat tone showed her not believing the sum of what I was implying happened in just one week. I didn't care.

"Yeah, a week. A helluva week. But can't we just talk in person at this point?" It hit me that the more open and accepting a person was going into this new world, the faster the results and change.

After a pause, "Sure. We can meet. When are you free?"

It was Wednesday and I had scheduled my next class the next evening so we decided on Friday after work to meet and have a drink together. I would have preferred privately but she insisted.

Regardless, I felt an almost joy that we were meeting and I knew now too I could express myself openly. I wondered if this was part of it all — actually feeling happy to *want* to express oneself. Well, I didn't dwell on it.

Another interesting effect is that a lot of worrying was gone. Worrying that I hadn't ever noticed before but once gone, I noticed. And I was happy to talk with her and meet again! I felt no judgment anymore.

I liked my newfound me.

It felt completely natural.

Episode 56 ~

I arrived a bit early for class, wanting to make sure I wasn't late. I entered and saw my fellow classmates and another group that looked like their first time. It was strange how I could pick that out. There was a different air between the two groups.

"Hey all," I greeted as I approached.

Everyone replied similarly and with enthusiasm. Before too much discussion, Josh corralled us.

"Welcome back friends! From what I can see, seems we all had some good experiences!" he declared confidently with a beaming smile. There were again many enthusiastic agreements. I counted eight guys and wondered if someone had bailed.

"OK! Well let's get started. Third room left. Be there in a minute."

So Josh was our trainer for the evening. I was fine with it and interested in hearing his take on things and next steps. Before I could follow the group, he pulled me aside.

"Got a sec?" he asked. He had such honesty in his eyes.

"Yeah, sure, what's up?" I replied curiously.

"Again, congrats on such a, how should I put it," he was smiling with a cocky smile, "fantastic, enlightening performance."

I didn't know what to say.

"Um, well, thanks. I think."

He laughed. "You *think*? Weren't you there?"

I laughed and looked down, feeling a bit embarrassed but only for a second. His demeanor was too trusting and friendly. "Yeah, I guess I was pretty good." I wasn't sure why I was being so tentative, so sensitive. But I

215

then said what I really wanted to say. "I mean it was fucking amazing!" I blurted out and feeling every bit confident in it.

"Yeah, well, I think you know that it's a bit rare to achieve everything in one lab session. But you did. So! Be that as it may, you really do not need to attend any more lab sessions unless you want to. It's always open, but we feel you should now, kind of do, home schooling."

"Home schooling." I repeated. Part of me was proud, part of me was disappointed that I didn't *have* to do lab 'work' again. Wasn't prepared for a choice.

"Yep. Here." He handed me a folder. "This is what we give to everyone after full achievement. Since you already reached that, this is yours. It has instructions on more ways to bring out your inner true self, and more ways for your inner intimate self, too. Hope you see now it's really all one experience together that makes you, you."

"It has ideas and suggestions on meditations and thought-provoking topics, on emotional exercises, as well as sexual exercises on different positions both alone and how to then work with a partner, male or female, and then in a group if you ever wish that. The mental, emotional, and sensual all must join together in you and others. But it's important to, how should I say, work *yourself* first. Learn yourself more, by yourself. Mentally, you'll be able to think clearer and deeper. Emotionally, you'll be able to find and express all true feelings. And sexually, you'll be able to achieve it all again and in different ways."

Knowing how important the *combination* of all really was, I still smiled inwardly at the demand for more masturbation and somehow, it was more exciting than ever. They say sex is one of the most powerful drivers in our lives. It's *healing power* is so underestimated by most of us. That I truly learned.

"We like to present all options and each student can then choose their own path individually as they see fit. More information you will receive after the classes, and some assignments, which are geared more towards our overall 'walls,' fears, and desires."

I suddenly laughed. Josh looked quizzically at me. I held up a hand to let me explain. "I have homework!"

Josh smiled and laughed, too.

"Yeah, you do! Don't fuck up! And after some time, when you feel very comfortable with everything, we can discuss the 'Advanced Lab Work.'" He put his hand on my shoulder and it was non-intrusive, like a brother would. "Welcome to our and your community!"

"Thanks! I am very happy to be a... member."

Advanced Lab Work? What was that and could I survive it?! I let it go ...for now.

"Member is a fine word," he smiled in agreement. "Let's join the others, shall we?"

"Let's."

"Oh, shoot, one more thing. A fun thing. There are also instruction in there on how to perform the 'cumless cum.'" My head slightly tilted as I hadn't heard that phrase since the beginning. "As you have experienced, it's not always easy to hold back, though it's critical to achieving the heights you now know we guys can — and even more, in different ways. The technique still allows orgasms and since there's no actual cum, you will find you rebound very quickly, if you wish to keep a 'session' going. Plus, amazingly, the orgasm is even more powerful."

I loved the word 'session.' But also 'more powerful.' Was that possible?

"Well, anyway, wanted to let you know, as that is something we do not train onsite. You're on your own unless you need assistance."

I loved then the word 'assistance.' Everything was simply open game, approachable, so frank and free to easily speak and discuss. I suddenly wanted to ask about the large area of the backyard that was fenced in so high, and no one could see from the outside. I held off as we were walking towards the classroom. But I was going to find out.

Definitely.

Episode 57 ~

When we arrived, I did another count and all were present. I was glad. I didn't want anyone to bail. Then the curiosity swelled up wondering how far did each achieve in lab. Before I could further contemplate, Josh started. I did notice that Teri was back in her seat.

"Welcome back again friends! We all are doing great! Remember, the door is always open for any questions, concerns, as a group or in private. And I want to give everyone a round of appreciated and well-earned applause!" He started clapping as did Teri and we all naturally followed.

"OK, now that our mutual admiration society is completed," he laughed, "want to begin with a bit of a statement."

We all quieted down.

"We're here to dive deep, to forget the rules, to pull out your deepest feelings, and your deepest *fears*, and the power that comes with it. With that, you'll be able to feel completely free to craft your mind, your body, your spirit, and what it really means to be you, a strong, virile, and *sensitive* male in complete control of your feelings, your real sensuality, and your life – your day-to-day living. And, as you may have already experienced, you'll also be totally *unafraid* to discover your inner *female side* with confidence, because gentlemen, you have a female side, as our ladies also find their masculine side. Have no doubt about it. A lot of guys will never admit it either. But it's there, in every guy."

"And, then realizing the *extreme* power of the two finally being *as one*, will open your eyes to what really is, and NOT what we're taught and constantly shown that beats us down every day, into a quarter of what and who we are! We're here to make you more aware of yourself, more than you think possible."

All were captivated by his confident, powerful, and sheer unwavering persona.

"Fucking free yourself from… *YOURSELF!* Free yourself from the bonds of everything you've learned since the womb. We are ALL male AND female. That's a fact very hard to digest at the onset. But there's ultimate power in it. Follow through and you will see more and more."

His astounding oratory energy was amazing and addictive. And all could feel he truly believed in all he said – and we did, too. The room was silent, and after a pause, he continued.

"Gentlemen, the truth will honestly set you free. And…as a famous American once said and is still true: *the only fear we must fear, is fear itself.* You have been chosen by us and more importantly, by your own self, to take this journey. Courage is all you need! Teri?" He motioned to her. She stood and all eyes met hers. The allure we all felt was utterly electrifying.

"Guys, this is so true. I am born a female and have learned so deeply my male side, better yet, my combined male and female self. It's not like one side or the other. It's all together. It's built in all of us. And it's important to know, we train our girl trainees as such, too. Before, you only lived *half* of your true self! Think about that! And you do NOT lose any of your masculinity. You just start seeing and *feeling* your femininity with it, as one. And then you are wonderfully whole! And with the fearless power that comes with it."

She paused, then continued. "It may be one of the hardest things to learn and bring out, as we are all conditioned to never consider it, to NEVER bring it out, *NEVER* ever admit it, and at times, many times, get ridiculed for even thinking it. Unless you find it, embrace it, love it, you will never be your complete self. You need to be inquisitive. You need to be brave. You need to want it."

She sat, smiling. We all felt her truthfulness.

'Complete self' drove deep into me. At that moment, I felt something break in me. Something fall apart, as something else emerged. I felt a deep honesty within myself. An honesty I knew that I would deeply know now from that moment forward. I was always going to be me, find more of me, and love what I find, *and* always *love me*, always. I looked up at Josh, and he was looking directly at me, lightly nodding his head as if he could read my feelings. I smiled back unabashedly.

"Great guys. Let's move on and keep that in mind. Now to some sexy dirty work," he stated with a bit of a playful evil grin on his boyish face. "When you love girls, attracted to girls, you are actually loving the female in yourself." He paused to let it sink in. "Same if you love guys. But there's one fact we all need to get onboard with, whether you like it or not." His tone went to serious. "Only a guy truly knows how to please a guy, and only a girl truly knows how to please a girl. Then we teach each other."

He sat and waited.

Episode 58 ~

Even though there was silence in the room, the feeling I could tell was that no one had an issue with what Josh just said. I don't know how many would have agreed with this idea prior to coming here. Or even in the outside world. In fact, I noticed some heads nodding.

Did that mean that the best sex possible between two is same sex? And not that I would do that, at least not right now, but the statement made sense. And such a statement would be fairly and pretty much immediately rejected among a lot of folks outside of our circle. But if I know best how to please myself, then it follows I would know how best to please another guy and know what he's actually feeling. Same for girls with girls.

"Now, please, by no means is anyone trying to say go out and have same sex, unless of course you want to, but we are open people here and sometimes some realities take a bit to digest and accept."

"But it's also so exciting with a girl to a guy and a guy to a girl as you may know." He grinned. "Because they don't know exactly the feeling they are causing and that makes for wonderful exploration to really try to find what makes their partner go crazy. That's why I say 'teach each other.' Just a lot of thoughts to keep in mind as you continue your personal, emotional, and physical journeys."

One of my fellow students raised his hand.

"Question? Good."

"Hey Josh, so you're bisexual, right?"

"Absolutely."

"So, you are speaking from direct experience." His tone was friendly but inquisitive.

"I would say yes," Josh replied with a chuckle.

"So, based on what you said about both experiences, which is better in the end."

"Both. Honestly, even though a guy may know better how to please a guy, each of us is still an individual and feel differently regardless. My point is a *starting point*, not an end all. Discovery is the best part, regardless of the partner. It's just from the onset, a guy will know better, but trust me, a girl can surely learn more! And vice versus. We *all* learn and gain!"

Laughter broke out at Josh's triumphant playful tone and I saw Teri cover her mouth trying not to release her laughter.

"OK, couple more things. First, you are getting an assignment." Some lighthearted moans heard. "Next, we have one more topic to discuss." He paused a second and continued. "Assignment is that on your own, in your own private time, you are to write down for only yourself to ever see, a minimum of three deep secrets about yourself you would *never* let anyone know. But now you are going to let *yourself know*. Title it: '*My Adventure List.*' Doesn't have to be sexual, though it can be. But take some quiet reflective time and being brutally honest with yourself, write them down. Deep ones. Five would be better but start with three. Yes?"

"Anything?"

"Anything. Could be something from your childhood, could be some hidden desire that completely goes against societal rules or expectations. Just be honest. We all have them. And writing them down is most important, so you can look right at them. Then, when you feel like it, expand on them. Get more descriptive. Give brutal detail. Remember, only you will ever see this and even if you wish to share with your closest friend or partner, do not. That's really important in order to be able to really let these out. And you may need to tear down some more walls or look over those walls to see the deepest ones. Again, the deepest, hidden desires, fantasies, and/or actions. Yes?"

"Can you give an example?" A bit of fun laughter again.

"Sure. I'll give a sexual one and a non-sexual one. Sexual. Wanting to have sex wearing woman's lingerie." Chuckling. "You'd be surprised," he playfully reprimanded, "how many burly, manly men have that fantasy... and act out it, at least by themselves. Another sexual. Being completely dominated by either a guy or girl – or both. Wanting sadomasochism bondage, even spanking!" I saw him glance at Teri. "Or simply shave your crotch because you always wanted to. So, non-Sexual. Wanting to take dance lessons and even ballet lessons. Wanting to skydive but are terrified. Get that tattoo you always wanted but was afraid of ridicule. Get some piercings if you're brave enough to take the pain. And no one should ever ridicule piercings if they have never experienced some of that pain themselves. It can be anything you *ever* desired. Yes?"

"And we keep this to ourselves? Why? Why not share?"

"Because they belong to you solely. Yours to *dare* yourself to actually do and when you are ready, just do it without telling anyone. Telling others is a crutch, usually looking for either approval or motivation. You must do these on your own and keep them to yourself. Once you actually do it, then have a field day telling others. At that point, you should be proud – and most importantly, free!"

"OK, now, for our last discussion of today. And this is specific to us guys and again, a hard concept for our conditioning – and not pardoning the pun." I and others chuckled. "Gentlemen, if you don't already, you gotta love your dicks. It's *part* of you. We have been conditioned to believe they are a separate thing, outside of us. You have to have a love affair with yourself, *all* of yourself, and accept you do. And you surely know this from the labs. We tend to treat orgasms like a slice of pie. One minute and done. Onto something else. Never take the time to savor, to REALLY treat yourself!"

"We don't even know how utilitarian we've become and we just fall in line with our own beliefs of our ourselves. A guy works out heavily, looks in the mirror at his muscles, and loves what he sees. He *loves* it. Trust me, our cocks and our sex are the same thing. And treat your equipment like a gun in training. Takes time to practice, to perfect. How many guys do you think,

223

even straight guys, ever have wanted to suck their own dicks?" He paused in the silence, and I think for the dramatic effect. It worked.

"Well, at least thought of it. How many ever wanted to or actually have tasted their cum? How many girls would love to lick their clit and vagina – even just to see. And to taste. This is not a gay thing or a bisexual thing. This is a human thing. It's great to be curious. Whether we want to believe it or not, we need to love ourselves both emotionally and physically to be truly one-hundred percent free. Remember, we are all both male and female. A male should sometimes play the female of himself and a female should play the male of herself. We know it's not an easy concept but it's natural to have these curiosities, *accept* them, don't hide from them, and then take them as far or not at all, as you wish. It's your *total power*."

He paused slightly and continued.

"We are so embarrassed to admit the realities within us. Remember, courage. Walls. Conditioning. Acceptance. Embracing your real self without guilt, without fear, and with the determination to find and behold your wonderful body and spirit. Be free! Let loose! And remember to always *engage* yourself and others!"

"And with that, I think we're good. Teri?"

She rose. "A journey is a journey. Sometimes we run, sometimes we walk, sometimes we crawl. But never stay still in one place out of fear of who you are, who and what you *really* are. The freedom is amazing! Have a great night guys!"

Spontaneous applause erupted.

I felt more alive than ever at that moment, in that room with a bunch of regular guys that I knew all felt the same way.

I still couldn't believe that when listening to everything, that it not only made complete sense, but was eye-opening for a guy like me to accept it *all*. I thought of the same but very different guy a couple weeks back.

I surely lost my virginity, my virginity of true male and personal self-awareness.

Episode 59 ~

I took the day off from work and decided to take a breather. I had not tried any techniques since my lab work even though I was extremely horny, constantly. I mused wondering if this was a curse, a nice curse to have. I also hadn't looked into the folder Josh had given me. I wanted more time to gather myself, process everything. Plus, I wanted to also gather my thoughts and feelings before meeting Melissa later.

As each day had passed, I found that with my newfound freedom of heart and thought, came even *more* wondering about myself. I found it amazing how once some doors are freely, and sometimes forced to be opened, other doors appear, ones I didn't consciously know existed, or things I had thought about in the past and forgot, all a continuing journey of self-discovery.

Regardless, I knew I was a very different guy from weeks ago and knew that I had embraced everything very quickly and I may say very happily, but still, like the old habit I had of having a cigarette after hot sex, I need to unwind, to decompress. Like lying motionless in a forest and just listen.

It was a really strange feeling how I saw myself now, even when looking in the mirror. Who is this guy! Are you for real? And inside there was growing a willingness to share myself like I never felt before. And share with everyone and anybody. It didn't matter who, as I saw all equally. As they had always said, it was so much more than just sex, this life driving force. I was just sorry it didn't happen earlier in my life.

Being not scared or worried anymore, I looked forward to having candid discussions with my friends and family. Would they even know me? But knowing so well how I was before, I also knew this would be a big hurdle and I understood why Fred wasn't completely forthcoming initially. Not because he had a problem with it, he just knew *I would*, or *may have* a problem, with such openness and candor. What guy wants to discuss sexuality with another guy — generally speaking. Or what guy wants to sit with another guy at a bar, having a beer, and discuss deep secrets, fetishes, fantasies, or just deep female sensitive feelings?

I really appreciated now the work and experiences Zach and team were providing. Could his dream of a new sexual revolution and new society revolution actually be completely achieved — where all are accepted regardless of anything, where all can express themselves willingly and completely, and be accepted and even loved for their free expression, for their differences, where no 'walls' exist anymore, and prejudices and judgements are a thing of the past. Can you picture that?

Where people can wear or not wear what they wish, where people can have any sex partner they wish, where people can express openly and be their true gender, where people can express themselves without fear of reprimand or alienization, where love and respect now rule and we globally evolve to the next level of higher existence, of higher vibrations, and then go further and work together to conquer inequalities, conquer diseases, maybe even conquer death. Maybe, possibly maybe, death is only a consequence of our continual, and many would say, primal behavior as a race. And maybe death is actually needed until we evolve past our greed, selfishness, and prejudices so none of these things can perpetuate forever.

I always wondered if there are intelligent beings, far more advanced races, watching us. Regardless of how advanced we think we are, do they see us as completely primitive due to our selfishness, our greed, our intolerance, our taboos, our false egos, our inability to accept each other as true brothers and sisters. Like us watching animals in a zoo. And if we ever achieve the levels of higher vibrations and higher life and living together, and truly conquer diseases and aging, would death then simply disappear. Do we cause death to remain? Or a natural or spiritual need to ensure evil cannot rule forever?

Shudders! Spasms! and Shock Waves! The Strokeless Orgasm

All my wonderings and studying of self-awareness I have done previously on my own, all the time before all of this, was actually being pulled into my new existence, all making even more sense. I had thoughts like these before, albeit fragmented and disjointed. In the end though, I always wondered, with all that has been written and taught over the ages, over the millennia, if we humans will ever change, actually wake the fuck up and change. All of us.

I opened my eyes from my contemplations and stared at the ceiling from my bed. I felt an intense freedom and a growing sadness – a sadness for ourselves. With that, I knew without doubt my inner commitment to the 'Society of Oneness and Ultimate Love.' I guess hippiedom wasn't dead after all. I actually laughed at that idea, not disrespectfully, but with respect that we had tried the experiment and it had become engulfed and stifled by the world, war, greed, and by deadly drugs. Maybe we're getting another chance. *Hippiedom – Part II, the rise of the Advanced Human Race.*

Propping myself up, I smiled how all this occurred with me starting from 'hadn't noticed!' and from the curiosity, more the need, to find myself sexually as a guy and as a person. Strange how a journey can take you in unexpected ways.

My sole thought was again 'onward!'

I was prepared to meet the girl I used to call 'my girl.'

Now, to me, it's 'our girl.'

Episode 60 ~

I forgot how much I missed Melissa's beautiful glimmering golden hair as I came up behind her at the bar. I placed my hands on her shoulders and planted a kiss on her cheek from behind. As usual and with complete composure, she showed no signs of being startled, as if she somehow sensed it was me.

She turned facing upward and kissed me on the mouth. I also missed her warm tender firm kisses. I started to think this may not be a good idea and to just forget it all, go back to our nice, uncomplicated relationship, and move on. And deep inside, I knew I wouldn't nor couldn't. But I knew I still wanted her and was determined to win her back, if 'winning' was the means or even the right word – and without compromising my new disposition. I was still getting used to this new Darian that she couldn't see yet, at least not fully.

"May I join you?" I asked courteously, taking the barstool next to her anyway.

"Sure," she replied with a broad, welcoming smile. "You look good."

"And so do you. In fact, you look absolutely lovely," I added, meaning it.

"Always the sweet talker. Keep going," she tilted her head and made a kiss with her lips. I leaned back on the stool playfully and intentionally eyed her up and down, with a serious analytical look on my face. She gave me her quick piercing squinted eyes and then pulled her shoulders back and her head, giving me the model pose I wanted. She had always been a fantastic sexy professional model before her fashion business.

"I guess," I finally said.

"Fuck you," she replied with her half-serious, half-playful tone.

"You wish."

"Only *if* I wish."

"Do you wish?"

"We shall see."

She now gave me her sweet 'I'm in control' smile and I liked it. There always was a fun aspect to our relationship where I had to win her, even hunt for her, and then the rewards were always exceedingly and deliciously hot.

I ordered a drink as we fell silent for a moment. I felt we each were trying to find the next thing to say. So, I broke the ice.

"Well, I'll have you know, I am now a sex-crazed fiend, a monstrous ecstasy-villain, a craving fuck-starved lunatic, a pussy-thrilling demon, seeking to conquer and take all that I want! Beware!"

She looked at me with her eyebrows raised. "You are, are you?"

"Damn right, m'lady, and you'll need all your strength."

"This I gotta see!" she broke into a short coy laugh and I could tell she was actually enjoying it — at least that the 'sex' discussion had started. I knew it was the crux of the whole issue between us, not because of any loss of feelings or emotions between us.

"So, honestly, since you brought it up," she continued with a more serious and inquisitive tone, "who have you been fucking?"

"Honey, that's not fair," I replied calmly, wondering why I didn't take the bait and pounce back hurt. "To be truly honest, I have fucked no one." Then it occurred to me. I had initially anticipated the lab training as a mutual type of sexual encounter with a participating person (or many others) and with *me* participating (ya know, coitus, cunnilingus, fellatio ...to use the cutesy technical terms) and it was none of that. No one else had any sexual experience at all. They were all focused on me, the trainee. In my happy afterglow daze, I hadn't connected the dots that Melissa could only think that was what had occurred. Who would ever think otherwise what really happened.

"Really? All this what, training you say, is for better sex, and you didn't have sex?" I knew there was more than a tinge of confusion she wanted cleared up, and now.

"I never said I didn't have sex. I said I didn't fuck anyone."

"Not even a guy?"

I gave her a mischievous leer. "Not yet."

"Ha! I knew it. This has all been because you are bi-curious. You wanted to experiment."

I had no idea where she had gotten that from nor where she was going with it. And I never ever mentioned nor intimated I was or was not. Then it hit me. This was a defense mechanism. A challenge to see why or how could I let her go so easily. I knew her well enough that her ego couldn't accept another female – or *wouldn't* at this time. We had talked about a threesome before. But to blame it on a desire for a guy kept the ego unchallenged. At least that's where my mind quickly went. So, I played.

"If I was bi-curious, I would tell you, when I am ready to tell you…"

She cut me off.

"So, you are then."

"I didn't say that and stop putting words in my mouth. And why? Do you want me to?" This wasn't going where I wanted it to go or thought it would go, but it really didn't phase me as it would have before.

"You'd rather have a dick in your mouth?"

155mm howitzer fired! Sir! And they are reloading! Sir!

I leaned forward and kissed her hard on the lips, she let me and I stayed up close, face to face. "I am interested in you. Please stop the inquisition."

She gave me a smirk back and a small smile grew on her face. She had completely intended this line of questioning. Damn. I shook my head and smiled back.

"Bitch."

"That's me."

Episode 61 ~

"So, do you want to know or not?" I posed, looking to get back on track and see if we were going to get back together or not. I was surprised by my sheer focus.

"Yeah, I suppose," she replied tentatively but I knew she meant it. And I heard the underlying curiosity. Also I was glad that the bi-curious questioning was over. I wasn't exactly prepared for that. And I knew many people always wondered it about themselves. Hence, 'curious.' I pushed the thought of Teri and Josh out of my mind and remained focused.

"OK, please have an open mind. First, and please believe me, really believe me, this whole experience, everything, has so much more to do with than physical. Intimate growth and understanding your own self, yes, is an integral part of the 'training' but it's really about self-awareness, digging deep and overcoming the walls that hide true feelings and desires. The sexual portion is…" I paused for the right words, "…is the *catalyst* that breaks down one of our largest walls, makes us have the courage to see our vulnerable self we hide, making it easier to break down other walls and *see* other walls. It's a holistic human experience of eliminating conditioning and inhibitions – about everything!"

As I spoke, I was hearing my own words like an echo that my mind was listening to after the fact, analyzing each word, trying to assimilate that it was actually me talking. I felt like a trainer all of a sudden. And it felt good.

I went on about everything except the explicit lab work. I didn't think that was any of her business, which I found interesting. Just like Josh's '*Adventure List*' assignment, there are some things if you wish to remain silent about, you have every right to be silent about. This wasn't about baring your whole soul to everyone – it was about baring your whole soul to yourself.

I could tell her interest was peaking.

"Where then is the sex part?"

I knew I couldn't avoid it.

"It's a deeply personal encounter where they teach you your own erotic power, and you have to completely let every guard down. Because it's so personal to each individual, I really am not getting into the details, nor am I allowed to, but I will tell you this much, I touched no one, no one else had sex, it was more like a… massage. If you want to know more, you will need to take the course yourself. Part of the rules."

I couldn't believe my adamant conviction. Truly none of your business and that's all you'll get. Period. And my use of the actual rules that each must make their own journey without interference by anyone was absolutely true. They must go in blind for the 'fear' factor to engage. 'OK, Darian, pretty good,' my sexy little angel said in my right ear. "Fucking, dude, it was still sex!" the devil said in my left. "I had fun," my dick chimed in with a nonchalant tone of complete satisfaction. Smiling inside, I think *Sir Dick* won again. What do we have for him, Johnny! And now, back to our program…

"So, what, do you feel… enlightened by all of this?" I felt the question was both sarcastic and genuine at the same time. What I loved about her.

"Absolutely. I feel free to express myself, to find my hidden wants and hidden cravings and look *directly* at them and accept them in myself and accept others as themselves – unconditionally."

I could see her reaction by her again raised eyebrows. I then realized I had never spoken like this before to her – so confidently, sure of myself, committed to a cause, a way of being.

"OK, where have you hidden Darian? And who the hell are you?" She playfully posed. After a momentary pause, she continued. "I kind of like this new you," she finally said with a quirky smile.

"You do?" I replied, taken aback.

"Yeah, damn confident bastard, even though I'm still struggling with it all. And you still haven't said anything about the sexual part."

"Why does that bother you?" I asked. I found myself surprised I asked it at all. I never would have tried to delve that deep into my or her emotions, always having remained more superficial. Never a need, or want to, before. And now, I wasn't sure why I had been superficial at all when it appeared normal to discuss anything now. Amazingly, our walls actually keep us ignorant of what really is.

"Because it does bother me. I am not one to share. But I see, I feel, you still care and love me. And I won't press anymore, at least not now. Is that okay?"

Again, I was taken aback if not shocked. I absolutely do not remember ever when she would back down and at the same time almost apologize. Was my demeanor that affecting?

"I honestly appreciate that. We can get into more details if you ever wish but it really is personal to each... student. It would be personal to you if you ever pursue it and I need not know. Again, it's like a sex therapist per se but ridiculously so much more. Take it as that with no intended hurt. I'll simply say, it really changes, or better yet, adds to your experiences, to your whole life." I knew that was a complete understatement but was willing to defer.

"You mean me?"

"Yeah, of course you. This isn't just for guys." Her eyebrows again. And I then saw a gleam in her eyes.

"I see."

"You honestly can. It just takes some courage."

Well, maybe a lot of courage but we'll start there. Most importantly, I felt some 'walls' were starting to be breached in her.

"So, maybe you can show me these superpowers you possess," she posed with a sensual smile, bringing her face close to mine.

"My pleasure my dear," I replied, knowing that it wasn't just jump in bed and boom! There was technique to learn, to have fun with. And I suddenly wasn't sure being back in bed with her was the right move right now. My thoughts suddenly went back again to Teri and Josh, and their proposal, their offer. I had to think.

"Dinner?" I offered.

"Naw, I gotta get back to some work I need to complete tonight and will grab a bite on my way." I knew she was being honest and not bailing.

"Sure thing. I'll get this," I said as she was rising from the stool.

"Thanks love," she said, pulling my shirt, forcing me to stand too. She planted her wettest warmest sexiest longest open mouth kiss on my mouth which felt like an eternity. Then she slowly caressed my crotch. As she pulled away, she made her good-bye.

"Don't forget that."

She released me, turned, and whisked away.

I watched her slender toned body sway out the door.

I turned back to the bar, saw the bartender smile at me, and suddenly and freely started to fantasize.

Fantasize about what, you may ask?

I'll never tell!

Episode 62 ~

The next day I felt relieved and apprehensive at the same time. After seeing Melissa and being very glad it went fairly well, ...well, better than I expected..., I found myself wondering my next steps. At least my next steps with another human, or maybe two.

Ever since the initial proposal from Teri, and then her second proposal, the thought kept crossing my mind. Of course, I very much wanted to experience her and her me, but the proposal included Josh. And knowing they were both bisexual and somewhat of an occasional couple, I toyed with the idea over and over again. What would that be like? Was I officially bi-curious? If you even just *think about it*, is that bi-curious? Or, being now completely openminded, literally opens the doors to all possibilities, without any fear?

Or could I just say okay and set my limit to be strictly heterosexual sex, being me and Josh with her and her with us? I'm sure I could state that and it would be accepted – or would it be accepted? We learned to accept each other but there was no rule to accept any proposal, just accept the person.

And if accepted, what would it be like – I mean with a bisexual guy. I never spoke of this, but I lost my virginity in a threesome after playing strip poker with my friend and his wannabe girlfriend. I was the unexpected but excited outsider. We ended up naked together and pretty much took turns, and then she masturbated us both, sitting between us. The dual-stroking image still makes me laugh. But he and I never touched each other nor intimated we wanted to. We always joked about it and accused each other of bisexuality but always was purely fun guy shit. Or was it?

Now, I was beginning to question that. I knew now well enough to see what is always underlying. Was it just 'fun guy shit' or actually our inner desires forcing themselves out through the many 'walls.' I honestly didn't know. Sorry for being explicit, but I knew I liked my cock, but that was *my* cock. I learned at least that much from Josh pointedly pointing it out last time. And he was right. And I don't believe just me, but I believed now that most if not all guys like their dicks. We have them, why not? Well, if they don't perform, we can still yell at them, right? We have a relationship. We do (lol).

But what would I do if in that same situation *with* Josh and Teri – even if claiming pure guy hands off – and they accepted that? And what really was their intentions, their intended actions? Everything conceivable? The sheer adventure of it was impelling. And as we know, I was now *Darian The Demented Adventurer*, always interested in a new adventure, a new journey. But I wasn't sure if I was really bi-curious. Then it hit me. I was *adventure-curious*. I didn't want any fear or inhibition to stop me from trying anything, at least once. Then I would know. And with Teri and Josh, I knew they would completely understand and be ever so helpful. I laughed. I am *sure* they would be ever so helpful!

My thought also was they would be a better first step being with my first *other* person or persons at this point, as they would know where I was at now and allow me to run freely through the experience. That I knew. And they would know my tentativeness. So, there was absolutely no barrier or extra effort to not to proceed. But did I want to? Experience something totally unique to me right in front of me. See my dilemma?

But at the same time, I wanted to really be with Melissa one-on-one right away too, which would be pretty soon after our last time that triggered everything. I was wildly curious about how it would be *now*. And found myself almost fighting with myself with who's on first. I literally broke into a snicker with the thought of *Abbott and Costello*'s skit which I love.

In the end, I found myself wanting to try both but knew I had to decide sooner or later who would be first. I was just wildly curious about everything now. I decided not to overthink it. Let it flow its own way into the reality that I really wanted. A benefit of the training!

In the meantime, I sat back on a lazy Saturday and opened the folder. The first page's heading was 'Guy's Post Training and Exercises.'

"Mmmm," came out of my mouth. Always interesting titles and wordings I thought amusingly. I started reading and perusing through. I stopped on the page titled 'Control.' I read on.

'You have been trained and conditioned by both culture and nature for instant gratification, immediate satisfaction. You have learned that there is so much more than that. You are at the starting point with what you have experienced here. Now, you will train yourself to control it, let it breath, let it fall and rise back, greater each time. Don't give in to the immense want to climax, as that is from the need for species to procreate. Procreation was the rule. Do it. Do it fast. You are now much more than that!'

'Learn the way to both subside the drive in order to control it, as well as learn the cumless cum...'

I paused. Ah, so finally.

'...which is a simple technique. When alone, as you build your sensations higher and higher from what you learned, and also as you more learn *yourself* on your own, when feeling yourself losing control, which will happen, simply take your middle finger and find the spot below the hump beneath you, right above your anus. Press upward and based on the amount of pressure, you'll gain control back to continue and can then release the finger pressure. Work at it. Time it. The more control, the greater the build, the greater the climax!'

The textbook wording of such a thing was calmly amazing, sounding like: 'the square root of the diameter of an isosceles triangle divided by the mean distance between...' OK, I digress. Back to the more interesting part of our story...

'That's for control to gently subside the climax before it happens. Now if you wish to experience a cum without cum, same technique but have to *time it* exactly when you are going to explode and can't stop it, then immediately press same spot upward. You will experience an even greater climax and voila' no semen! And you will be recharged faster than normal for round two, as your hard-on will pretty much be maintained unless you wish to stop.'

I was definitely going to master this technique! Thank you *Dr. Cumless*. And could see why it had to be outside the lab as no one would really know exactly the point when a guy was actually going to climax, and then the moment to engage *the brakes*! More great guy stuff and I felt no embarrassment at all. It was cool to me. I was amazed how much I had been missing out on.

And amazed how everything of such content sounded so much again like a textbook, a textbook of ecstasy! I fumbled through more pages, each page or set of pages was a different topic, and some were reiterations of classroom discussions, as reminders. Very thorough I thought. Shame a lot of guys would never take this plunge, I also felt. But press on!

I came (not really) to a section I knew (was hoping?) had to be in here. Page title was '*The Orientation Theory and Methodology*.' 'Theory?' 'Methodology?' I read on.

'As we all know, in life we characterize ourselves in so many ways by categories. It's a natural human response for identity. And a lot of times, *rigid* categories. For example, 'I hate apple pie.' Until maybe I taste a certain apple pie that I end up liking. 'I love roller coasters.' Until maybe experiencing the one that made me throw up. As humans, with our analytical structured minds, we find *order* in categories, they make sense to us, and we can plop ourselves into the ones we like and exclude the ones we don't. And a lot of the times, there's no gray area – yes or no – period.'

'The theory can then apply to sexual orientation. And these ideas are purely our, the school's, outlook on the subject, and you may agree or disagree, which is completely fine. But for argument's sake, let's take a look! For a simple example, let's start with the 3 commonly discussed orientations, even though there are more with no doubt. 'I am totally straight.' 'I am totally gay.' 'I am totally bi-sexual.' How we view ourselves is extremely important to our self-image, our feeling good about ourselves. So, it's not unnatural to keep a solid image we adhere to, which again, is totally fine (us being 'totally' something). No argument. However, when you look at it from a different vantage point, an interesting thing can be theoretically derived.'

I felt like I was now readying a psychology textbook but it was capturing me in its non-jargon way.

'First, there are times when someone gay will intentionally 'crossover' for a quick alternate experience and enjoy it. There's absolutely nothing wrong with it. And it's healthy in our opinions. And then forget about it. But it does happen. So, why? Well, in our studies, research, and experiences, it's because all sensual experiences are beautiful, regardless of preference or shall we say 'main preference.' It also applies to a straight person being bi-curious. There's a safety in the word 'curious.' I'm only *curious*, I'm not bisexual. Well, simply put, being curious means the person is actually thinking to try it, or at least what it would be actually like. And being so, then they are by default attracted to it. 'Curious' allows for the keeping of the distance until maybe someday, they take the plunge. And a lot of times, will run away scared, vowing never to do it again, only to return and do it again. You have learned through your training that that is simply their 'wall' about the experience starting to fall.'

'Then, a proclaimed bisexual will experience both worlds and maybe sway more one way than the other, or depending on mood, will indulge for a while with straight and then another while with gay, feeling the total consumption of whichever orientation is occurring at the moment – meaning when engaging same-sex, they may see themselves completely gay – and vice versa. Totally fine and to us, very much engaging the many possibilities of fun, pleasure, and intimacy.'

'In order to make sense of it all, and without any hard category boundaries (though completely respecting anyone's hard boundaries), in order to promote all possibilities and all viewpoints, we see the whole level of possible experiences as one *human spectrum* that we think helps facilitate any and all possibilities, and promotes as much enjoyment as possible without strict boundaries. Of course, anyone can dispute this and are welcome to dispute it. It's just our thoughts to review, digest, and take as you wish to take it. Acceptance across the board of all ideas.'

'So, picture a straight line. For simplicity sake, at left end, it says Straight 100%. At the right end, it says Gay 100%. Of course, there's Transgender, Non-Binary, etc but we are intentionally being simplistic for the sake of example. If someone gay occasionally, very occasionally crosses over, in our mind, they may be to the right at maybe 98% instead of 100%. If someone straight is experiencing bi-curiosity, they would be to the left maybe 96% instead of 100%. If you see where this is going, the point is, we feel that *just maybe*, there are *no* 'absolutes' with the human race. Food for thought.'

'And if anyone sees themselves absolutely 100% all the time, it is their *perfect right* and needs to be respected. And finally, bisexuals may be *anywhere* in between at any given moment. And the beauty of it is that the 'meter' *can move* and never has to be fixed. Complete freedom of expression at *any moment in your life* with no hard fast categorizations. This is our theory and method. We find pure beauty in this way of seeing ourselves. Hope you find something for yourself, too!'

Wow. Never thought of it that way. I sat back and let it sink in.

I wanted to just let it... sink in.

Episode 63 ~

A week passed and I did my normal day job at home. I found it nicely (and boringly) distracting from all the excitement and all the deluge of information and ideas. Incredibly I thought, how mundane routine activities have a soothing effect. And then of course excruciatingly boring again.

I had no contact with Melissa. I think we both settled back for a bit to let our meeting and feelings go through its process of mutual understanding. At least that's what I hoped.

Even though I did not participate in more labs, I found myself beyond curious as to where my new sexuality would take me. I still refrained from another's contact in order to continue my exploration with myself. Yes, I mean masturbation! My masturbation! Gotta do something.

I read more and applied techniques and then found I was modifying them to my way of feeling. Teri, Josh, and all were right. We are shown the way and then take the rest of the journey *our own way*. And still had that roller-coaster insane feeling that I'm actually doing all this. Every fucking repressive taboo was literally thrown out the window forever. Nothing bothered me. No guilt. No hiding. No fear. Everything was game and we all were of the same mindset. Nobody judged at all. Truly amazing. Truly free to do. Truly free to be. *Paradise*, inside *and* outside, *everywhere*. Way more than just sex! Sex was just a 'trigger.' It was deeply personal. I felt like dancing all the time.

And I experienced those shudders again, the spasms, and the amazing 'shock waves!' I was able to command and guide my pleasure as my mood fit. I had no embarrassment at all. In fact, it was uninhibitedly exhilarating! I was my own sex tour guide! And as a guy!

I had wanted to find out and did finally experience 'shock waves' by actually stroking and teasing, versus the strokeless way – which I was also really beginning to master, too. I felt the humor of mastering the masturbation! But it wasn't at all like before. It was an ever-creative experience and experiment of myself, even spiritually, and I found myself wanting more – more ideas, maybe realize fantasies and maybe, even, fetishes. Fucking doors were opening up as never before.

And I finally started feeling the want to now move to the next step of a partner or more than one. I wasn't sure but I knew in the end, it really didn't matter. I knew now it will happen as it happens, and how I feel at that given time. Literally, no expectations and therefore no concern at all. So many possibilities now. Freedom to be, however, whenever. Literally freedom to be free. Maybe it really is a new sexual and even personal revolution.

I was also fascinated, *completely fascinated*, by my uninhibitedness. Even my exhibitionism. Dare I say voyeur? There! I said it! (...and meant it! ...sticking out my wicked tongue!) Like doing it in public with the exciting fear of being caught causing insane pleasure. The freedom was so addictive. The adventure was so addictive. The addiction was so addictive. And I felt no less a man than before. And as I continually learned more and more with my experimentation, I was a greater man *and* person. I felt actually more masculine, as if I found the lost *'Fountain of Ultimate Man-Power!'* (That would be a cool button.) And I knew my newfound feminine side combined beautifully and made everything even more exciting. I felt I could finally breathe freely. I had entirely no fear or embarrassment of anything. What could be more free!

I continued the final classes and in the end, found such close and trusting friends. I vowed to work on my current friends to be as honest as I could be, and be as open as I could be, even if I get push back or even ridicule. I know I can stand my ground and truly be me. I actually found myself wanting to bring them onboard, to help realize a more expansive way of being, and knowing full well, there would be the natural, if not intense, resistance. Somehow, it always comes down to courage, personal courage.

I also finished the Josh *'Adventure List'* assignment and was able, albeit still sometimes difficult, to *surrender* myself to my true self and be honest with myself.

I came up with my initial five 'adventures.' Some things I wrote on my private paper did not surprise me as my desires, but when greater expanded, did have an eye-opening effect. And some things I wrote, and it did take real courage to admit them, shocked me that they were really me. And I knew why they said keep it always to yourself until you finally experience them. And I knew, eventually, I was going to experience them – all of them.

As the graduation time and ceremony approached, it all came together. Being a guy or being a girl was so much more than most of us know or experience. It's being *human* that matters – being who we really are and breaking down the 'walls' – all the 'walls!' And then seeing each other in a new accepting light that natural camaraderie *just happens* - naturally.

I was ready for graduation and what lies ahead.

The excitement of the continuing adventure was overwhelming.

Life felt like *Life*!

Episode 64 ~

The last weekend of summer had arrived. The air was still beautifully warm. When I drove onto the property, my car was parked by a valet. The graduation ceremony was held outside on the expansive mansion grounds. Tents were everywhere and a special area for the post-reception where there were long tables of food being prepared and multiple bars. I thought again that Zach knew what he was doing and always did it with taste, style, and class.

We were to wear a white top. It didn't matter if a shirt, blouse, tank top, bikini, whatever — as long as it was white. I chose surprising to myself, a white tight tank top. I figured, that's what I felt and what the hell!

There was an enormous stage with three huge large screen monitors. It felt like one of those meetings you see with big tech companies. Flowers of all different kinds and colors were exquisitely positioned everywhere, accentuating the grounds' palm trees. The feel and mood was beyond festive and one could only see smiles and hear laughter. And above the stage was a colorful rainbow banner that emblazed against the open blue sky the simple word: "*SOUL!*" that spoke everything everyone was feeling.

I looked up and felt the spectacular heat of the sun on my face, but the air was semi-dry and it felt wonderful. As we entered under a flowered trestle, the graduates were each given a lei of flowers to wear and a small name tag on them. Additionally, we were each given a small envelope that said, 'do not open until home.' I obeyed but was crazy curious.

I hadn't realized until then that there were many guests participating. And to my surprise, though after seeing them, I really wasn't that surprised, was Fred and Katie. They were beaming smiles at me as I strolled up to them.

"Well, well, well, if it isn't Freddie Mercury!" Fred exclaimed holding out his hand. I looked at him quizzically and then realized I was dressed as Freddie was at the Live Aid concert. And I had on light blue jeans, too. I took it as a huge compliment.

"Hey!" I replied as he pulled me to him for a hug. Katie then made it a threesome hug. "Hey, Katie!"

"Well, Darian, you look adorably sexy!" she also exclaimed. Somehow I wasn't offended by the term 'adorably.' I actually liked it.

"Didn't expect you or any other non-graduates here," I said as we all broke free.

"Are you kidding! This is always a wonderful time and every alumnus is invited and see that," he pointed to the large screen. "And the alumni from around the world."

"Wow. This is serious! And all about sex!" I replied with a hint of humor, thinking back to Fred's party which seemed eons ago.

"Well, you know now that it's way more than just that, my man," Fred added.

I noticed Katie eyeing me coyly and wondered.

"Shame Melissa isn't here. How's she doing?" Katie asked still with that coy look.

I always wondered what it would be like making love to her. I shut that away, for now.

"She's doing fine, really fine. We met up recently and had a great talk. You know, working things out."

"Good. I'm sure you will convince her," she added with her finger gently running down my cheek. This was a side of Katie I had not ever seen before.

"Shall we!" Fred proposed as he held out his arm to move to the general area.

"Let's!" Katie answered.

I walked with them as I digested this unexpected turn of events. I was feeling like a schoolboy and it was like Fred and Katie were my proud parents. It even wasn't a bad feeling. I embraced it. Openness was everywhere.

I suddenly felt two hands come across my crotch from behind. Instinctively looking down, they were girl hands and I knew. I turned intentionally abruptly and was literally face to face with Teri's shining face and eyes. Her boyish bob haircut simply made her stunning in the sun, with the glitter on her cheeks enchantingly sparkling in her eyes. I was beyond captivated.

"I'll catch up with you later," I called to Fred and Katie as they continued on. Fred raised his hand in acknowledgment.

"Lovely to see you!" Teri said with such attractive enthusiasm.

"Lovely to see you, too!" I replied similarly.

As always, she never stopped surprising me and planted a wet open mouth kiss on my lips and mouth, pulled away quickly, and simply bounced away. "See you around!"

Stunned, it took me a second to reply. "Yes, definitely, see you around!"

She waved and I stared at her beautiful bare thighs below the shortest miniskirt I have ever seen her wear as she disappeared in the crowd that was gathering and getting bigger. I took a deep breath and looked to find where to go. It was all a dream.

"This way!" declared Zach as he put his arm around me for a second.

"Hi Zach. This is amazing," I greeted back as I followed him. He was dressed in an exquisite all white suit. There was something about it that I could only explain as 'Angelic Aura.'

"Isn't it! I love a party!"

"Well, it's amazing," came out again as I didn't know how else to put it.

"You are over there. Anywhere there is fine. See you afterwards." He glided away towards the stage. I followed his directions and was among my classmates and other graduates. It felt like a reunion, even when meeting some folks I hadn't met yet. Girls in bikini tops, tied blouses, lingerie teddys, and guys in polo shirts, tanks like me, waist-tied shirts, and one even with only a white bowtie. And somehow it all felt normal and real, each expressing themselves freely and all accepting freely. Everyone had a smile. I still was amazed at it all and was exceedingly glad to be part of it all and one of everyone.

There appeared to be at least 200 graduates and even more guests. The grounds were huge and accommodating. No one felt squeezed in. And I also again noticed the large tall fence where I assumed a pool area was and wondered if that was part of the ceremony. But this time there was no noise of activity there and probably for a rare time, it was closed. But what I did notice was the large sign above the fence gate where I only saw 'Your...' before. I felt an uncontrollable big smile grow on my mouth. It read very appropriately: *'Your Garden!'*

I heard an echoing tap of a microphone and all eyes turned to the stage. There stood Zach with Sam and Maxie on each side, the same way I had first met them. Then the three screens lit up and there were many squares of what looked like other outside and indoor gatherings, with one square all of us, and the center square Zach from a video camera setup in the middle of the aisle. I assumed these were the remote gatherings.

We all sat and a respectful silence fell. Sam and Maxie took seats to either side of Zach and a bit behind him. He stood alone, watching over the audience. Then he smiled.

"You fucking *DID IT!*" he screamed into the mike which echoed wildly everywhere.

A thunderous applause exploded from behind us from the guests and from the large speakers from the monitors. And we all started applauding and cheering, too. It was mesmerizingly intoxicating. People were whistling, cheering, calling out names and it went on for about two minutes until Zach calmly raised his hand and the focus returned to him.

He waited until full silence again, standing there again as an angel in the sunshine, his white suit glimmering.

"Honestly," he began in a quiet voice, "I am always insanely proud of all of you for willingly taking this personal journey into your own heart and souls. You could have always left and wonderfully, no one did!"

Again applause and cheering, then respectful silence.

"I'll be brief," he continued and someone yelled out "Right!" He smiled. "Well, I guess you do know me!" he laughed a boyish laugh. Then he paused a moment, seemingly collecting his thoughts. He had a way of commanding the stage and in everything he did.

"I sincerely wish to welcome all of you new graduates to your well-earned lifetime membership in the '*Society of Oneness and Ultimate Love.*'" A reverent soft applause ensued which caught me by surprise after the boisterousness. I realized this was a serious thing for Zach and all knew that. He continued somberly.

"I grew up in the inner city, more the slums. I had abusive parents," he started with a solemn tone of sadness. I was again mesmerized by his openness. "I was a troubled child and rebellious teen. Hateful. Angry. Resentful. Pissed the fuck off all the time. I blamed everybody and everything. Had run ins with the law but managed to not ever get into real trouble. I saw no end to my miserable, lonely, despised life. Completely hopeless as a young man. Nowhere and no one to turn to. Desperation didn't even matter anymore. Until one day, walking down a filthy city block in the neighborhood where I lived, I see it clearly even now, with my head down, staring at the oily grime and trash on the street, I heard a voice. I heard someone calling to me."

He paused and took a sip of water. The silence in the warm sun was stunningly amazing. No sound at all, not even a shifting in a chair.

"I looked around me and there was the most beautiful car I had ever seen, even on TV. Not knowing until later, it was a Rolls Royce, a gleaming white Rolls Royce."

"It was surreal and scary. All my street-smart fears and flags were going off. I thought 'predator' and instinctively inched away down the block, keeping my eyes on the car while trying to pick up speed in my stride. There was no way this was going to be good. Then I heard the door open and out appeared the most beautiful girl I had ever seen. She appeared my age. I stopped. I couldn't take my eyes off her. She wore the most exquisite white dress I had ever seen, wrapped tightly at her waist and flowing down all around her. If she had wings, I knew she was an angel. Why was she here, on this street, talking with me. She looked so very young but with a face of awareness, of maturity. I waited cautiously, ready to pounce or run. I was frozen."

"She walked slowly towards me, fearlessly, never taking her eyes off me. I wondered how she got there, why she was there, didn't she know how dangerous it was? And I knew I must have looked scary to her, dirty, or at least pitiful. But there was courage in those eyes. There was compassion in those eyes. There was strength in those eyes. There was kindness in those eyes. There was *power* in those eyes. At about five feet away, she spoke."

"My name is Samantha."

Episode 65 ~

A low hush sound flowed through the graduates as Sam stood up on the stage and went to his side. My heart rose up my chest as things fell into place. I felt the love between them and how they looked at each other. Then the applause slowly erupted and a standing ovation. Sam smiled at Zach as a sister would to a brother. Finally, the applause subsided and all sat.

"Well, you all know her as my Sam. Without going into the morbid details," he impishly said as she playfully slapped his arm, "this angel saved my life. There was no other reason than absolute selfless unconditional love for another person, a complete stranger. Why she picked me out, only she knows but it must have had to do with this gorgeously handsome boyish face!" Another hard slap and then a kiss on his cheek. Laughter rose and then subsided again.

"And she changed my life, in so many ways. And patiently taught me how another whole world can and does exist. Not a world of riches or selfishness, but a world of real people, loving people, loving souls. This is the world you have willingly entered."

I was flabbergasted at these revelations and at the same time honored to be among them and to have been accepted into all of this, by them. We must have all felt the same as we turned and looked at each other sitting there, some with tears. Then we looked back.

"So, as she has generously and lovingly passed on to me a new life, so we pass on to you. This is our bond. And our sincere wish is that you too pass on to those you feel are ready."

I thought of Fred and felt even now a stronger brother friendship. Zach continued.

"This makes me think of the *Plato's Cave* analogy where all the world is in a dark cave with no outside light, everyone chained together arm and arm, legs and legs, necks and necks, all facing the back wall. Behind everyone are candles that cast the shadows of everyone against the back wall. No one can turn any way except look at the shadows of each other on that back wall, only seeing images of each other, all chained to one another without ever really *seeing* each other. Only images."

"Then the enlightened person that was previously freed by another and lives in the sunlight outside the cave, feels compelled to travel back into the dark cave and finds a way to release another and works to convince them to leave the cave. It's a difficult thing to do as the cave is all the person has ever known all their life and is fearful to leave into the unknown. This is the great resistance. But the enlightened person does convince them but knows to only show them the light of the moon so as not to blind them with the instant sunlight after being in the dark cave."

"As the person adjusts to the moonlight, and adjusts and starts to see another whole world, they desire more and are then shown the sunlight and all the beauty and freedom around them outside the cave. And there are no more images but only the true reality of life and love."

"This same person, this newly enlightened person, then feels for the others still in the cave and does the same as was done for them."

"This newly enlightened person is all of you!"

Wow. That's exactly what I had thoughts about before – finding a way to help others realize. And now, this analogy of *Plato's Cave* was the exact answer to a desire that had grown in me over the past weeks and I knew I can realize it into reality!

As we the graduates all sat there in almost a daze, all the guests stood and gave a huge round of applause to us. The level of emotion was indescribable. I turned and saw Fred and Katie smiling at me. Above the din, Zach continued.

"So, welcome to the world and society of enlightenment, of truly loving human beings! As you already know, you are among awesome, real friends.

This is no cult, no brainwashing. Each of you have experienced 'shock waves' in many ways! Yes, first the intimate one, but more importantly, the human one. We are planting the seeds of a new evolution of people. We can no longer support the current way of this world."

The applause continued and from the speakers of the monitors.

"Remember this: no society, no religion wants you to be wise, to be intelligent, to challenge the norm with true individualistic thinking. We are the budding change, an internal change, of a *new* society – *YOU!*"

He paused to let it sink in and waited until it fell silent again.

"A month ago, most if not all of you would have laughed at such a thing – or never believed it possible. I never believed anything was possible until I was shown from a true tender heart who cared about *me*. Honestly cared. That is why this all exists. Because I and everyone cares about *you*."

"We are not power hungry. We wish to rule nothing. We wish only to continue to be the spark, the fire, the lightning that ignites and allows the spread of love, real human love. As this beautiful girl did for me. And I'll always be eternally grateful."

"You have learned how to break out of your imprisoned comfort zone. You have learned to find and let your feelings fly. You no longer need group conformity! You have learned what your deepest, even craziest desires are you'd never tell anyone. We pulled it out of you. You have learned to eliminate your self-imposed resistance. You have found and are still finding your true self. This is ultimate power. This is *your power* no one can take away. You are done being repressed, redirected, conditioned, reprimanded, and the fear of being made fun of. Those are the seeds of prejudices, of hatred, of dishonesty, of elitism, of intolerance, of repression. We seek to change the world one person at a time and have our family grow. A new society slowly growing, slowly encompassing all who are willing."

Silence as he paused.

"We want to send a clear message to the whole world, not from the pulpit, not from politics, not from skywriting. The message is 'YOU

CANNOT CONDEMN ANYONE FOR ANY REASON FOR BEING THEMSELVES!'"

Cheers erupted.

"You and I and everyone are one together, each an individual, each with your own tastes and desires, each with an unending discovery of your heart and soul, and yet still as one, together. We make no judgments, we hold no inhibitions, we are both personally and socially free, we support each other, and we love each other."

He stopped at that and held his head down a second and then looked up towards us. I thought I saw a tear.

"Wherever life takes you, you will always be family. You will always receive our emails and mail about upcoming events like our monthly get together, future graduations you will now be invited guests at, and so many other things, and... especially ... entrance to a bit of paradise!" His voice lifted as he pointed to the fenced in area.

Cheers erupted again and a growing applause.

"So, with that, and in a sincere effort not to bore you any further, I close this graduation down and again welcome you all and now let's party!"

The sound of cheers, whistling, and applause was deafening. We all started hugging and kissing. I even got a couple kisses from some fellow graduating guys and just didn't care as the swell of emotion and happiness was overwhelming.

We all started leaving the seating area and I felt a tug from behind.

"Congrats brother!" Fred exclaimed as only Fred could.

"Thanks! I can't believe all of this and about Sam and all!"

"Amazing isn't it. He'll tell you more someday I'm sure if you want. Let's get a drink and party!"

"Well, I have to drive."

He looked at me with a 'come on seriously' look.

"No one drives out. The rules. For safety. You have a choice. Stay overnight or the limos will take you home and your car will be delivered to

253

your door. Compliments of Zach and team so you can party all you want! It's your day!"

"OK, wow, that's really cool!"

"Hey lover," I heard as Katie squeezed my ass.

"You are fucking bad," I answered.

"Wouldn't you like to know," she added and went straight to the bar.

"She's crazy," Fred said looking at her walk away, not caring at all about her actions.

My only thought at that exact moment was 'I wish Melissa was here.'

Episode 66 ~

The party went on all night. Colorful lights lit up the grounds everywhere. An island band was playing constantly. And the festive atmosphere was intoxicating as well as the well-made top-shelf drinks. Some folks were even getting high as there was a table of various types to choose from.

We all started dancing, and some were touching and others were kissing, and there was no rules or inhibitions. I got a taste here and a taste there, as if enjoying hors d'oeuvres. I got completely caught up in it all and loved every minute. Free love and free friendship everywhere.

Later I found a comfortable lounge chair and just laid back soaking in the continuing festivities. I closed my eyes and my mind wandered to the thought of 'I wondered if there was a way to break through to all guys and all girls in the world' and then Zach's cave analogy appeared in my mind.

"Watcha thinking?"

I opened my eyes and there was Teri standing next to me, her thighs at eye level about six inches away. (Sorry all! By now you know that I am enthralled by them! I'm completely addicted to them. Licking my lips... Alright. At ease Darian. Back to the tale...)

"Right now?" I coyly replied, just gazing at her thighs.

"Right now!"

"Of taking my mouth and tongue and running them all over these sexy thighs until you scream..."

She cut me off.

"OK!" she blurted and playfully pushed me a bit to the side as she sat down with me.

"Oh, I didn't mean here," came stuttering out of my mouth from the surprise of her readiness and offer.

"Well, why not?" she asked tilting her head as her short hair hung to one side. I just wanted to kiss her. I knew anything would go and be fine.

"Well… well… I don't know," I muttered, feeling again like a little boy who had a crush on his teacher. And I knew I did.

"You are so silly sometimes. Okay, we can wait. But promise?"

I had absolutely no choice but to say, "promise!"

She took my hand in hers, slowly brought it to her breast and pressed my open palm against it. "Now, our promise is sealed!" She then took my palm and slowly guided it down her thigh, lifted it, kissed it, and gave it back to me.

"Bye! See ya at the pool!" And she was off.

I was still utterly amazed how such a girl could be so bouncingly cutesy and such a strong personality and teacher all in one. One moment I'm in awe of her open, firm classroom discussions as a college professor and the next I'm quivering like a schoolboy unable to speak.

And I love every second.

Instinctively I turned in the direction she had left and saw her back as she was in a tight embrace kissing a guy. As I watched, the guy broke from the kiss and looked up at me smiling a teasing smile. It was Josh.

I found myself smiling back.

It was just so natural.

Episode 67 ~

After waking up in the same lounge chair, I realized it was the dawn of the morning. I saw most of the people had left and there were others like me asleep on lounges, on the grass, and many were in embraces.

I got up and walked among the extraordinary peaceful scene, got to my car, found my keys inside, got in and slowly drove out of the grounds. A part of me was sad feeling the nostalgia of everything that had occurred was over, almost as if a dream.

I finally returned home and it even more felt like a dream that I had lived through and now was back from the land of imagination. Neighbors were the same, the houses were the same, everything was the same – except me. 'I guess I'm back home, mommy,' I thought with an inward chuckle. Nothing was wrong with it, I just sincerely felt an immense difference.

I also thought of Melissa again and how she was still the same, too – or was she? I glimmer of hope rose in me that maybe our talk together had ignited at least a real curiosity in her, as it had in me, which had caused me to undertake my insanely wonderful journey. I suddenly wished she was here right now.

I closed the door behind me and then it occurred to me. That small envelope!

I found it in my jeans and held it up, staring at it. I then opened it and grinned broadly.

It was my pass to the pool! It read 'Paradise Pass to Your Garden!' I let out a "ha!" and then the excitement rose, and a bit of apprehension. When would I go? What do I wear? And then it hit me. All of that was solely my decision! Without hesitation, I decided to go that very same day. It was Sunday and I was feeling pretty good even after the amount of prior day and night drinking. It was early, so I took a quick nap, then a cup of coffee and a shower.

The pool area was open 24/7 with the food to order until 2:00 a.m. and all was still free. The bars opened at noon through the night and early morning. I planned my arrival for about 2:00 p.m. I got dressed very casually as if going to the beach, shorts just above my knee and an open short sleeve thin cotton shirt. Felt it probably was somewhere in the middle of what I was about to experience and see, though again, still a bit of a mystery, and always apprehension. Well, a lot of a mystery and apprehension knowing Zach and team! And that anticipation of the unknown thrilled me. It was a magnet.

I found that every encounter was an eye-opening, surprise of *freedom*. I didn't know any other way of describing it and was satisfied with my thought. And of course I was hoping Teri was there and somehow, someway, I knew she would be. Instinct. And probably with Josh, and many other newfound friends. A strange feeling of going home came over me.

As I drove, I contemplated how I will be with my bar friends and family. I thought of Fred and Katie and how they always seemed somewhat different than others, always more outgoing and accommodating. And maybe that's how it really is – just be me and not care. But I knew the first time would be maybe a bit tentative. And then immediately, everything kicked into gear and I felt that again reliable feeling of confidence surge in me and the concern simply melted away. I guessed each wall, whether tall or little, still had to be crossed and removed, sometimes with remnants still to eliminate.

At the same time, I also now felt the strange need to win people over and almost to preach a new way of being from the conformities and prejudices we live in. I told myself to take that one slow and again remembered *Plato's Cave* and showing the moonlight first. I vowed to always wait for the right moment with anyone I encountered, manage my enthusiasm, whether I knew them or not. I was suddenly extremely thankful for Fred.

I finally arrived and parked in the member parking lot that was shown to us the other day, that was hidden around the huge mansion. I wondered if this is where Sam had actually grown up. So much more interesting discoveries to learn and be part of.

I heard the unmistakable fun noise of the pool area — laughter, splashing, boisterous discussions, and of course island music. As I approached the gate, I still couldn't see above it. The attendant was an older gentleman with gray hair and dressed in a flowered open Hawaiian shirt which showed off his muscular body. He greeted me with a wide smile.

"First time?" he asked. I noticed what I thought was a Jamaican accent.

"Uh, yep, first time," I replied tentatively to his playful tone. What did he know that I didn't know and was about to find out? It only added to the beautiful, almost scary suspense.

"Great," he exclaimed and took my card. "I've seen you around so all good, we just take the card so no one loses it in there. You'll find towels, suntan, and everything you need."

"Thanks," I answered to his still smiling face.

He unlatched the gate and held it open for me to enter.

I nodded and walked through.

The site was amazing.

Episode 68 ~

Happiness. Fun. Exhilarating. Joking. Toying. Playful. Touching. Kissing. Lounging. Games. Water. Suntan. Umbrellas. Palms. Flowers. Splashing. Floating. Cocktails. Songs. Singing. Paradise.

A pure paradise was before me. The feeling was exhilarating. I was immediately drawn into the ambiance and the feeling of intense trusting friends and family.

I looked up at the arch inside the gate which said: '*Freedom Lives Here*' and then a girl strolled in front of me, topless with a string bikini bottom. She smiled and continued. I walked past two guys talking with a girl, all were completely naked but just talking and laughing. They waved. There were three pools and two hot tubs. There were large screen TV's tastefully placed so as not to distract from the scenery nor to infringe on anyone who didn't want to see a TV. I saw sports, movies, comedies, and figured it was completely up to the folks to watch anything they wanted or nothing at all.

I walked around the first pool, having no idea where I was going and didn't care. I was taking in the sights, the pleasures, and the fun.

Two ladies were hugging in the pool and then playfully pulling at each other's bikinis until they kissed. I continued past folks on lounge chairs, some smoking, others tanning – both clothed, semi-naked, and naked. I continued and the scenes were just amazingly open. I saw two guys in long shorts sitting at the side of the pool, hand in hand. They smiled at me as I passed and went back to talking. Against a shaded tree, a girl and a guy were standing with towels around their waists, softly caressing each other as they watched the scenery. For the first time in my life I saw a transgender girl with a penis spread out on a lounge soaking up the sun reading a book. It was all normal to me whereas before I would have taken a huge doubletake. I smiled. She winked.

The music was seemingly making everything sway, adding to the sense of peace, openness, and togetherness. Then the images of the murals shot back into my mind and here was the exact enlivenment of them, an endless idyllic paradise of pure freedom. There were no rules except respect. We were like children, forever young. A *New Garden* was before my eyes. The dreamlike atmosphere was intensifying with every moment.

Approaching me as I continued my walk past palm trees was a guy in a string white bikini and a lei around his neck holding a tall glass of champagne. He was sleek and slender but toned. I never looked at a guy that way before but the bikini forced me to as I would a girl in a bikini. I couldn't go past him. He walked straight up to me, stopped six inches from me, looked me in the eyes, and offered the glass. I instinctively took it, he smiled and ran his forefinger down my chest, laughed and walked away.

I saw him end up on a double lounge with an absolutely gorgeous black girl in a lingerie teddy and they went on talking and lightly touching as if nothing happened. In the second pool, a game of water polo was in progress. It was a coed game and the guys here wore long bathing shorts and were very aggressive, as were the girls. I noticed all ages and all races but everyone again had a youthful look and attitude regardless of their apparent age. Inner youth overtook age. Everyone intermingled as one.

I stopped and watched the game for a bit, sipping the champagne when hands folded around my waist from the back and I knew it was Teri.

"Hey handsome!" she whispered.

"Not fair again sneaking up!" I whispered back over my shoulder.

"Glad you came," she said suggestively.

"Not yet," I played back.

"Ha!" she batted back and came around front. I knew my mouth was agape. "I see Tony likes you!" she declared softly, eyeing over to the guy who gave me the glass. I didn't know how to answer.

Still trying not to look at her semi-nakedness, I blurted awkwardly, "I guess so." She had a bikini top on and that was it. And I glanced at her shaved crotch and quickly looked back up at her. She laughed.

"Still shy I see," she rebuked me with a smile.

"Yeah, still getting used to everything."

"How did you feel when Tony touched you?"

Again speechless.

"Come on, I think you liked it. I was watching," she sweetly accused, cocking her head, searching my eyes.

"I'll never tell," came out of my mouth before I could stop it. I knew it gave the hint of the possibility and it came out on its own. I decided to not fight myself and just say what I wanted to and knew that was the rule anyway.

"So, there's the possibility you may try it, may like it?" she challenged the door I had inadvertently opened.

"Ya know what? Sure, it's a possibility. Isn't everything here a possibility, always?"

"Ahhhh very good!" she kissed me lightly on the cheek, as I figured a reward for my honest openness to new things. "Now, let's see what you are wearing."

"What do you mean?" I tried to divert.

"I know better. I can read you. You didn't come here intentionally just wearing those shorts. Especially not to go in the pool. Maybe just nothing under? Maybe something? What are you hiding? If you don't, I will!"

"Who said I was going in the pool?" I ignored her last comment, diverting again.

She just put her hands on her bare hips, cocked her body, and gave me her 'seriously?' look that only she could do so well. Then without warning, she started playfully tugging at my shorts to bring them down. With glass in hand, I had no real defense. I noticed others starting to watch and some were applauding, egging her on.

I tried to push her hands away with my one free hand but she was too good. My only salvation was that the shorts were fairly tight at my waist. I was wiggling to avoid her hands getting too good of a grip and was being successful, until…

Episode 69 ~

Suddenly, the cheering and applauding grew louder and louder. It was so not my intention to draw such attention to myself my first day, or any day, but there was no choice and she was having a blast with it.

The next thing I felt were larger hands pulling from behind me and without much effort, those hands succeeded in dropping my shorts.

The applause and cheering peaked and the only thing I could do was graciously bow, which caused it to get even louder.

Teri was eyeing me with a sincere approving stare as I stepped out of my shorts on the ground. I felt an arm come around my shoulder and next to me was Josh, the smiling culprit who had succeeded in exposing my white men's bikini bathing suit. All the tugging and pulling had actually somehow aroused me somewhat in front of everyone. The tightness of the bikini surely didn't help.

"I think I need to sit down," I said with urgency.

"Why? Because of this?" And with that question, Josh cupped my starting to bulge crotch. A blast of pleasure shot through me and I immediately retreated to the nearest empty lounge. I think if a robot had cupped me, the same sensation would have occurred due to my already excited state, but as I sat forward trying to hide and subdue it, I also felt in my body the fact that I had liked his touch. Under ANY *other* circumstance, I would have been completely mortified by his action and the public attention. But I felt another 'wall' start to drop, slowly. I knew then that the seal was being broken and the door was wide open if I wanted to pursue. I pushed the thought back – for now. I was between complete embarrassment and exhilarating voyeurism.

Teri and Josh had followed me. I looked up sheepishly.

"Nice outfit!" Teri coyly but cockily noted.

"Yes, I'm impressed by your courage to wear that. Never thought you were the type," Josh added with friendly sincerity.

"Well, it's all your fault anyway!" I toyed back, looking at Josh. He was wearing loose fitting short running shorts with overlapping splits on the sides for running freedom. I would have thought it would have been much more skimpy or naked, and again, it came back to me to never judge what others may be or do. Just live and find out.

"What? Me? My fault?" he replied with an innocent, yet guilty tone.

"Yeah, you!" I retorted, putting the glass on the table. I stopped hiding myself and relaxingly leaned back on the lounge, fully exposing my bikini-clad body. And I knew I looked good. I was happy to flaunt it. Teri instinctively sat at the edge of the lounge. Her legs were partially spread and I tried not to look but then, again, the frankness of it all made me take a sincere gaze. She noticed and ran her finger up it. Surely didn't help my bulge.

"Not helping!" I joked.

"Sorry," she smiled.

"Anyway," I continued as I felt a wonderful surge of unguarded freedom come over me, "your assignment."

"Ahhh, my assignment, your *Adventure List!*" Josh replied, his face lighting up understanding, though somehow I knew he knew.

"Oh," added Teri, pointing to my bikini, "this is one of you inner, hidden desires! You always wanted to wear one and in public!"

I smiled broadly in agreement.

"Honestly," I again continued, "never! Never would I *EVER* think to wear this before and NEVER EVER in public. The staring and the ridicule would have been unbearable. But I always wanted to wear it and show off my body! I work hard enough on it. And it just feels sexy." I thought of my newfound feminine side.

"Seems like you do work *hard* enough and it does looks sexy," Teri commented as she leaned forward and pointed to my crotch, her fingertip lightly touching for a second. Another jolt of …enjoyment.

"I didn't mean that, little girl!"

"Well, anyway, congrats!" Josh said. "You obviously made a big hit here and on your first day. Question, if we hadn't dropped your shorts, would…"

I cut him off.

"Yes, of course. Just when I was ready and not right in front of everyone. Probably behind a tree," I posed laughing, "but I know now that was silly and should have dropped them myself right when I walked in."

"I know Tony would have liked that," Teri laughingly posed. "He's looking over and so is his girlfriend," she noted, motioning her head. "I think they both are admiring."

I looked over and saw what she saw. Then suddenly the girl stood up and slowly, sensually, strode over to us. Without pausing, she leaned down and full mouth kissed Teri, slipping her hand inside Teri's top. My crotch reacted immediately.

Then she took a step closer to me, her gorgeous dark skin shimmering in the sunlight. I couldn't move as she full mouth kissed me, slipping her hand inside my bikini. "Name is Jasmine," she slowly stated, looking directly into my surprised eyes. In an instant it was done and she was walking away, back to Tony's arms.

I couldn't stop my full hardon showing sideways tight in my bikini and didn't care. I was about to say something but Teri beat me to it.

"Now you listen, we're first, period. Then you can have your rounds with them, or anyone." She was looking at me with a pure ecstatic look I wasn't going to disobey and didn't want to deny either. I knew she was playing and at the same time nicely reminding of their multiple offerings.

"No worries," I replied. With her note of 'anyone,' my mind suddenly and unexpectedly went to the transgender girl. Teri interrupted my curious thought…

"Where's your phone?" she asked. I took it out of my bag that had been hanging on my shoulder. She took it and typed a text. "There, you just texted me. When you're ever ready!"

"Thanks," came out of my mouth.

"Well, enjoy! We'll be around!" Josh finished with and then they both left, arm in arm. As I watched their backs move away, and the cool look of their combined outfits (one topless and the other bottomless) both complementing each other, I started to see less difference in our bodies, and that in the end, the sexes were more the same than different.

And it didn't matter anymore. All bodies were beautiful and sensual both in their similarities and their differences. It occurred to me then that we make too much of the difference and not enough of the same. Both sexes, and Teri and Josh, were perfect examples that the 'whole' was the highest form.

I watched myself with wonder how I could even be more free with myself. I was starting to lay back to soak up some sun when I noticed a husky guy passing by in a long, below the knee bathing suit. A stereotype flashed before my eyes. I glanced down at myself. My fear of exposure in public rose in me. A part of me wanted to cover up my much more highly visible nakedness and remaining semi-hardness but before I could, he was walking right in front of me. I froze.

"Hey dude," came out of his mouth, with a wide, disarming, exceptionally personable smile.

I was caught by surprise as I expected an immediate judgmental, condemning, unapproving glare at what *I* was wearing. But it was like we've been friends forever.

"Hey man, how's it going?"

"Cool. Thanks. Have a good one." He just continued walking past me.

I then realized how still conditioned I was to the immediate expectation of ridicule and nonacceptance of a human choice and difference. But he just showed me up! And I was both embarrassed by my *own* stereotyping and inner fear, but was also inwardly grateful to him. I wanted to apologize for *my* judgment!

Again realizing that remnants of conditioning and resistance may still take some time to be fully eliminated, I knew going forward, courage and belief in myself, and my desires, were going to rule. Before I finally laid back on the lounge, I glanced at the back of the archway. It read '*Acceptance For All*' and I smiled. This was a world, *the* world, I wanted to be in.

I downed the remaining champagne, laid back in my white bikini, my crotch had subsided, and as I felt the full blast of the hot sun on my skin, my mind went to one thought.

Who's hands actually had caressed me during my 'shock wave' first experience in that room? I toyed with the idea.

My crotch started to bulge again as I re-felt that eternal pleasure.

I let it do whatever it wanted to do.

I was in the *New Garden*, *My* Garden, *Our* Garden.

I was finally at home.

Episode 70 ~

The rest of the day was perfectly wonderful, made more new friends, talked for hours, went swimming with some playful people, got a lot of phone numbers, and finally said my farewells and headed home. My drive was one of peaceful awareness of the world and everything around me. Everything somehow had new meaning and felt different.

Where I would have found myself tired from such a day, I actually felt rejuvenated. Once home, I made a cocktail and went outside to enjoy the late summer day. And I laid out in my bikini. I hoped my neighbors enjoy it as much as I do, I mused humorously but innocently.

My phone then buzzed. I looked. It was surprisingly, Melissa. She had sent a text.

'hi! just wanted to say I was thinking about you. and about me. i'm sorry if I have been somewhat terse with you lately and challenging you on everything. you are free to experience what you want. i just want to be part of it. and I'd love to be taught by you, for you. you inspired me. and I'm thinking about joining. love Melissa.'

Wow was all I could think. I read it again and felt her desire to make amends. And felt her sincere wish to take the daring plunge. It struck a sincere chord in me and I also felt a bit apologetic for being so forceful with her. And now she was being accepting. And accepting of maybe her own hidden desires. I was widely curious by such a simple text! I suddenly wanted her here right now.

But the day was getting late and a workday tomorrow. I also learned not to be as impulsive as I usually am, and decided to sleep on it. Not that I wasn't going to get us back on track, because I definitely was going to, it was just how and when.

I texted back a very nice thank you and let's get together soon and loved her, too.

For the rest of the day and into the night, the resolution of everything – the training, my new outlook on life and adventure, my new friends and real friendship love and acceptance, my relationship with Melissa, my love for her, and the open proposition from Teri and Josh (and others as a matter of fact) which reinforced the true oneness felt by everyone – all somehow fell into place. I want all of it. I want to experience as much of life as I can, explore as much as I can, share as much as I can, help as much as I can, and most importantly, experience all of what *I* desire. It is like a large table full of many different fascinating desserts and you know you want all of them but have to start somewhere.

And I knew now it was time for my first time with someone else other than myself since I started this journey. Somehow that first encounter was very important to me. I felt amused that I was now a virgin in this new world, even with Melissa. I liked the feeling. It was exciting and new adventures again.

Maybe that's what was missing before, before that time at the bar with Fred. And maybe that's what's missing in a lot of folks' lives – that ongoing feeling of constant adventure. Truly *Living the Life!*

I clicked off the nightlight and smiled to the nighttime.

My thoughts were that maybe we're all demons and angels at the same time, nothing to do with good or evil, nor the knowledge of, just as night and day exist together, and cannot be one without the other, with a demon's mischievous curiosity and an angel's outpouring of love, just expressions of our *total* unique being. Maybe we never actually left the *Garden*. Maybe just our vision got blurred by our own misconceptions and what we have been erroneously yet innocently taught. My newfound friends were just pointing this out beautifully.

My last thought crept in unexpectedly. It was more of an image, a vision than a thought. I saw all the wonderful trainers, all standing around me. They were glowing, emanating light, all around them and behind them, with the most peaceful yet powerful visages, gleaming at me as if from another world or place. Were they real Angels? Or actual visitors who have come to break our chains of ignorance, of prejudice, of intolerance, to raise us all up to the true spirit of existence, the true spirit of Life. I smiled. They nodded and smiled back.

I fell into a fast, pleasant sleep.

Final Episode ~

I awoke refreshed and ready for the workday. Got my coffee, went through email, took care of other business, and then got on my first call.

As the day went on, I continued my thoughts on who would be my first dessert. I knew my mind and my heart a lot of times went in different directions, as well as my crotch (lol). I simply let all the factors play themselves out and present their cases to the judge and jury, which of course was me. I also had fun playing the side of both lawyers presenting their arguments!

At midday, I had no meetings and decided to take a walk. As I strolled in the warm air, I finally made my decision. The judge and jury agreed. And honestly, I knew it was going to be that decision the day before and just wanted it to blossom fully in its own way. I knew always now to give myself time to let the real desire and feeling come out on its own. And then it was plainly obvious.

And for some reason, it was really important to me who my first experience was with outside of myself. I needed to level set myself this first time and knew with whom. Then afterwards, gates are open and game on. But the first was truly important to share with.

I made the call and after hanging up, felt good about it. It was the right thing to do. On for Friday evening! The excitement enthralled me!

After the week went by, I spent the late summer Friday afternoon cleaning up the place and getting ready. I felt excited and apprehensive at the same time.

An hour before arrival, I made a drink and lounged outside on the deck. I contemplated how so much has occurred since that fateful night when I heard 'hadn't noticed' and knew the journey I had decided on to find my real self, albeit wasn't always easy, and the new and sexy friends I made, and the ability to be open with Melissa, all came together at that moment outside in the warm breezy summer air.

I breathed it in slowly and deeply, allowing myself the moments of satisfaction with myself and the new world I have found. I vowed never to go back to not expressing my true emotions, thoughts, and feelings openly, my masculinity and femininity as one, and that being a guy didn't mean I had to hide them and hide *any* desires or *any* experiences I really wished for. I felt more of a whole person than ever before. Plus, I now knew the true, full meaning of *life's* 'shock waves!'

And another dawning happened to me right then and there. When that fateful moment when Melissa nonchalantly said, 'hadn't noticed,' I had taken it as an afront, as well as that something was missing in me, sexually.

And my exquisite journey took me to *this* day – right now, where yes, I found my true sexuality and knew it would only grow more. But the actual *real* dawning was that I 'hadn't noticed *myself!*' It was *me* I was looking for, the whole me, the true me, the adventurer me, the seeker me, and the courageous me.

I looked at my watch and it was five minutes to go. I figured was going to be on time, so I got up, went inside and sat near the door. The excitement rose in me. Suddenly, I felt like a little child on Christmas morning.

Right on time, the doorbell rang.

I got up, paused a moment, took a breath, and then slowly opened the door.

Our eyes met.

I'll always remember our smiles.

THE END

Gabryel Kevyn

(…and please stay tuned for Darian and Friends next extravagant, exhilarating, arousing, stimulating, *adventure installment*, along with the suspenseful exciting *Advanced Lab Work*, and many more *personal hidden discoveries*!

…and of course, the rest of the *Adventure List*!)

Afterword - Author's note:

And so, as you can see, Darian has ventured willingly into another world, courageously into this new unforeseen innocent world, a reborn, transformed forever ecstatic guy who has learned to truly *Live Life*!

Some may say a world of fantasy. Some may say a world of the surreal. Some may say a world of inspiration. Some may say a world of true magic. Some may say a world of pure imagination. Some may say a real possible world.

It is for each of us to decide. May your adventure begin.

What is it that *you* desire?

www.ingramcontent.com/pod-product-compliance
Lightning Source LLC
Chambersburg PA
CBHW031103260626
47172CB00001B/203